944 Hidalgo

A Novel

944 Hidalgo

A Novel

By Jack Davies

**ROUNDFIRE
BOOKS**

London, UK
Washington, DC, USA

CollectiveInk

First published by Roundfire Books, 2025
Roundfire Books is an imprint of Collective Ink Ltd.,
Unit 11, Shepperton House, 89 Shepperton Road, London, N1 3DF
office@collectiveinkbooks.com
www.collectiveinkbooks.com
www.roundfire-books.com

For distributor details and how to order please visit the 'Ordering' section on our website.

Text copyright: Jack Davies 2024

ISBN: 978 1 80341 835 3
978 1 80341 837 7 (ebook)
Library of Congress Control Number: 2024935615

A CIP catalogue record for this book is available from the British Library.

Design: Lapiz Digital Services

UK: Printed and bound by CPI Group (UK) Ltd, Croydon, CR0 4YY
Printed in North America by CPI GPS partners

We operate a distinctive and ethical publishing philosophy in all areas of our business, from our global network of authors to production and worldwide distribution.

Contents

1. Ingrid   1

2. Uley   22

3. Sami   45

4. Francesca   107

5. Hidalgo   117

6. Ruth   119

7. Max   150

8. Alice   156

9. John   201

10. Irma   213

1

Ingrid

April sun
bend your arms back
fireworks

Saturn is less dense than water. It's the only planet in the Solar System like that. Its Greek name was Cronus. It was on its day, Saturday, that Ingrid wrote. By Saturday, two weeks later, a piece of asteroid 944 Hidalgo, near Saturn's ring, was heading towards Earth. Three days later it would kill everyone.

Cronus was the son of Mother Earth, in Greek mythology, who castrated his father, Uranus, and threw his testicles in the sea. Aphrodite appeared from the white foam from Uranus's testicles. Cronus ate all his children thinking they might depose him, except Zeus, who forced his father to throw up his brothers and sisters, and castrated him. Family can be tricky at the best of times.

Love is an even rockier road. I knew the mountains and lows of love's fetid canals, the leaking refrigerator in the plum tree of blossom. All of that I understood, all that mattered was Ingrid's letters, which I, a man with fire for hands, scooped up like Fabergé eggs rolled down Ladbroke Grove, and I had a hat as big as a bus to catch them.

The mining space station in orbit around Saturn revolved, so that even if she wanted to, it was impossible for Ingrid Bester to see her home of London, England as the timing was all off. This was Ingrid's first trip in space. She wrote to me every day. We were in love.

She wrote to explain, "The viewing platform is on one side only, the side that faces away from Earth we see through our scopes. Sometimes I sit and peer out just to catch a glimpse, but as Europe comes into view, we turn another inch, and England is lost."

She said all the other employees could see home, but not her. They were from different countries, different backgrounds, she was having a hard time fitting in. There was a gap in her understanding of who she was, without seeing where she came from. That gap was like the gap of not knowing her parents, or of falling over a waterfall and in mid-fall knowing that as the whirling pool below came up to meet her, she was alone, never moving forward.

She said she was hating space. Hating the repetition. But finding time to not hate. To be herself, despite herself. She said the mining corporation she worked for had identified a new near-earth asteroid, 944 Hidalgo, in the belt near Saturn and they were planning to launch a mining ship soon, on an intercept; to mine diamonds which had been detected was the purpose of the mission, of all space missions, wealth. Of course, she wasn't involved in manning the ship, her job was purely admin, though she knew more than anyone really how these things worked, she had studied hard and gained her degrees and a PhD in astrophysics; it was just, things got in the way of her progression, mostly other people and their attitude.

Why did they feel the need to compete all the time? She never felt the need. But, anyway, she felt good to be part of the mission, in any capacity.

She wrote, "The time for knowing is past, what the future brings is shaped by the destiny we bring to our future. I wish I could have found love, but then, for what purpose? The purpose of me never depended on you. That purpose is more than the shame you talk about."

She wrote, "You have such good qualities. Up here the weather is always the same. But I am changing. Maybe I am becoming what you want, docile and placid. That is not what I want. No one wants that." She said that when the world comes around we are always pointed in a different direction.

She wrote later, "Thank you for your message, I am glad you are happy now, I hope you do not give up your thoughts, your actions. I feel that I have given too much. I had a dream about the shell from the Jokaca Sea. The material to coat inside, the green moss that grows only on the Kerselsha mountainside. The locksmith, Teraxa, you talked about. I constructed my own box. I have it here with me. I am not alone. I store my shame, word by word."

She said life on the station, in the black night or in the light of the blinding awkward sun or hazy glow from Jupiter, had helped her to contain all her thoughts, and she was careful not to let them leak out like a stray tear. She wrote that she was exercising and meditating, that work was exciting now the launch date was close. She said she had set aside time to reflect on herself, as though she was standing on a mountainside and far below she could see herself, her actions, her thoughts, and not judge them. Words no longer hurt. Impatience was becoming less and less. She had time to allow other thoughts in. She said she could now confront herself like a stranger. As the mining lander launched she felt anger melting away. She had let go of herself, like a large balloon pricked and deflating and happy to see it float heaven-wards.

She said she loved to write with a pen, even though she knew the ink became binary numbers as it hit the page-screen. She thought of days when she would type on a keypad, the touch of that was so different from the grip of the pen. Maybe the art of communication was shaped by the tools we use, like a tongue fitting in behind the teeth in a curl, pronouncing a word so very differently whether said with a smile or a grimace.

She wrote again to say the mining ship had landed on the asteroid. They had begun drilling. All was well. She would be home in another year.

She wrote, "The pen I write with now, that beams the numbers, splutters out every now and again, digital ink falls in a blot on the page-screen. Yesterday it formed a pool of blackness, with a beak and spindly legs that looked like a raven."

She said how she longed to see an animal, to hear its voice. To touch a tree and feel earth under her feet. There was a longing for a home she had never experienced, as though her memories had been stolen and hidden in a cave, that the rocks themselves had absorbed her thoughts and were patiently waiting for her return to download and decipher them.

Two weeks later she wrote to say the mining ship had drilled deep into an asteroid, 944 Hidalgo. That it had extracted ore of platinum and cobalt, but then there had been an explosion which set off a chain reaction that ricocheted through the honeycomb interior. The ship lifted off just in time, with no loss of life. They were monitoring the asteroid. It had broken in half. The two pieces were drifting apart.

She wrote to me to say, "John, please listen. Update on the situation. I have smuggled this message to you. All communication has been banned. The asteroid, 944 Hidalgo 2, has found a new course, latest predictions are that it will enter Earth's atmosphere in two hundred and fifty days. They estimate the main bulk of the debris will fall across Ireland and Britain. A sub-zero winter will come, the sun be blocked from view for five years. They say all life not underground will perish. Please, get underground, move to the hills in Scotland, it will be the safest place in Great Britain. There will be massive flooding, a deluge, a wasteland, it will affect the whole world. Millions will die. I will send more when I can."

Later she wrote, "I hope you received my last message and you are on your way to Scotland. Please go. I told them in no uncertain terms, I could help them, that I had an idea, but they wouldn't listen. They told me to go back to my room, take my meds, be a good girl. How can I be anything if I don't speak up?"

"I stare out at the stars and wish I could dive deep into them. It feels like someone is watching out there, as though the stars were holes in the sky like peepholes through which someone or something peers down at me in my capsule room, padded with white like a mental health facility. I have just a tiny desk over my narrow bed, room to only sit up, one sliding drawer for artefacts, mementos from home. There is a fir cone we collected from the standing stones site in Portugal, remember, we had gone there to see forgotten megalithic stones, recumbent mostly, some caught in a tangle of wild brambles, others with trees that had grown around and over them. The fir cone is a strange fit in a world of white walls and metal, in this cylinder floating in space. I put it in my palm and looked into its hard, thick scales, its presence a reminder of home, of all that will be lost. The stones may well survive, Earth will spin around another day, but in three days people I know will be dead, and millions more. This thing will tear out our humanity, claw at the earth and all I think of our small things, those memories of sensations lost to the future. No more peace in those small pockets of my homeland where once I felt something, treasured a moment, laughed, cried, was connected to the landscape. No more all those precious things that make up the glue that holds lives together. When a place is fractured, how hard it is to bury the past when it must be buried with those memories lost in time."

The fire of a gas stove is blue fierce red. A coffee pot boiling sends streams of smoke and makes a bubbling sound. I looked at the palm of my hand, I held something tiny, it delighted me with the way it glinted. I tied my laces. I walked. The door latch opened to let me out. Out to a London spring day. Slow, the street motion behind me was slow, my frame blocked the sky. Face in shadow, sun behind. I walked the western streets, a road of shops, cafés, smells of the Moroccan food on the street stalls, people I'd seen before, though never talked to. I thought of Ingrid in the sky. The asteroid hurtling towards us. My job as a fireman, the boys in the clubhouse. The ring of the bell when a fire broke out. My love of putting the fire out. Sensations of everything affected me. Small things, sounds, colours, smells. My brain ran through stories all the time, events that hadn't happened, disasters in the making. The wash of thoughts, the monkey mind, always jumping from one thing to another. I tried to quell it. Tried to count, thinking only 1, 2, 3, to clear my mind. Make the monkey come and sit beside me. But it never worked, and it wouldn't now, now that we were all coming to an end and still I hadn't used my power.

My van journeys took me all over the capital, along the Embankment, through the city, tangling up in traffic, stopping slow, edging up through gears, never reaching fourth gear. There were few places to cut free, put my foot down on the gas. My bulk squeezed into the seat; I always had the bulk since a child, as though someone had injected me with a serum to make me grow. I felt like a man-child, bursting at the seams, unable to contain spurts of crazy energy, clumsy with it. My hand can span a dinner plate, hold a basketball upside-down. My arms bulged from shoulder to wrist, legs like balloons ready to burst. Even my toes shot out in thick primordial clumps. I moved slow, aware of my weight, my presence, my shutting out of the sunlight. But I wanted to be unnoticed, to fade into the red brick walls, to shrink my shadow into the world. My secret held great embarrassment and pain. To hide what I had, and yet to be unable to hide because of my size drew me deeper into myself, as though a giant finger was always pointing down at me, marking me out to others, pushing my soul into a cramped corner of myself. It was a good thing people rarely talked anymore. Language had mostly become obsolete; it suited me fine that way.

The plague that had swept through the country had left many of my friends dead. I felt isolated and alone. They had blamed it on the aliens, but there was no proof of that. They had banned the aliens, thrown them out, barricaded the country, allowed no one in. Still the effects could be seen. Buildings that had been burnt to the ground where aliens had lived. To 'purify and contain' as the saying went, a scorched earth policy. The piles of stones on the corner of the street reminded me of a row of teeth with one knocked out after a drunken fight. Their absence spoke of intolerance but also of a missing piece in the jigsaw of society.

An antidote had been invented to rid the population of the plague; it had been used worldwide, except in Italy, Venice, where it still raged.

I walked through a concrete arch, along a walkway, down stone steps to a green patch surrounded by graffiti and apartment blocks. Up above the Trellick Tower, an edifice rising skywards. I must be careful here. This was an area set aside for the aliens, when they were still here. No one knew anything about their practices but they left the area alone. A patch of green, graffiti on the walls all around, an upturned supermarket trolley, a light that never went out in the shape of a crescent moon on top the trolley. A marking in the grass that never grew back in the shape of a figure, a person. It was said that they worshipped here, a long time ago, a religion based on a gateway and a 'star', but that's as much as anyone knew. Like the megalithic stones that Ingrid spoke of, maybe they were for ancient religious ceremonies the same.

I picked my way through, took a step, and stopped suddenly. A chill ran through me. Was it fear? The boys who sprayed the graffiti, they had no fear. Suddenly I threw myself to the ground. I could feel a searing heat suddenly pass close over my head, like the exhaust of a jet plane. I pushed my face deep into the earth, buried my hands and legs as much as I could, gripped the soil between fingers, holding on tight. Eyes closed, I prayed, let me survive and I'll be good. That is all. Let me prepare for what I must do. Let me hear the words from the Tower and act on them in good faith. Let me not fail.

The heat field passed, the discharge caressed my body but did not burn, a cool, thick air hit my face. I breathed deeply and stood. I was alone, as always, stood in a small patch of earth surrounded by concrete. I crossed quickly to the low entrance, stopped, opened a padlock with a key, entered.

I stood in the centre of the basement room, squeezed my hands together, concentrating all my force into them. I held my hands up, palms slowly opening and facing out. Concentrated everything into the palms of my hands. My hands ignited and spewed out fire. A thick stream of flame that came out like the rush at a sluice gate. It was hard to stand upright. Two thick tunnels of fire hit the opposite wall with a blaze of flame. Black smoke billowed out, filling the room. The last of the flame scorched out from my hands. I dropped back, sunk to the floor, and buried my face in my hands.

Shame followed shame. The tinderbox. My shame box. And the fire God said, "Lift up your hands. Make friends with the Sabbath. You were born to be a hell starter." Everything was black inside, like the crater of an extinct volcano. What are you when your superpower is full of destruction? You are nothing without an adversity. That's where my thoughts laid. I had this terrible power and I didn't know what to do with it. I pitied myself but I wasn't a twelve-year old boy anymore, creating a world where I could feel special, getting the attention I deserved. I was a two hundred and forty pound, six-foot six guy, with fire for hands, worried about touching anyone, worried about touching Ingrid who I had to wear gloves with, and even then, controlling myself so I didn't turn her suddenly into a kebab. I laughed to myself. Though the thought of it was horror. I stayed away from the world because I didn't understand it and I was afraid to hurt it. But most of all I wanted to fight the ugliness I found inside myself. That need to destroy was all that I was, to drive headlong into a wall, to tear apart, limb by limb, the fabric of a society, hell-bent on destroying humanity from the inside out. But now. Now I had a purpose. I could use my power for right. I must go soon, maybe I can stop it. Maybe there is a purpose for this power, something to believe in, something to prove. I looked up and saw a face at a window. The face of a teenage woman, hair fringed her face. She stared right at me. I have to kill her.

Ingrid felt alone. But knew it was up to her to penetrate the mystery of what could be done. She had been to see her superiors. She had a plan to stop the breakaway asteroid. It required an enormous amount of power, a fusion reaction, something that the scientists on Earth had never mastered. Her dream had opened up a connection, the bubbling lake, the monster held within. Already rockets from Earth had hurtled into the meteor, to no effect. What was needed was a plasma discharge, but channelling it was the problem.

She went to see the captain of the station and he shot down her plans. There was nothing they could do, and no one else to speak to who would listen. They were lucky to be alive, to have the chance of survival, he said, they could exist in space for many years, they had already made plans to find a new planet.

"Everyone I know would soon be dead, but then, I don't really like people," she wrote to him, though of course she didn't mean it, it was a reaction to circumstances outside her control and so altered her speech that blurted out at moments. The blunt manner of her speech always went down well with her friends back on Earth, they laughed and admired her directness. Here though, it didn't work the same. She was on unsafe ground. It came over as defensive, without care. She resolved to try and be more sensitive.

She wrote, "I am without words anymore. This place drains words. It sucks them out to space, they become useless in the air, the stars grow out of them and on their bright points, rich phrases, meaningless. I pick them out and spread them on the shore of my lap, they are like crumbs from a rich cake."

She took the walkway to the observation deck, sat on the curved metal bench. Earth was there far below. She could see Antarctica and Australia, the pure blue water in-between. A drifting cloud over New Zealand. There was the ever-present whine of oxygen being filtered around the spaceship, the crushing enormity of what lay outside their tiny capsule. She suddenly felt a huge pang of homesickness, a nostalgia crept up on her, her thoughts of the past, or him, of what she needed to survive this; the inner reserves it would take to overcome her fear flooded through her.

She remembered walking down a path to the sea together. Feet sliding down the sand, a sharp wind whipping up the sand on a Portuguese beach they had driven to early, a cold front of cloud and rain passing overhead. Huge, monstrous rocks darting up from the beach like a giant had stumbled and kicked up jagged stones the size of houses. The Atlantic sea had sucked up deep mouthfuls of water and spat it on the beach as though in a fit of childish glee. Mist rose in gulps overhead, flattening the horizon.

They walked to the end and she needed to pee so he stood guard, watching for any intruder coming around a thick skyscraper boulder. She saw a bird gliding out to sea, thought of tiny crabs underneath her scuttling away. She stood up and dressed herself, went down to the sea and washed her hands. Mussels thronged in clumps across the rocks. They walked back and ate clams and prawns in a tiny beachside café and waited for the fog to clear. She caught him looking at her and smiled.

There was something about that day and his face watching her and the dry wine, and the wind that turned flags around poles and dried wetsuits hung over balustrades, as men with knotted sacks brought mussels back from the sea, that whipped her passion and love.

She slipped off her sandals and felt the cool stone underfoot. A clatter of pots inside the open kitchen. A paper tablecloth, a metal tureen of seafood, a glass of wine. These things she did not want to forget. She closed her eyes aboard the spaceship, let her mind dissolve in memories like a warm, scented bath.

The drive home through twisted, narrow roads in their Fiat 500, shallow fields either side, as though scooped out like a furrow of ice cream, whitewashed buildings in the villages, blue sky.

Later in their apartment in the hills of Sintra she woke at three in the morning and could feel the presence of a ghost, an old man who malingered in the corner of the room, a heaviness in the air which sparkled in the darkness like the sparkle of the stars looking out from the ship. There was nothing more anyone could do, but watch the destruction of the earth, a bystander, in limbo, ghost in the machine.

She went to her cabin and slept. To wait it out and cover her eyes with shame. To retreat and hoist a white flag surrendering all her energy to sleep. If she could reach out and hold onto some kind of firm position without her shifting mind creating landslides then maybe there was a solution. She placed her eyes in the crook of her arm to protect herself from slipping into an opened portal of the nostalgia.

I ran after her, hands still hot with flames extinguished, I saw the heavy fringe, the small stature, the ripped jeans; skull and crossbones earring. She was alien heritage, light green skin, scurrying away, up steps, running, looking back, panicked. Her name is Alice as I was to discover.

My hands, wicks of hands, smouldering. I had to kill her. I picked up speed and she flew around a corner. She slipped and fell and I grabbed her, dragged Alice back, screaming, and kicking. I pushed her across the graffiti yard, down through the door into the basement. Black stained wall at the end from the fire. Hot in there. Smelt of pigeon shit and thick damp.

"Who are you?" I demanded, pushing Alice to the floor, her elbow scraping on the concrete.

"Nobody, I didn't see anything," Alice said, backing away across the floor. I turned and squeezed my hands together. Alice's eyes opened wide, she got to her feet, ran to the blackened wall, searched for an exit, but there was no escape. She turned back to look at me, my hands glowing, pressed together. I raised both hands towards her.

"What do you want?" Alice protested.

"Nothing."

"What is wrong with you?" Alice shouted.

I breathed deeply, "Nothing you can know."

"Try me," shouted Alice.

I walked towards her, she backed into a corner.

"Are you going to kill me?"

I stopped, I looked at her, she was just a kid, was I really going to kill her? I drops my hands. "I'm not going to hurt you."

"You were," said Alice.

"Not now."

My temper had cooled. I backed away.

Alice wiped sweat from her forehead, her hands shaking.

In the corner of a Portuguese café, Oporto, I told Alice everything. The power I'd had since a child, the woman in the lighthouse and how she contacted me in my dreams, her messages to me to find an alien man, the asteroid and approaching Armageddon, the whole damn story. And Alice believed every word because she knew who the woman in the lighthouse was, it was her mother. She just didn't let on to me. Not yet anyway. Some things had to stay secret.

"So, what's the plan?" Alice asked.

"I'm not sure, the soothsayer in the lighthouse has not talked to me for the last day. The last thing she told me was that life and death were in equal balance and the fate of the world lay in small twists of fate."

"That's quite a dream."

"It was."

"I mean, it seems so classic, like a Greek drama, life and death and the fate of the world…"

"I know, I thought I was going mad."

"When is it going to happen?"

"In two days."

"Cutting it a bit fine," joked Alice, "Where is this alien now?"

"I'm not sure, in the North, I think, but he may be on the move."

"Haven't any of you heard of email, or … maybe a phone call? Texting?"

"He's strictly off-grid. I would be if I was him."

"Why, what's so special about him?"

"He's one of the newcomers' chief scientists. They've been working underground since they first arrived, to find a way back to their own planet."

"I thought that was destroyed, I thought that was the whole point of them being here?"

"They left because they were forced to, they weren't wanted there, but they knew one day things would change and then it would be time for them to go back. To reclaim their rights."

"How can we find this alien?" asked Alice.

"It's his son we want, a boy, he holds the real key to this, we need to find him, take him to the drop zone," I said.

"What's that?" Alice asked.

"A body of water," I replied, eating a slice of pie.

"Where's the boy?"

I drank my coffee, looked up at Alice over the rim of the glass, "Why did you follow me?"

"I, I ... it sounds dumb. Not dumb. It's just, I can see. I see can inside people."

"What?"

"I saw the fire inside you."

I raised my eyebrows.

"You have a superpower of your own then?"

"No. Not really. I always wanted to, you know, have something special, but ... you know, when I was kid I thought that if I could be a superhero I could save people.

I used to dream every night of being a superhero, I know ... weirdo.... I used to fly around and fight evil in my dreams. I was strong and fearless. So, I decided I'd become her. I made a list of things I needed to do..."

She tells me of when she was a twelve-year-old girl and scribbling in the back of an exercise book a list entitled: "Things to do". The list read: "Martial arts — judo/karate/krav maga, chemistry/biology/forensics, survival techniques, hand to hand combat, guns — handguns, advanced driving techniques, hostage rescue..."

Alice used to make a tick against each skill.

"I was determined, headstrong, I enrolled in every course, pulled favours, pushed myself in every way."

She remembered being on a log bridge of an assault course, armed with a fighting stick, halfway across over water. She was wearing blue sweatpants and a blue jersey. Petrov, her instructor, twice her size, thickset and Slavic looking, edged forward to meet her, armed with a pole. His expression was grim, fixed. He advanced and they hit sticks, Alice executed a parry and repost, Petrov didn't hold back and lunged at her. Alice stepped to one side and guided Petrov's blow away. Petrov overbalanced and fell headlong into the murky water. He disappeared under the grimy surface. Alice stared down at the bubbles bursting on the surface of the water. A fist emerged from the gloom, one thumb up, and then the smiling face of Petrov appeared.

Another time, dressed in full combat gear, she remembered hacking at dense jungle growth with a plastic machete. Suddenly, she dropped to a knee, lowered the machete, and took out a pistol she had made from wood. She scanned all around, then stood and pushed forward, stumbling out of a bush in an atrium in Kew Gardens. A gardener, sweeping up, barely lifted his eyes at her. She nodded to him and he nodded back in complicity.

On a mountaintop, she remembered being in a small tent perched on the craggy summit of a foggy mountain. She opened the tent flap, tipped out a steaming pan of water, she looked up at the sky, assessing a possible oncoming storm, licked a finger, and raised it to test the wind direction. Alice, huddled up inside the tent, drew a line through an entry entitled: "Survival Techniques". She sighed, put her book away and disappeared under the covers.

In the laboratory of a university, young Alice, dressed in an oversized white lab coat and goggles, poured green liquid from a test tube into a beaker. There was a pop, a small explosion and a stream of smoke curled into the ceiling. A small group of older university students, sitting in a semicircle around her, looked on in amazement and clapped.

"So how come your parents let you do all that stuff?" I asked.

Alice painted a picture of her home life, "Not parents, just the one, Dad."

Inside a terraced street, late afternoon with golden sunlight slanting through, Richard, Alice's dad, gelled quiff and Levi's jeans, cigarette drooping from his mouth, open black shirt, sat in an armchair, noodling on a guitar, completely absorbed.

"Thing is, after Mum left, Dad kind of went into his shell," continued Alice.

Young Alice, dressed in her army camouflage gear with green and black face paint on, covered in mud and exhausted, walked in behind her dad. She looked at him, trying to get his attention but Richard was in his own world, oblivious.

"So, I wanted to be a superhero? Seems a reasonable ambition. But MI5 thought otherwise."

"You tried to get a job with them?" I asked.

"Yeah."

"What did they say?"

"They don't say," said Alice.

"Just show you the door and that's it?"

"I failed on the psych test, they tend not to explain why you're too mental."

"You got that far though, that's good."

"I failed, that's all," said Alice, exhausted by her own memories and lack of success. "Anyway, it's ridiculous, I look at myself back then and think, what an idiot, how could I think I could save the world, just childish dreams and fantasies. I don't know ... and then one day, after the plague, I woke up and I could see things."

"Maybe you can help me save the world."

"Really?" asked Alice, her eyes lighting up.

I told her about Ingrid in orbit, about her warning of the end of the world and how I knew I could help to save it. She asked when that was, why hadn't anyone been told. I said I received the message 247 days ago, but I had no means of changing anything, but last night I had a dream, the same dream, a woman in a tower, but this time the woman told me to come to her, so that is what I must do. But I told Alice that I was worried and she might help me with her X-ray eyes to see inside people, to know what lay inside them and did she want to come with me? I could only take her with me if I handcuffed her, and if she ran away and told anyone I would have to kill her. She thought about it, pulling on one green ear, then cleaning her upper teeth rack with one finger staring out the coffee shop window at a man with a placard that said, "The End of the World is Nigh," and agreed. And winked at me, which didn't seem appropriate.

"You took your time to do something, 247 days?" she said.

"Yeah," I answered, "I was thinking."

"I think you need to think faster, speed up the process. Where's this tower?"

"Yorkshire."

"Do we need passports?" Alice enquired.

"No, I got some fakes, I can put your picture on one."

"So, you had a few, were you looking for a partner?"

"Maybe. Anyway, the whole Yorkshire passport thing is a bit ridiculous."

"No Irish, no dogs, no aliens, you forget I'm green."

"Yes. Oh yes. I'll smuggle you in."

"Maybe you'll eat me."

"It's a possibility, I get peckish around this time."

"Confined to quarters," she wrote, "they didn't want to hear my plan, and then I took matters into my own hands, whilst they slept I went up to comms and turned a transmitter towards those who might be able to help. I had another dream, I dreamt of a woman in a tower. I tried to contact her, to transmit, but I was caught and brought here to the brig."

"They don't want to try, they want to start again; there is a sense of delight in their omnipotence. When one knows the specialness of your place in the world, then a certain hubris takes over. Last man alive, and all that junk. One chink of ego excites the Universe and it comes rushing in to fill the hole with outrageous ambition. The tree withers and dies as the seed grows right next to it."

She wrote, "There are patterns to our love, like a fern curls up inside itself, or an ice crystal forming, cracking under the weight of expectation. There is a window in my cell. It looks back to Earth, I am swamped with a great longing for firm earth, for my feet to hold fast, for non-regulated air in my lungs, for the catastrophe of life, with all its faults. To reach for the peace of not thinking, to burn down all the libraries of the world, with all the thoughts, to have only one thought, or no thought. Is that the peace of death?"

"I long for life, for all the souls. I am homesick, nostalgic. Looking back when forward, out there, the future can only lie. I don't even know if you are receiving these messages, I write in secret."

"There has always been a question that we've never answered, up here. With all the developments, all the progress, all the aspirations: what are we here for? I don't mean in the philosophical way, I mean, here, in space. What is the purpose of all of it, what have we learned? Down below nothing has changed. We haven't been enlightened by looking outwards, by exploring space, mining asteroids. Where did the mission go wrong, in the largest sense? Right now, decisions are being made without me, we are making for a new home. Can we call somewhere home without roots, without the smell and tastes of home? Time will tell."

She wrote to me to say there was a rescue mission underway. That a journey had been planned to a star 3.4 light years away at a distance of 20 trillion miles. There was a star there, more massive than the sun, but just fifteen miles across. It spun at a hundred times a second, and orbiting that star was a diamond the size of Jupiter.

She wrote, "Nearby is a planet, that is our destination. It will take 23 years to reach but we will be in a deep sleep. The planet has the conditions for life, liquid water. It is blue, like ours. We are trained for space, we are already here in orbit, away from the politics of Earth, without the distraction of choices. We have been asked if we wish to take someone with us. Do you want to come with me? My parents are gone, my brother also. I have concluded that a life worth living is one where I find a reason for being, maybe you can help me. Will you come?"

She wrote, "I will meet you when you arrive and we will sleep. I cannot stop thinking of a story I read in a book called *Zen Inklings*, about a butcher in Japan who all his life, cut up meat. He had started as a boy, scrubbing the chopping board, then moved onto cutting out the entrails, then to killing itself, cutting the throats of pigs."

"One day, a day like any other, he was slitting the throat of an animal, pulling out the stomach, his hands deep in the blood. Outside, it was a bright autumn day and he could see, through a window, flowering grasses in a meadow. He looked at his hands in the blood and the guts and a feeling came over him. He was at one with the meat. I know, it sounds so odd."

"He stood that way until nightfall, hands in the meat, eyes on the grass, and at dawn he left, never to return, he never killed an animal again. He walked up into the mountains and there he stayed. He wrote a poem which became famous:

'Just yesterday, the soul of a demon,
This morning, the face of a bodhisattva.
A demon, a bodhisattva…
There is no difference.'

Only he knew there was no difference, and that was the difference." She wrote, "We will sleep. Stopping time. Allowing us to breathe and think and to dream. Will this be a death that defines us? Can we reach a higher place with the knowledge that we might never wake? Without the constant flow of time, will I mistake myself for someone else when we wake up?"

I wrote to her, "I think our paths lie in different directions. How funny to say that when you are a million miles away. I am an anchor to this earth that you need to leave behind."

All she wrote was, "What about the cat, she'll miss you?"

I wrote, "Maybe Fluffball has more chance than the two of us."

Alice was handcuffed to the steering wheel in the car park of a motorway service station looking pissed off. She was alone, looked around, no one about. She rattled the handcuffs trying to break free. I walked back to the car with sub sandwiches and drinks. Got in. Unlocked her handcuffs and passed her food.

She ate. She looked at me, "You have family?"

"What do you mean?" I bit my sandwich, looked at her.

"You have a mum, dad?" asked Alice.

"No. What's that got to do with anything?"

"Why not?"

"It's a story that is long."

"It's a long drive."

"You don't want to hear about sad things."

"I love sad things."

"We were out driving in the forest. I was in the back seat. We stopped at a light. They came over, tapped on the window."

"Who's they?"

"Men, gangsters. My dad was a cop. Investigating them. This was in Japan. They started firing and ran away. I heard them shout a name, I..."

"Shit. What did you do? Wait, how old were you?"

"Ten. I took my dad's gun. Went to their place. My dad had showed me where they hung out. I knocked on the door. A man answered. I asked for I — he came to the door. I shot him. They took me in. Not such a long story really."

I ate some more of the sub sandwich.

"What about your mother?"

"She was in the car as well."

I drove. Spoke, "I became one of them, learnt how to do what needed to be done to earn the money I deserved. Nobody hurt me again.... When I was eighteen they gave me the job, to kill someone, but I did not do it."

"Did you ever use your fire hands?" Alice asked.

"I did not have them then. They sent me to work in a sokaiya. You know what that is?"

"Is this the Yakuza?"

"Yes, they sent me to London. Out of China Town. We invited Japanese businessmen to this club, got them drunk. We acted like investment brokers, gave them a good time, then took them to this other place, there were girls there, we photographed them with the girls."

"So, you were like a pimp?"

"All we needed was the photographs with the girls."

"The prostitutes?" Alice insisted.

Ignoring her I carried on, "Then back in Japan we turned up at their shareholder meetings ... we've bought stock in their business ... and one of us stands up and shouts Banzai! And they know who we are, what we have on them. If not, we send them an envelope with the photos, what they've been up to on their business trip. The money comes quick after that, the shame is too much."

"Nice business," Alice said sarcastically.

"Good money."

"That's all you're about, the money?"

"What else is there?"

Alice stares out of the window. I looked out my side window. There were things she didn't know, like how I'd helped a woman working there and had to run when she ran, how they were still looking for me. About how the woman died, nailed to a tree in the forest.

"Where's the woman in the tower?" she asked.

"You know I can't tell you. She's up North."

2

Uley

A world where faith is given only to those who are born into it. Words are given only to the few. Those words are sacred, only to be spoken by priests. A world without words. Objects have no label. Zen turned into fascism. In the beginning was the word, and the word was never to be spoken. The word became forbidden to be uttered. And finally, all wrong words were outlawed. And we rarely spoke. There was no escape.

I do like to remember the past; if I go there, it's just fear. I remember a ditch at the edge of a park. But then my mind flees from that. Supplants it with the time in the same park I was caught by two boys who held me whilst the other used a knife to scrape up and down my arm because I had kissed an alien girl. Or again, the time I was caught with my sister in the demolished bomb shelter (when the threat of aliens was inflated by the Nationalists), and boys threw sharp stones that clattered around and spun in the collapsed doorway cutting legs and arms. And later the torture with those that wanted to experiment. In a dark place, with no limits.

In truth I'd had enough of this life. I could try 'Relife', but there were no guarantees. Who knew, after they had your money, whether your soul really did go into a new-born being. They said it did, but no one ever remembered their actual past, documented real life. They said that was the way it worked.

It was as though insanity had struck the country and everything was stood on its head. The roots of this were in plain view but nobody talked about it. The English talk about the weather instead, I thought. I looked over at Alice, she was asleep, curled up in the passenger seat. She still had the handcuffs on. I couldn't take any chances. My secrets needed to stay that way, and hell, she could be an infiltrator, like they said.

We passed Harewood House, the place where they made an old television show called *Downton Abbey*. The House was built with slave money the government had paid out when slavery was abolished. The Earl of Harewood, owned 2947 slaves and 22 plantations on the islands of Barbados, Grenada, Jamaica, and Tobago. By the time of Emancipation in 1833 the family still owned six estates in Barbados and Jamaica, consisting of 3264 acres and 1277 slaves. Under the terms of the Parliamentary scheme to compensate planters for freed slaves, the 2nd Earl of Harewood received £23,309 in 1835–6, which they built the House with. The Earl lobbied strongly for the continuation of slavery, saying at a meeting held in 1832, "I, among others, am a sufferer; but I am not a sufferer equal to those who may have nothing but their West India property to depend upon." When slave ownership was abolished by Britain in 1833, the government paid out a total of £20m, the equivalent of £16.5bn, to compensate thousands of wealthy families for their loss of "property", and on the back of that money many of the stately homes were built.

The problem is, I thought, our collective subconscious desire is to grow up and get over it, the Empire, the slavery, but we are held back by a sacred wrong belief that pride is the only way forward. It's Lawrence of Arabia all over again, a man in the desert leading a band of Arabs into Aqaba, only to be caught when brazenly walking into the Turkish camp at Deraa, and being tortured and raped. We head towards our torture with open blinded arms. Can the soul of a nation regenerate?

We scooted around the Humber River, a great dirty serpent, rolling over and over in excrement. We couldn't cross the Humber Bridge, it lay like a beached, broken octopus, slumped in the middle, iron tentacles splayed out. The Nationalists had never repaired it. They thought they had created a fortress in Hull, the city on the other side, a fortress from the aliens, but they never came that far and the plague dissipated over time. Now they had a bridge that led into the sea.

We skirted past Goole and arrived at the border outside Hull. I remembered Hull well. During the dark times I lived here, worked on the *Daily Hate* as a journalist, Hull section, "The Free Hull Supplement — Life Without Aliens". I lived up near Pearson Park; each day, after delivering my copy I would go to the tiny reptile house and look at the axolotl in a glass case. They were a bit sad, I thought, as though they never fitted in anywhere. Not a fish, nor a mammal, an amphibian, but they had gills and lived in the water. And they walked on land. They injected them with iodine in research labs, or with thyroid hormones, to make them grow into adult salamanders. They had a neural plate and tube similar to humans. Their greatest feature, I thought, was their ability to regenerate. They did not heal by scarring; they could grow a whole new leg when severed off, and some could grow bits of their brains to replace lost portions.

They could take transplants from other animals, including eyes, restoring alien organs to full functionality. Sometimes when they grew an extra limb to repair what they thought was a damaged one, they get an extra leg, so became the only five-legged beast. None are left now in the wild. Deep in Lake Xochimilco in Mexico, under Mexico City, there were a pair left. But some dumb fisherman stood on one of them and the axolotl tried to revive the first, lending it its leg, its brain, its heart, moulding with it, providing pieces for all the broken and torn bits, but it did not work. In the end its heart gave out, and the other axolotl gave up living through the loss of the only kind of itself.

I had read about the last of the right whales, they said it roamed about singing its song but there was no female to hear it. That was very much what I thought of my writing at that time. I gave that all up. I became a fireman in London. It seemed more a force of good, less harmful all round, except the bloody nose I'd left the editor with on the day I left for some trans joke he sputtered out and wanted me to include in my spew of hate. So now I was back, with an alien in the boot of my car. This meant one of two things but as the second thing was accepted by a corrupt border guard, namely a wad of fifty pound notes, the former, an imagination of torture, cold cells, rape by hairy men and dragged behind a shitting horse until final hanging and bowels thrown outside the body to dangle didn't happen, there was no point dwelling on such things; and I drove on and through Hull in Yorkshire and out the other side and to a spit of land that curved as the Humber River hit the North Sea at Spurn Point. I stopped. Let Alice out the boot; she gasped for air and stretched her legs extravagantly.

I looked towards Spurn Point. I recalled coming here before, when a road led out to the lighthouse, a spit of land curving out for two miles into the Humber Estuary. North Sea to the left, with waves crashing in on stormy nights, mud flats to the right, deep, thick mud that might drag a man down as soon as he stepped in. I remembered a book called *Softly Tread the Brave* about a man in the Second World War who tried to diffuse a sea mine out there, and the bomb started ticking. The mines had anti-tampering devices designed to kill the bomb diffusers. They had to use brass tools because the mines were triggered by magnetic touch. The bombs were fitted with light sensitive switches, so when the bomb was pulled apart it would trigger the detonation so they had to cover up the switches. That day the man at the mine heard the trigger go, the clock tick-tocking its way down to death. He ran, headlong, in thick mud, like some great giant slowed down, a film jammed in the machine, clawing at the mud to propel him forwards whilst the loudness of the clock, the thirty seconds he had, thrust him onwards, his only chance in the inches he could travel, the footholds his feet could find, the quarter mile needed to have any chance of survival. The mine exploded with the force that could rip a whole ship apart, gouged a hole in the earth and sent down a hundred weight of mud high in the air. It came down and flattened and covered the man. He was buried in it and had to be dug out. But he survived.

I remembered driving out here with a friend, when I was young and my friend was older, the same age as I am now. We ate bacon and egg sandwiches at a café in a trailer at the end. We found birds caught in netting, birds captured to be tagged as a survey on migration. We found a box on the beach as big as a small house. And a dead deer washed up. My friend took photographs with no film in the camera, conserving no record except the eye and brain. The local militia caught him. Didn't like the way he looked. People had spoken about him. He was suspect. His answers under interrogation were not satisfactory, and so they brought him out here and tied him to a ducking stool in the muddy Humber and ducked him until his mouth filled with mud, and choking he asked why, and they ducked him again and held him under, and when he surfaced he was dead and someone shouted, "Because you suck..." Or, to be honest, it could have been, "Because..."

Now the road was washed out due to floods from Global Warming that eventually, laughingly everyone had to accept or look like King Canute, and so travel by car impossible. I looked out at the distant lighthouse, out on the Spit, our destination, to meet the most hateful person alive. That was how I saw the old lady, her reputation, how she came to me in dreams. I told Alice I was going alone. She nodded.

I climbed the fence. I must walk the approach to the lighthouse. A shuttle service, an old sign advertising such, lay flattened and faded in the mud. Nothing had come this way for years. Maybe the ogre in the lighthouse put them off, maybe, as so many other things, the grinding gears of progress had rusted, slipped full back.

I climbed the fence, and stumbled and fell. Face near the earth, ankle twisted. Hands plunged deep in the shifting sand. I head a cackling. Alice was laughing and I felt ashamed and then stupid then funny. I laughed with a mud-filled mouth. And then I heard a clacking, a rhythmic striking and tinkle. Above a sand dune appeared an old man with a fishing rod, silver lure at the end, tied in but making a sound like a tiny bell. The old man was festooned with a long, grey beard, deep creases at his eyes and a mustard sou'wester hat pulled down over straggly, long, grey hair, so that the patch of eyes and cheeks showing were just an eyehole in a world of grey and yellow. With folded down wading boots, thick corduroy trousers, a check shirt, and a fishing keep-net slung over his shoulder, he made headway for me. I walked towards him, gesturing for Alice to stay behind the fence. "Slipped down, friend?" asked the man.

"Yes ... I seemed to." My words choked out, my voice harsh like a rasp of an electric saw, vocal cords atrophied.

"It's heavy going." The fisherman approached, stopped, held out his hand, "My name is Eric."

"John."

We shook hands.

"What are you headed?" the old man asked.

"To the lighthouse."

"Are you to see the woman there?" asked Eric.

"Yes."

"Be careful."

"Why?"

"She may not be what she seems."

"Why careful, is she such an ogre?" asked I.

"It's a tragic story it is, you know of it?"

I confessed I did not.

Eric continued, "A young woman, married to an older man, with two young children, girls, they live out there in the lighthouse. She falls in love with another man in town. She is caught in between them both. Headlong in love with the new man, devoted to the first. She does not know who to love anymore. So, she runs away, out here, climbs to the top of the lighthouse, out there, and jumps to her death. But she is not dead. Just horribly crippled. They carry her into the lighthouse. She cannot be moved, her heart would give out, so there she has been ever since. Both of the men, her husband, and the lover, take off, leave the poor woman alone. Her daughters, who knows! Some say one stayed with her father, or died, and the other ran away to Venice." He turned and pointed to the lighthouse. "So, there she is. Holed up in her castle, sad story. She won't see anyone. No sir."

"I shall try. But please do not tell her I'm coming."

"I don't care for secrecy. But who would I tell? I'm nobody but a silly old man who can't catch a fish, ha, ha."

"Is fishing not good here?" I asked, because I did not know what else to ask.

"It is! Ha, ha. And look at me, a fisherman who couldn't catch a crab! You'd better get going, the tide's turned, this all will be under the sea in half an hour." He pointed at the path, and with that took up his rod and tinkled his way to the fence and over it to the road.

I continued on as layers of thick cloud drifted in, dark at their underbelly. I crossed a thick soup of sand and water, steadily filling in the hollows in the path from the insistent sea. Ahead I climbed a shifting dune, crested it, feet sinking down the other side. There were pockets of thick bracken, a sharp wind that blew through, a change of temperature, dropping down low, the taste of sand in my teeth.

I thought back to two years ago. I had met a woman and fallen in love. Before Ingrid, another. Sophie. The spring breeze that year had blown her in as it had shaken the blossom from the trees. I fell for her, she released me from a torment of unloving and the roots of my sadness had been exposed, cleaned, and shaken free from mud, lifted up and gleamed in the bright summer sun. We had spent that summer in a tangle of rollercoasting emotions, and then one day she was gone. It happened quite suddenly, the plague got to her, she went down hard, the disease crippled her and finally killed her off. The tide came in and out. The possession I felt, the un-eye-opening tunnel of obsession which stood in for the unity of man and all things, that cockeyed enlightenment, had vanished. There was a unique irreplaceability of my love, in the act of possessing her I had of course already lost her; and when she went I lost the physical aspect but not the religion. In making her my own, I had given myself focus, lifted myself out of the soup of a life wasted, but now I was back, swimming around in a bowl of muesli. I stopped on the crest of a dune, walking towards the lighthouse, and laughed to myself. I saw myself doing backstroke in the muesli, dodging the raisins, knocked over by the nuts.

Now she was gone and my heart shrivelled to a dense stone. I knew I must move and move fast, in whatever way the wind took me. So, I took off and travelled. Walked in the only direction I knew, south to the sun, to a small cove on the Côte d'Azur in Southern France. I stayed with an old friend in a house that had once been home to Greta Garbo, a grand pink stucco pile in the Petite Afrique area of Beaulieu-sur-Mer. Here I lounged around the terrace looking out on the bay and boats, ate fresh fruit and drank brandy.

The turn of events I dwelled on incessantly, I took to walking around the jutting point at Saint-Jean-Cap-Ferrat. I swam in the bubbling, rushing waves, sat on the dried seaweed flotsam's high tide mark, thought of who I might kill in revenge. The approach was made in a lonely bar in Nice. A middle-aged

French man in a peaked blue sailor's hat had sidled up to me, started the sort of conversation that seemed innocuous at first. Sport, the weather, where did I come from, did I work, need money? Over a few hours, a few more bars, a few more cognacs, I had been made an offer. For money would I go on a little trip, across the border to Italy. To do a job, not hard, quite simple. I needed only go to a man's house, knock on the door, be let in, and then when the man's back was turned, pull a trigger. I would be paid handsomely. That was all. And I, well, I jumped at the chance. Why not, what was there to lose, this man meant nothing to me. I needed the money. No one would know. After, I would escape back across the border. Maybe move on, try Spain, stop down there for a while.

On the drive to Bordighera, I felt my heart slip. It fell into the pit of my stomach, detached, heavy as a stone. It soaked in the bile. Took away shame, guilt, remorse. My feelings for the world, any sense of beauty, seeped away. My soul hardened as I drove into the small town, down a wide avenue, stopped, had a coffee and a piece of Crocetta di Dolceacqua at a tea shop.

The wind was blowing in, the mistral. Cutlery and ashtrays clattered off tables outside. The pain beat down inside me. The sun felt heavy on me. On the seafront, with a few out of season restaurants still open perched on wooden stilts over the beach, I walked the promenade, the waves crashing under an oyster sky.

The man's villa lay on a narrow street leading away from the sea. I walked through a palm grove, the palms they say were left by Phoenician pirates, the palms named Phoenix Dactylifera. The latter part of the name meaning "I bear"; though dates never grew this far north. Monet painted Bordighera and the date trees. I walked in his steps.

The villa had a low wall at the front, green shutters and sandy orange painted details on the brickwork that reminded me of a gingerbread house. I opened a gate and climbed a few stone steps. I remembered the gun in my suit jacket pocket as it thumped against my leg. The man had given it to me outside in the car park of the bar. Showed me where the safety catch was. It was an old Luger pistol. I gripped it firmly now. My hand was dry, forehead wet in the humid sea-crusted day. I felt no fear. Just a sense of destiny. A hangnail irritated the side of my little finger, I bit it off. I rang the doorbell. No one answered.

I walked back down the steps and looked up at the shuttered windows. Maybe I had been sent on a fool's errand, but for what purpose? I could hear the trickling of water. I walked around back of the house. There was a bark of a dog and water splashing. Italian words spoken slowly, with a lilt and smile in the voice, "Ora, stai fermo." I rounded a corner, an old man with a grey beard was washing his Yorkshire terrier with a hose pipe. The brown doe eyes of the dog looked up at me. The old man followed the dog's stare with his own large brown eyes. I looked at both of them. "Che cos'è?" said the old man; he was dressed in a singlet, slacks, and a battered pair of sandals.

"Someone wants you dead," said I, and walked towards him, handed him the pistol.

The man took the pistol by the barrel. He spoke, looking me in the eye with sorrow. "Not me. Mi dispiace."

I turned. At the bottom of the drive a man in a powder blue baggy suit and shiny patented shoes, like he was on the way to a summer wedding, held a revolver in his hand pointing at me. I have no idea why someone would want to kill me, except perhaps for what I was born with but had never used until now. It was possible, I have since learned, that certain aspects of my childhood, certain experiments that I have no memory of when I was a child and roamed about and was taken, may have been the cause. The journey is often backwards when moving towards nirvana. But now, with death knocking fairly loudly on my door, it was time to act as I only could. My hands came up as the man in the powder blue suit placed his finger on the trigger. A spew of flame came out and travelled the short distance in half a second. Two lines of flame the width of a can of peaches. The man was frazzled dead, burnt to a crisp, dead in ten seconds. There was a rolling around, screaming, singed flesh, the smell of a wet dog and burnt roast. Flames dripped from my palms. I turned around. The man behind with my gun was frozen. He dropped my gun. He turned and ran. The little dog yapped.

I reached the lighthouse at nightfall. The last rays of light hit the top of the tower. The wind had died down. I was in a hollow, sheltered, staring up at the tower, in amongst a few outposts of houses long since crumbled and left open like carcasses to the wind. I knocked. It took three more knocks and the door opened. An old woman, wispy grey hair, bent over double, but with the face of the Buddha, cheeks blooming out of her face like ripe apricots, stood before me.

"Yes?" she asked, easing out the words, somewhere between a question and a discerning acknowledgment of my presence.

"My editor sent me, he's been in communication with Uley, I have a meeting with her."

"Uley sees no one, I'm afraid."

The woman shut the door slowly and benignly.

"I've come a long way." The door stopped just a half an inch open. "I'm from the *Daily Hate*. I understand Uley wishes to speak to us, to tell me her story."

From within, "Her story is known. She does not speak of it."

The door closed. I stood staring at the door. My breathing was slow; though my heart beat fast, I did not know why and checked myself, repositioned myself, shifting my feet on the cold stone step, shoes wet through, toes scrunching inside my shoes. The deception I had enquired with was true to an extent. I had made a call, talked to this woman, in fact, told her my credentials, of course false now. The story was, an interview with the woman who hated the most, or in the *Daily Hate*'s style,

"Meet Britain's Most Hateful Woman — Wicked Witch of the North." I knocked again. This time the wait was longer. Finally, the door opened a crack. I stretched an arm forward, placed a hand in the door jam, dangerous if the heavy door were to close suddenly.

"It's not her story I need to know, it's ... I need to know if someone can hate more than I do," I pleaded.

The door slowly opened; the old woman's face was solemn now, "I doubt that is possible, sir, I've read your work. Your old work. I understand that you are not employed by that newspaper anymore." The old woman smiled. "You see, Uley doesn't hate, she does not have the capacity for that, Uley sees. And you are a fake, which bothers both of us."

"Did she see me coming?" I asked.

I waited, the old woman's expression changed as she seemed to peer into my soul. "Come in," she said.

Inside there was a spotless clean floor, whitewashed walls, an old apple crate, turned upside down as though this was where the old woman sat, waiting for such a visitor as I who might come calling, and at the back of the circular room, a spiral staircase with a lit kerosene lamp hanging from its metal stepped entrails. The room was dark with no windows.

The old woman led the way, wordless, up the spiral staircase. I followed, my wet feet squelching on the metal staircase ruts. The next floor was much the same as the previous, except a bird, a bluebird, in a cage hanging by a metal chain from the ceiling. The bluebird danced around on its perch, hopping, and changing its head by degrees in different angles so each eye could see me. The floor underfoot was dirty, a thin film of sawdust or sand over a greasy floor; it smarted under my step.

"I'll leave you here," said the old woman.

She turned and walked back down the spiral staircase. I was left in the dark wondering if the old woman had returned to her apple crate to wait endlessly for another caller in the night or whether she's left and gone on some night errand over the sand, a letter in her hand that let the monkey people with the wings to stand down and not chase the foreigner away. Or maybe a pint of porter at a pub was her thing, feet up on a stall, a black thin pipe in her mouth.

In the blackness of the room I could see little by the light of the kerosene lamp which sent up plumes of ochre light and dropped a rich stream of burnt oil to the floor. I walked to the bluebird in the cage. It hopped about, then stopped, dead still, so you might imagine it had suddenly died on the spot. With nowhere else to go, I climbed the spiral staircase.

The light receded as I headed up into the gloom. I reached the top step. Another room the same as the last, circular, cast in black, no windows. Opposite, the edge of a bed. I was deeply apprehensive. My breathing tight and irregular. The room smelt of ink and soot and a thick acrid smell, like burnt tin. There was also an animal quality to the smell. A deep-rooted nasal ancestral memory I felt to my core, it invaded the nose by degrees, at first offending and then slowly burying deep within my subconscious, awakening thoughts of cave pits, animal skins, rotting flesh.

"Come here." The voice was from the throat, with an inflection it was hard to discern, a sliver of Baltic pronunciation in the vowels, soft and low. I obeyed, as if the voice could tell me to jump here, or climb there or to eat a poison apple, and I would do as it said. My eyes adjusted as I stepped closer and then I stopped with a jolt. Uley lay on the bed, naked, hands behind her head, propped up on a pillow. It was hard to tell her age, maybe forties, maybe younger, could be older. She was slender, her hair short, black. She had one knee raised. I realized the smell came from her. Her body-hair was extensive, armpits, down her legs, at her belly, thick dark hair. There was a smile on her lips. Her mouth was cruel, uninterested. Her eyes green, deep set, her cheeks had dimples, which seemed incongruous;

her laugh, which came now in full throttle, was at a higher pitch than her speaking voice, like a child lurked within. "Come closer, I need to see you," she said.

I obeyed and stepped around the bed so she was looking up at my face.

"Do I shock you?" she asked.

"No," I lied.

"Visitors are few and far between, but are always shocked. By what, I do not know. Why should someone be shocked by what is natural?"

I tried to think of an answer, but could not, so stayed quiet.

"Please, sit down," she implored.

I looked around for a chair, there was one against a wall. I pulled it to the bed, sat, took out a notepad and pen from my jacket side pocket.

"How quaint," she said, motioning to my pen and notepad.

I smiled briefly. "I find it easier than data," I replied.

"Yes. So, you wish to know if your hate matches mine, but my Dottie has already told you I do not hate."

"She said you 'see'?"

"Yes, I see, beyond these walls. Are you shocked that I have no injuries to speak of?"

"I had wondered," replied I, shifting in my chair and trying to look only into her eyes.

"It's only my heart that is broken, irreparable. The other limbs broke but mended, the skin heals. Where are you broken?" she asked.

"I'm not sure that I am," I replied.

"We are all broken, out of the womb, we break free only to find the world a place that crushes in other ways. The first freedom is the last."

"You speak to me," I said, sitting back in the chair and putting the notebook and pen away, "You speak to me in my dreams. You told me to come here."

"Yes, I did, didn't I," Uley said, arching her neck and picking up an apple from between the ruined sheets, "You wish to know where the boy is, well, that can wait. Did you think I would be an old crone, a witch?"

"I had no thoughts on your appearance."

"Boldercrap! Of course you did. But that is by the by..."

I lay upstairs in a room above hers in the dark thinking through what she had said; she had said so many things, some of which seemed impossible. She talked of ways of seeing, of connections outside my comprehension.

I looked through my notes, long descriptions of planetary systems scribbled in the margins, diagrams, and half-finished symbols that I had drawn according to her instructions. And all this while trying to keep my gaze on her green eyes that would suddenly seem to darken into purple, then back to azure, then to a deep ocean blue and finally black. I would avert my eyes away from those dark pits and back to my notebook, but then be drawn to looking at her, covered in thick hair and what seemed like a thin film of luminous gel. Glutinous and sticky. As were her words. They clung to my brain, my reasoning, like a dirty lichen growing deep inside the crevices of my mind. She talked of a boy of the Prinshj People, the alien race, of destiny and fate for all concerned. She saw into the future, into the lives of humans and those recently arrived; all of this to me was a mystery unfathomable.

Fear, she said, led to hate. Nothing more complex than that, fear of the other. This fear could be easily manipulated, as it had been in past wars and political campaigns. She said something terrible was coming, an unstoppable force, though there was a chance that it could be altered and I was to be the recorder of the events that would determine the destiny of us all. I said I knew of the asteroid and she smiled. Told me I was a two-timing little fuckwit. That the whore in the sky was a messenger of hell, not an angel hovering for my benevolence. She said I would find the boy, but to bring all the ingredients together a sacrifice must be made. I knew that I was here for the long haul, that maybe I would never leave. The thought troubled me. Alice was waiting, some thoughts of protection stirred when I thought of her. There was a planet to save, god damn it, and here I am listening to a woman who smelt like a fox in heat. Which was surprising, but not knowable; she had cast a spell over me and I could not, did not want to escape.

I stretched my arms, it had been a long night. It was day outside, I rose, rubbed my eyes, peered down the spiral staircase. My room was above hers. The smell had gone and I sensed that Uley had gone too. I climbed down the stairs. Her bed was empty, the bluebird had gone, the cage door left open. I descended another floor. In the room below, the old servant woman was not there. I was alone.

Outside the sky was a thick low bank of heavy clouds stretching to the horizon. The Humber River dirty and surging, so full of methane now through global warming it bubbled up in thick belches; no bird song, just an incessant wind, whipping at the sand dunes and sending sand into my teeth. I walked past the derelict houses, up over a sand dune and down to the beach. The sand was wet. The sea had flooded in, dragged at the beach, reclaimed what was lost during the night, taking it down deep back into the ocean, scoured it like skin from flesh.

There was no one on the beach. I hugged the sand dunes, trying to shelter from the incessant wind. I reached a crumbling bunker left over from the war, a pillbox, its door missing, picked my way over fallen masonry to shelter inside. I peered out through a narrow slit. Stamped my feet to bring blood back to them. There was a hollow sound beneath my foot-stomps. I crouched down, felt around, my forefinger found a round metal ring, I flipped it up, pulled at it. A trapdoor opened up, with a ladder leading down inside. I hesitated, took one last look out through the slit at the crashing sea, and descended, lowering myself through the trapdoor back, and letting it close back down over my head.

At the bottom of the ladder a tunnel led off into pitch darkness. I took out a lighter and flicked it on. The tunnel illuminated in patches; there were markings on the walls, thick wavy indentations coloured with charcoal and ochre in the mud walls studded around with shells. There seemed to be an organization to the placement of the shells, as though the wavy lines were a current that eddied around them, and here and there, larger shells, conches, were star formations or nebulas that the shells radiated out from.

I walked on through the tunnel, picking my way slowly, and then I heard the sound of a deep croaking like the clicking of old bones. Suddenly, underfoot, I felt something slippery, I lowered my lighter to the ground and saw hundreds of frogs hopping towards me. One after another, they covered the tunnel floor, their croaking grew louder, they dropped from the roof of the tunnel into my hair and swarmed at my legs. I stumbled back, trying to shake the frogs free but they stuck to me, climbed up my legs. One on my chest. I was against a wall, put my hand back and hit a mossy, slimy wall. A centipede crawled over my hand. I shook it away with disgust, righted myself and trudged through them, slipping, sliding as they squelched beneath foot, blood and guts spurting out.

I reached the end of the tunnel. There was another ladder down, cold and metal to the touch. I descended and found myself in a cavernous space. I could see glimmers of its width, more markings on the far walls. I stepped forward, and suddenly the ground beneath me gave way and I fell deep into the earth, rocks tumbling after me, hit the bottom. My head smacking flush on a rock bringing a burning to my eyes. As I lay, injured and close to unconsciousness, I heard the low, guttural sound of a huge animal, its feet trampling the earth towards me fast. I passed out and awoke in a different room. A very small room, damp space, no light, just four walls, closed in. I sat up and hit my head on a wooden lid. Pushing at it, the lid opened. I stood, reached for my lighter and got it going. I was standing in a coffin box. The room around me was stone clad and on the walls were bookcases full to brim with fat leather tomes. There was a smell I couldn't identify, acrid, putrefying, curdled milk or meat that had long gone off. I stepped out of the coffin and moved close up to the books. I realized the smell was coming from them. I pulled down a book by its spine, opened it up in my hands. The paper crumpled and folded, curled and floated up slightly, and then down to the floor where it turned to dust. The smell was more intense, more like rotting dead animals; it was the smell of death I realized, like a decomposing body. I dropped the lighter at the recognition of the smell. The flame caught the spine of a book on the bottom shelf. Then the book caught alight. I pulled the book out with my shoe and tried to stamp on it but it sent up sparks that caught the whole bookcase on fire, a wall of flame. I backed away quickly, turned to search for a way out. I found a low door, turned the handle. The door opened an inch, but there was something heavy behind it. The flames crossed the floor and licked at my heels. The bookcase groaned and a shelf fell in. The room filled with smoke. I frantically pushed at the door with all my weight, it shifted another inch. I pushed again, the flames caught my trouser leg. I shook my leg, but the flames ignited and spread further up my trousers. The pain surged through, like some stabbing at my leg, my leg on fire, burning. I heaved and pushed at the door with everything I had. The flames came nearer, there was a crash on the other side and the door gave way just enough to squeeze through. I fell to the floor on the other side and patted my leg with my hand, burning my fingers, but my trousers were still on fire. I pulled off my jacket and smothered the flames, and wrapped the jacket tight around my leg. Smoke seeped from my jacket. I lay back on the floor. The fire blazed around the edge of the door. I could see what had been holding the door shut, a pile of human skulls. I crawled, leg smarting from the burns. I crawled to a place in a dark corner, leaving the skulls behind. I realized the room was much bigger. There was a bed there. I climbed on it. The bluebird flew around overhead. Uley lay on the bed. Her eyes shut. I moved towards her and she took me in. I was entranced, enchanted. I thought that if I lay with her, the spell might break. I would be revealed to myself. All would be revealed. That promise hauled me closer like a ship laden with cargo being drawn into dock by ponies on a length of rope. She turned to me and fixed me with her eyes like the depths of a moor's lake. I made a pledge to stay with her until the spell was broken, waiting until the meteorite hit, the waters rose, the land was destroyed and everyone with it; here was safe, all thoughts were gone, all pain, all purpose directed towards one aim, to please her, to find what I was searching for, to become an opium eater, to list and lay at fallow, to be shipwrecked, but at once as that thought manifested I knew I was leaving, would be gone.

I stirred in bed. Awoke. Underground there were no sunsets, no dawns, but my body felt the pull of a new day. She was not here though her smell clung to my skin. The pile of skulls was still against the door, I could see no other way out. I was hungry, but there was no food, just a plate of grape stalks. I tried to rise but my legs were heavy, and when I tried again I realized my ankle had an iron clasp around it with a chain attached to the metal bedstead. I fell back into the bosom of the sheets, my mind chewing over the past; I thought of a river I once swam in when a boy growing up in Ireland. My mother waiting on the shore. How I dived down deep and found a gold locket in the river and brought it back to show her; she opened it but there was nothing inside. How I fished with my uncle in the same fast-flowing frozen river further down one Christmas and caught my first fish. It had the marks of talons from a bird of prey on its back and we killed it and cut off its head, and inside were maggots we had spread in the river to entice the creature. I thought of a waterfall and a bare mountaintop, a fuselage full of dripping candles where they hid out during the bad times when the wars consumed everything. I thought of the graveyard and my father dropping slowly into a waterlogged hole. I remembered the time I denounced a friend, the friend in it for the money, and we were to split it but they took him away and his head appeared on the large bridge on a spike. If we had to denounce someone, they said, to make the world a better place, to protect the leader, it was only because it had to be so, to fix things. The great project must go on, people must be saved. And yet, here, with the stack of bones, the toppled skulls, something about this place dented my self-importance, told me I was nothing and my mind turned in revolt, trying to reconstruct my psyche. I would stay here whether I liked it or not. I felt like a shot-down pilot, a prisoner of war. I thought of those men and women held captive, paraded through the streets. Of their 'confessions', recorded under duress. I thought of their arms black with torture; it had been a time of pain; 'all pain, no gain', I thought, and smiled at the slogan, like a fitness regime motif, corrupted for use during the war on ideas corrosive to the State.

And then the door was pushed opened and Alice appeared. She smiled quickly, putting a finger to her mouth. Alice knelt and looked at the chains, at me.

"She will never you let you go, you will never find the boy."

"You know about that?"

"She is my mother, god help me."

"Your mother?"

"There must be a key."

Alice stood and searched. There was a large clang overhead, like a metal door had been fixed shut. Alice picked up the pace, looked under the bed, through a debris of things on a small low table; she opened a box and pulled out a key, crossed to me and unlocked the manacles around my wrists.

We left quickly through the skull door, went into the library, thick with ash. Alice pulled at a burnt bookcase; she stepped back just in time as it fell forwards and smashed into pieces on the cold stone floor. She pushed at a door behind, it opened to reveal stone steps leading up. I followed after, and when we reached the top she opened a trapdoor above her and climbed out. I followed. We were at ground level inside the lighthouse. Escape was to the left, through the door I had first entered. Alice walked towards the spiral staircase and stopped as I had stopped, looking at her quizzically.

"Leave if you like, I have business with her. We need to know where the boy is."

I nodded, strode forwards. Alice led the way up through all the floors. Uley's bed, the empty cage, my empty bed, and then a door I had not seen before, hidden in a wall, led to another staircase and then we were at the top. Alice opened a door and the view across the Humber filled the doorway. We stepped, one by one, outside onto a narrow walkway around a huge lamp which swept around and out to sea with a terrific beam we could see in the diminishing light.

"This is where it will happen," Uley said, rounding the corner of the walkway, and pointing out towards the Humber Estuary, the wide mud flats below.

"Why did you chain me up?" I asked.

"To stop you running off, of course."

"Why would I?"

"The future is always in flux, dependent on our actions, on chaos, on random acts of hate and kindness. Emotionally changed events can imprint the mind, and we try to flee from it. But you are adjusted now."

Alice butted in, "You make it sound like you made him some kind of experiment."

"You must look deeper than the surface. Do you ever look into a mirror deeply?"

"I try not to," said Alice.

"What you are looking at, it's not you, it's a reflection, inverted, transposed, a flat representation of yourself," Uley intoned, looking down at the dirty brown mud flats below, "People see a mask, skin, eyes, a flash of teeth. But they do not see beyond. Sight confirms, but does not define. Who are you when you stop talking to yourself?"

"I wish you wouldn't talk in riddles, it makes my head hurt," I said.

Alice wasn't having any of it, "You caused this, you abandoned me. I hate your feeling that somehow you are special. Where is the boy?"

"Your father knows."

"I haven't seen my father for eighteen years."

"You will. He married again after dropping you in at the sad orphanage. Did you good I suspect. He married a full blood this time, and they had a son and the son carries what is needed to stop this. Though he does not know."

"Where is he?" Alice implored, "We can stop this, if that's what you really want to do, or do you want all destruction brought on us, to kill everything because you are some sad broken whore?"

"My part is to direct the focus, to correct, to channel towards obliteration. The mind must be destroyed before it can be rebuilt," Uley said, lost in her thoughts.

"Where is the boy?" I asked.

"Well, can I say, I'm not sure?"

"You can say," I began, "but then, why are we here, why call me to do this, why?"

"You know I remember before this life," said Uley, "I was a kamikaze pilot in the Second World War, I remember the silk scarf around my neck, the smell of oil from the plane, the noise, the fear, the glory, the whirling propeller; I remember setting off, siting the American aircraft carrier, banking down, aiming for it, and then KAPAM!" Uley said, making a gesture with both hands exploding.

Alice rushes towards and slapped her across the face, "Where is the boy?"

"Crossing the Channel. You'll find him in the end, at the beginning. Someone has already been assigned his guide. You must find his father first, Gerad. He is everything if you are to succeed. Drive to Bridlington, you are to meet a man there, his name is Liam, he has been sent to kill Gerad, you must kill him. Then, drive to Lindisfarne, Northumberland. Gerad is there. Your father. There are some who do not want to be saved, who want this Earth scoured of people, so that they can emerge from their hidey-holes free and clean of the unwashed. Not that I wash much these days." She smiled, "You will only know these things in death, John, only then will you see and know what needs to be done and you will gladly give what was not meant to be taken, you will gladly build a new future in the ash of the past. Dream, John, and know what is meant for you."

3

Sami

Two eggs were cracked into a bowl by a pair of hands belonging to Mike. Another pair of hands intruded. Smaller hands, Joe, ten years old. Mike talked to his son, "Want to beat them?"

"Yes," answered Joe.

Mike let Joe beat the eggs. Poured a little milk in. Mike took a slice of white bread from a packet, slowly dipped the bread in the beaten eggs.

"You got to get it on all the sides, and the edges..." said Mike showing Joe, pivoting around and slowly laying the bread into a pan sizzling with melted butter, "And lay it down slowly. Okay, your turn."

Joe picked up a slice of bread, dipped it in the egg, making sure to coat it all over, and slowly laid it next to his father's slice.

At a small kitchen, with a table next to a window, Mike sat with his back to a closet to the boiler. Joe sat with the hallway behind him. Dim London light came in the window. They ate their eggy bread from plates with knives and forks. Mike's phone was on the table. Mike looked at Joe.

"Taste good?" Mike asked.

"Yeah," said Joe.

"You don't want mine?"

"No. Why?"

"Well, you cooked yours, mine might be better."

"Nah."

"Sure?"

"I'm sure. What's wrong with mine?"

"Nothing. I'm just messing with you."

"You're not good with people, are you?"

"No," Mike admitted.

Joe had been building up to ask a question. He looked up from his plate. "Did you kill people?" he asked.

Mike's answer took a while to come, but when he spoke he did it looking Joe straight in the eyes. "Yes," said Mike.

"How many?" Joe asked.

"I don't know."

"You must know." Joe shifted in his seat.

"I don't know," said Mike with regret.

Joe changed tack, "What's it like?"

"Not nice."

"But you had to, right?"

"That's what I was paid for," Mike said with a gruff indifference.

Joe was thoughtful, "It's weird people paying people to kill people."

"Well, not just that," Mike said, straightening his back, "protecting people, rebuilding the country. Getting the bad guys out of town."

"Like a sheriff?" Joe said, smiling broadly.

"Yeah, just like a sheriff."

There was a pause. The real question that Joe has been worrying about asking came out a bit awkward, "What happens after...?"

"What do you mean?"

"What happens when you die?" asked Joe.

Now, a longer wait for a reply. Mike thought it through, "I don't know."

"Really?" Joe made a face.

"No one knows," Mike sort of shrugged his shoulders with the answer, "You been thinking about this stuff a lot?"

"A bit."

"Some people say there's a heaven. But no one really knows."

"Well, what happens, then if no one knows, I mean...?" Joe is exasperated by Mike's loose answer.

"Well, it might just be, well, nothing," explained Mike badly.

"Nothing? Just black ... like sleep, dreaming?" Joe asked.

"No, maybe not dreaming. I don't know. You're just not here anymore."

"That's very depressing," Joe isn't liking any of this.

"But then, maybe there is something?" Mike said with a smile.

"Well there is or there isn't, I mean... You don't know?"

"No," Mike answered, "No one does."

"What? All these people ... all those lives, and no one knows? How many people have there ever been?"

"I don't know, billions."

"What, billions of people, and no one knows?"

"That's right."

"It doesn't make any sense."

"Eat up your food before it gets cold."

Mike finished his plate, stood, crossed to the sink. Mike put the plate down in the sink and turned. He stared at Joe's seat. It's empty. On the table was a plate with the eggy bread on it, untouched, knife and fork either side. Mike raised a hand to shield his eyes, holding back grief.

Mike snapped out of it, walked from the kitchen into the bathroom, on the same level. There was a set of stairs outside, leading up to the lounge. Mike took off his belt, made a loop with it, tied one end around a hook on the back of the door, threw the loop end over the top of the door. He came out, opened the loop on the belt and put it over his neck to form a noose. He buckled his legs and pulled down, hanging himself. The door opened under the weight and Mike swung in with it.

In the empty corridor Mike was hidden inside the bathroom. There was the sound of gasping and then something broke and a crash. Mike appeared with the belt noose around his neck. He took it off. The hook had broken. He went up the stairs, through the lounge and into the bedroom. He came out of the bedroom with a hammer in his hand, came down the stairs, his teeth gritted. A large nail held in his teeth.

He entered the bathroom and took out the nail; there was the sound of a nail being hammered into the back of the door. And then he repeated the process. Belt tied around the nail, over the door, noose over his neck, buckling his legs, the nail held fast, the belt held tight, he swung in the doorframe.

And then —

Mike's phone rang. It rang and rang. Mike got out of the too tight necktie and walked to his phone, looked at it, withheld number, thought of his lousy suicide attempt, laughed, thought of his time as a soldier in the Middle East, laughed at it, thought of his dead son, answered his phone.

Mike sat in his truck on a street that ran along the south English coast on a blustery night. Money was laid into his hand by Jennifer, a woman in her thirties. The bills stopped, then more were added, fifty-pound notes at a time. A crash of waves outside, dimmed headlights illuminated a coastal road ahead. The call had been from Jennifer. A removals job, that was what he did, moving people's things. But this was not that, this was something different. Mike still had his son, Joe, in his mind. He looked up and thought he saw a shadow figure in the cool night air ahead in the gloom of the street ahead. He shook his head free of it, looked back at the money and at Jennifer as she bribed him to go through with it.

The wind was up. The sea treacherous. Waves lashed in. Mike stumbled with Jennifer over a dark beach. There was a scattering of light from a nearby town, up over the sand dunes. Mike's U-Haul truck was parked back up on the coastal road. Mike was thinking, "What am I doing here?"

Jennifer stopped walking, took out a small torch, flicked it on. She looked out to sea. Mike peered out after her, just a dark, black-blue nothingness. Jennifer flicked the torch on and off again. Mike kept looking but could not see anything; then, far out at sea, a light came on, then off. Jennifer strode down to the shoreline. Mike stayed where he was. She flashed her light again. The light at sea flicked on and stayed on, coming closer, rocking with the waves.

Mike could see a boat. People on board. And it was coming faster now, in on the tide. With a judder that shook the ground, the prow crashed into the beach, two people jumped overboard. Jennifer ran into the surf, grabbed the prow of the boat, people jumped out either side, pushed the boat up the beach.

They clambered out. Fifteen of them, all aliens, women, men, children. They called them "Greens", Mike didn't, but then he'd never really thought about it, never really seen them except on TV, and occasionally in the background when he was clearing a house. The law was passed decades ago, no Greens in the US. Of course, there were some here. They used them in nuclear reactor stations, their physiology meant they were immune to radiation sickness. But they kept a tight rein on them. And those in service, house servants, used for domestic duties, were never let outdoors. Then there were the ones who came over the borders. Why? thought Mike. What was here that was so worth all that pain of getting here, plus the worry of being discovered?

One face after another, caught in the pale light, green faces of different shades, some light skinned green, others much darker, but unmistakable. Each was held for a few short moments in the torch beam. Mike stared at them, some bent over, some with a smile, they came towards him one by one as though he was an official. They each took out their card, held it up to him. He swung his torch up, looking at the cards. They were their all clear, to say they did not have the plague. Mike nodded at each of them with a painful smile. Some held a hand out to shake his.

His thoughts intruded on him, what has he got himself into? These people, where had they come from? He took one step back. And his hand raised to shake hands with the new arrivals.

Then, one last face, the face of a boy, aged ten, Sami, green face, smiled. Sami's eyes locked eyes with Mike's. He held his card up diffidently and then he was gone with the rest, herded by Jennifer towards the truck.

They drove. Jennifer in the passenger seat, Mike at the wheel. They worked their way up from Hastings to London along the A21. Quiet at this time of night. Suddenly there was a bang from back inside the truck. Mike flinched.

He pulled up to a green light at a crossroads. A police car flashed through, no sound, just lights flashing. It was as though Mike knew it would be there, like a dream he had dreamt again. The lights changed to red. They waited. Jennifer looked nervously over at him.

The words came slow from Mike, he was used to slowing things down, hell, he savoured the slowness of being right there in the middle of the storm, time ticking like a snail. His background was war, infantry, driving a truck mostly, he was used to the shit, better to sit back and look at it from a distance, as though from the top of a hill. "Let's take the M25, better that way if they have the road blocks up again."

"Okay. Good idea. Where does that take us?"

"Come in through the A3, cross the river at Putney, they shouldn't be looking too hard."

"That's okay, right?"

"As long as you don't look scared, we'll be okay."

"Do I look scared?" said Jennifer, looking scared.

Mike blinked slowly, "Nah." He smiled.

She smiled, realizing she probably looked terrified. They pulled away as the lights turned back to green.

They were parked up opposite a run-down warehouse building near Wormwood Scrubs, the drop-off point. There was a main door to the building, with a light on inside, across the way. Jennifer was trying to decide whether to go in, unsure if the coast was clear. Suddenly they saw the door opening and a man sauntering out, followed by another, this one with a jacket on that said: "Police". They loitered, as cops do. Legs apart, that little bit too wide, one eased his thumbs into his kidneys, either side, stretched his back.

Jennifer opened the door, "I gotta go."

"Don't be crazy," said Mike.

Jennifer turned to Mike, looking, well, just a little bit crazy, "I've got to see if they know ... what they know, I..."

Mike put out a hand to stop her, but she was off out the door, the sudden gasp of air came in and then snapped off shut as the door slammed behind her. Mike was left watching her cross the road towards the cops. He shook his head slow. She was history. He watched it unfold.

Jennifer talked to the cops, they listened; they had their insincere smiles on, their assurances as they escorted her inside, hands under each of her arms. The door shut barely a second, and then banged open, Jennifer running out, twisting free, running into the street, tripping, falling, and they were on her, pinning her to the floor.

One cop reached for his firearm, the other bent with a knee in her back —

That was all Mike saw, he dropped down into the passenger seat. Out of their view. And there he waited.

The cops stared around. Just a dark, quiet street. They hauled Jennifer off towards a car.

Mike drove solo. He had no idea where he was going. He pulled over into an industrial complex of low-rise storage units, desolate. Got out, walked to the back of the truck, unhitched the tail lift, and let it drop. It banged down. The sound echoed off metal everywhere. Mike looked around quickly, but nothing stirred.

Mike unlocked the shutter on the door roll and pushed it up. He poked his head in. Strained his eyes. There they were, the huddled "Greens". Fifteen aliens, blinking in the weak light.

Mike asked, "Anyone speak English?"

A voice from the gloom, the voice of the boy, Sami, "Me."

Sami sat up front with Mike who drove onwards into the night, up through Cricklewood, his way.

"Where are you from?" Mike asked.

"That's kind of obvious," said Sami.

"I mean, where have you been?"

"All over."

"And where are your parents?"

"Mum is dead, Dad, Ireland. I left, he had his own things going on."

Mike nodded a bit, thought of the kids in the streets where he saw service in North Africa, raggedy kids with no home, he had walked right past them; karma just came around to bite his arse, he thought.

"Do you know where she was taking you?" Mike asked.

"To that place, back there, I guess," said Sami.

"But after?"

"No."

Mike sighs.

"How long do we drive for?" asked Sami.

It was a good question, and Mike had not got much of an answer.

They were back at Mike's place. He ushered all fifteen of the aliens in, one after another, they collapsed on his sofa, motioned to ask if they could use the toilet. He shut the door behind the last of them. He made coffee, there was a crowd around him.

He opened cupboards, pulled out what little food he had and handed it to them. There was a lot of thanks, some sullen looks, like, is this what I paid all that money for?

The women tucked up a line of kids in Mike's bed. Mike sort of smiled, looking in from the doorway. There were pillows and sheets on the floor in the lounge, one guy in an old sleeping bag of Mike's. An alien man got up from the sofa as Mike came in, motioning for Mike to sleep there. Mike waved him back down and the guy stretched out on the sofa, put his hands behind his head and beamed, best seat in the house.

Mike sat at the kitchen table and ran a hand over his face. He looked up. Sami was sitting opposite — how did he get there? In Joe's seat. Like a Ninja sneaking in. Mike rubbed sleepiness from his eyes. Sami had the green skin of the aliens that had come here. Had landed one June and turned the world upside-down until it no longer became strange, more it became a new 'other' to blame for the plague and the desperation of men in high places making lots of money out of people in low places with no volition. They put the aliens to work in the nuclear reactor stations because they didn't feel radiation.

"New family?" said Sami.

"Like hell!"

Sami smiled, he knew the score, he had looked around, lonely guy just got upgraded with the full force of having to give a shit about a whole bunch of people.

Mike relaxed his face, he thought, just relax. Didn't someone say that once, just relax, it makes everything better?

"You're a hell of a kid," said Mike.

"My name is Sami. Now you can't kill me."

Mike narrowed his eyes, then he laughed. Like the boy was a hostage and he had just personalized himself to Mike, the jailor.

"You're all right ... Sami," said Mike.

"You do this all the time?"

"Do what?"

"Take people from boats?"

"No. First time."

"How's it going?"

"What do you think?" asked Mike.

Sami was stone faced. Then smiled. "Not well."

"Look, I do removals. Furniture, wardrobes..."

"Wardrobes?"

"I move people, my name's in the book. But she didn't say at first what it was, just someone had let her down. Then she tripled the money, and..."

"You said yes."

"I said yes."

Mike's phone rang. Withheld number. He answered. It's Jenny. He grabbed a piece of paper and a pencil.

Kent vineyards, farmlands, orange groves. Sami sat up front with Mike. It was still night. Mike marvelled at now that England had got hot they could grow most anything, of course no one abroad wanted to buy it. The plague had started here, everyone knew that. No one wanted tainted produce, plague fruit.

Mike turned down a gravel track towards farm buildings. Narrow road, flanked by a lima bean crop, dark and foreboding in the gloom.

The back of the truck was parked up at a wide entrance to a processing plant. Lights on inside. A middle-aged white guy with a white goatee beard stood with a clipboard as a line of the aliens, men, children, women, bleary-eyed, piled out of the back of the truck and entered the plant.

White guy ticked off the number and held up a hand to say, that is enough. Mike checked a piece of folded paper and walked back to the cab where Sami sat.

Another farm. Just after dawn. Mike unlocked the back of the truck, pushed the door up. They were parked up next to a tractor and an expanse of white-topped cotton bushes. There was a young farmhand in a baseball cap, with his hands in his back pockets, chewing gum. Mike stared at him without a smile, and not without a little malice. The door clanged open. Four "Greens" jumped out. Sami climbed down from the cab and joined Mike.

"The boy?" the farmhand said.

Mike took out the list.

"No."

Sami looked up at Mike and smiled.

Mike and Sami walked along a sidewalk in a rough part of North London. The truck was parked a little back down the street. It was early morning, no one around. But Mike is aware of the threat of being reported.

"I can go there alone," Sami said.

Mike checked the piece of paper, looking up at the house numbers. It was a mixture of run-down, old, two-storey terraced houses and vacant lots, plague buildings in rubble.

"I'll walk you there," said Mike.

"It's okay." Sami stopped and held out his hand to shake. "It's been nice to know you."

"Likewise." Mike shook his hand.

Mike smiled at the formality of the exchange. Sami looked at the cracks in the pavement, the rubbish in the gutter.

"If it's not right … in there…" Mike began.

"Not right?" said Sami.

"If it's not the right place … Jenny may have given me the wrong address." He held up the paper.

"Oh."

"So, I'd better come along."

"Yes."

They reached the right house number and entered through a low gate held on by one hinge. There was a cracked hole in the corner of a downstairs window, patched up with cardboard and tape. Dog shit on the path. The front door was peeling with paint. Mike rang the doorbell, looked over at Sami, who was putting a brave face on it. A short, unshaven, pot-bellied man in his forties, Dougie, opened the door a foot. Looked them up and down.

"Yeah?" Dougie said, not nice-like.

"Jenny sent us," said Mike.

"Don't know her."

"She likes walking on the beach at night?"

Dougie looked up and down the street quickly. Opened the door for them to come in.

A filthy corridor, rooms off either side. Mike noticed a padlock and clasp over the corner of one door. Stairs up ahead, a kitchen yonder. People were moving about in the kitchen, but kept out of view. The whole place reeked of hopelessness.

Dougie went back, into the kitchen, shouted a few words. There was a scuttling of footsteps, like cockroaches when the light comes on. He returned with a dirty envelope, handed it to Mike.

Mike opened it like you would a turd wrapped in an old banana skin. It was stuffed with fifty notes.

"It's all there," said Dougie.

Mike had not expected payment for the boy. Guilt flooded him when it came down to this. He looked around, properly this time. Looked up the stairs. Back to Dougie.

"What's he going to be doing?" asked Mike.

"Helping out."

"Helping out with what?"

At the top of the stairs, on the landing, an alien boy with a green face and body appeared. Mike looked up, noticed him; a young teen, wrapped in a towel around his waist, terrified, he scooted out of view quickly. Mike looked down at Sami, whose brave face had cracked. Mike handed the money back to Dougie.

Sami

"We're leaving," Mike said to Sami and took him gently by the hand, leading him towards the front door.

"No way," Dougie said.

Dougie approached from behind, grabbed Mike's shoulder, pulling him back. Mike turned around, a hand went straight up to Dougie's throat, caught him suddenly with a grip tighter than a vice.

"There's no reason, for you," Mike said. He squeezed tighter. Dougie's eyes bulged, Mike backed him up against a wall. The envelope of notes dropped to the floor. Sami tugged at Mike's shirt. Mike looked down at him. Sami was shaking his head no.

Mike released Dougie, who dropped to the floor gasping for air. Mike left with Sami, a protective arm around his shoulder.

Mike drove. Sami was in the passenger seat. They were in Mike's car now. The van too obvious. There was silence for a bit. Mike was thinking.

"What's it like, where you came from?" Mike asked, though he regretted asking the moment his mouth had opened.

"Not fun," said Sami. "I mean ... wait, you mean, where I grew up, or home planet?"

"Both."

"Well, I have no idea about home planet.... And I grew up in the squalor of a reactor centre. That's what you want to hear?"

Mike did not know how to reply.

"Actually, that was just part of it. We moved around a bit. How long you were married?" asked Sami.

"How did you know I was married?"

"We 'Greens' have special senses," said Sami mysteriously.

Mike looked at Sami like he might believe him, he had heard stories about the aliens. Sami pulled a face, like, you really believe that shit? "Ring on your finger, and your place doesn't look like a woman's been there for years."

"Ten years."

"Okay, so, you just stopped being together?"

"Something like that … yes."

"Why wear the ring?"

"Don't know, just haven't felt like taking it off."

"Oh." Sami looked out the window, "What about the boy in the house, what's going to happen to him? We should have done something to help him."

"You saw that?"

"Yes. We tend notice each other, our lot…" he put the last two words in his own inverted commas.

"Is it true about 'Greens'? I mean, your people, they can read each other's minds, or…?"

"No, that's bullshit."

"I wish I knew what some people thought, it would help," said Mike a little dejected.

"You should call the police, that's my magic projection."

Mike made a call at a payphone in a service station on the M4 at Membury. Sami sat in the car in the car park, sloping down in his seat whenever a car drove past. Mike talked on the phone to the police. He hung up, returned to the car and got in. "I told the police about the boy, if that will do anything."

"Thank you."

Mike did not say any more, but a thought crossed his mind, the same thought that he had back at the house. What were they using that boy for? He shook the thought from his head, it was horrible to contemplate.

Mike took a turning off the M4 and took the Bath Road. Sami stared out the window.

"Why come to England?" asked Mike.

"I have to get somewhere, here. Can you drive me there?"

"Where?" said Mike.

"The North. Who are we going to see, anyway?" asked Sami.

"I thought there might be someone who can help you."

"I know, you said, who?"

Mike and Sami stood outside a visitor centre in Avebury looking at huge sarsen stones in the distance. Mike's car was parked up, a few people milled about. Sami ate an ice cream.

"Want to go inside?" Mike asked.

"What's inside?" said Sami.

"Tourist stuff."

"Not really. I saw this before, somewhere else." Sami looked at the view of standing stones, "Why bring me here?"

"Don't know. Thought you'd like it."

Sami bite into his ice cream, got brain freeze, clutched his head.

"You get that too?"

Sami nodded, in pain, open mouth full of ice cream. Mike laughed at him. Sami spat the ice cream out because he was laughing too much, "It's not funny."

Mike drove through the suburbs of Bristol. He was looking for a house. Sami was withdrawn. He knew something was coming and he was not going to like it.

"You have many friends?" Sami asked.

"Some," Mike replied, "Why?"

"People need friends. Someone to look after them."

"I do fine on my own."

Mike missed the point of the conversation. His social ability was pretty much down to zero. Sami was angling for help. Mike was oblivious. He pulled the car in and they got out and walked to a door.

Mike rang the doorbell. They were outside a semi-detached house on the southside of Bristol. He rang again. Another doorbell that Sami did not want answering. No one came. Mike wandered off to the side of the house. Sami followed. There was a side gate. Mike tried it, but it was locked. Then the front door opened and Mike scooted back, Sami in tow. On the front porch was Linda, roughly the same age as Mike. They recognised each other immediately. Linda's face kind of fell.

"Hey, Mike," said Linda with lacklustre.

"Hey," said Mike brightly.

Mike stopped on the front lawn, kept his distance, like he had been told to before.

"How are you doing?" Mike asked.

"I'm fine, Mike. How are you doing?" she said it in a gritted teeth way, with a smile. And under that there a deep sense of pity, a lot of pain and a smorgasbord of guilt and unresolved issues.

"Who's your friend?" she asked Mike.

Sami perked up at this — "friend" — that was what he had been implying all along, whilst hoping Mike would help him get to where he needed to go, not this pitstop, leading, who knows where?

"This is Sami. He's ... he's new to here."

Linda's eyes narrowed.

"New? How new? He's vouched for right, has papers, registered?"

Sami's face falls.

"Can we talk inside?" asked Mike.

Linda took a moment to think about that. And nodded, slightly.

Mike and Sami sat on high stools around a breakfast bar in Linda's house. Linda busied herself with making coffee, opening the fridge, pouring juice for Sami, anything not to have to look Mike in the eyes.

Mike was talking, "So, it was just a thought really..."

"What was?" Linda asked.

"You ... I mean ... it's probably not the best thought, but..."

"Go on. You said, 'you', what about me?" asked Linda.

"I thought ... did you ever think we might...?"

Linda stopped in her tracks, milk in hand, fridge open. She looked at Sami, "Do you want to play outside?"

"What's outside?" asked Sami.

"There's a swing in the garden," said Linda.

"A swing?"

"Yes, you know, you sit on it, and swing?"

"I know what a swing is. It's for kids."

Mike smiled. Sami got off the stool. Wandered to the kitchen door and into the garden.

"Smart kid," Mike said.

Linda put the milk away, holding in the anger, "You want to run that past me again, the 'we' part?"

"I was thinking..."

"That's not a great idea —"

Mike cut her off, because, damn it, he's angry, mostly at himself, "Okay. Look. It was a stupid idea. You can't replace ... it's not that we can ever ... I know ... but ... it was a crazy idea, you're right..."

Mike got off his stool, he walked to the front door, kind of forgetting about Sami. Linda came out from behind the breakfast bar.

"What are you playing at, Mike?"

"Just, you're a good person and you could take care of him."

And then she realized, his back to her, his head down, that maybe he was crying, or ... she softens a bit, "Where's he come from?"

"I picked him up from a boat."

The information made Linda stop mentally in her tracks for a second, "So, he's an illegal alien?"

"Yes."

"What are you still doing with him?"

Mike turned around. He had not been crying, or if he had wiped any evidence away, "I got suckered in, then I got stuck with him."

"You thought I might want him? Really? Mike, I've got two kids and another on the way. Look."

Linda turned to the side, she had a bump on her belly.

"But don't say ... don't say 'we', please, it hurts, and don't think this Sami could replace Joe, please."

It was Linda's turn to turn away, and when she did she had tears in her eyes, and Mike knew it for sure, and he felt just about the worst individual to ever walk the earth.

Sami stood in the garden. He looked at the swing. He looked back at the house. He could see Mike and Linda inside. Sami knew that bad news was coming. They both did not want to help. Sami sighed. But then, he had a job to do, so ... He saw a board in the fence that had been pushed aside. Probably a cut-through kids had made. He looked back at the house. Mike and Linda had moved out of eyeshot. They would have talking to do. He took the short cut.

Sami walked along a pavement next to neatly mowed lawns of terraced houses or pebble chips. All was peaceful. He walked past the high hedges of a park, past the ruined buildings of plague houses, a burnt-out library, a shopping centre. He turned a corner.

Sami walked along a pavement next to a row of shops, hardware store, barber shop, boarded-up businesses. A pickup truck passed by, a guy stuck his head out of the window to get a good look at Sami. The guy had a toothpick in his mouth, unshaven, he shouted, "Dirty, stinking, alien."

Sami crossed the street, walked past a gift shop. He stopped in front of "Brown's Shoe Shop". He looked at the shoes in the window, then down at his own raggedy shoes. Entered the store. Sami idled behind a rack of shoes. Up near the counter, the store manager, Ralf, late twenties, in an oversized suit and bum fluff moustache, spied him. Came striding down to Sami.

"Get you anything?" said Ralf.

"No. No money," answered Sami.

"Right."

Ralf folded his arms.

"Except this," said Sami.

Sami leant down and rummaged in his sock, pulled out a dirty fifty-pound note, crumpled up, handed it to Ralf, who looked at it with disgust.

"What can I buy for this?"

"Your parents around, or you from one of those reactors?"

"Both dead."

"Oh ... Look, what do you want?"

Ralf handed Sami back the fifty.

"Shoes like Michael Jordan."

"Not for fifty quid."

"Well, fake ones then."

"We don't sell fake shoes here, son. Now where's your host, your manager, you're not supposed to walk around unaccompanied?"

"I'll take my business elsewhere," said Sami with a dignified air.

Sami turned to leave.

"Hang on. You registered?"

Sami did not look back as he made for the door.

"You legal? Hey!"

Sami got outside and took running down the street. Ralf had his mouth half-open. Sami ran for his life all the way down Broadwalk, fists pumping, heart racing, shoes slapping the sidewalk. At a junction, a car door opens, right on cue, right in the way and the guy with the toothpick got out his truck and stopped Sami with a giant hand across his chest.

"Where you going, kid?" asked the toothpick guy.

The guy looked up and saw Ralf running towards him. He looked down at Sami.

"You a thief, alien?"

Sami shook his head no.

Mike drove with Linda, searching for Sami. He was frantic, holding the worry in. Mike took corner after corner. He hit Broadwalk. Pulled over suddenly.

Linda hit the dashboard, bracing with her hands, "Whatcha doing?"

Mike pointed up ahead. There was a crowd of people. A police officer taking Sami by the shoulder and leading him to a cop car, putting him in the back seat, shutting the door.

"Damn it," said Mike and punched the steering wheel.

Apple orchard, Somerset. Two apples on a tree branch. A hand went in and picked them, one by one. This was Rufus, a man in his seventies. He put the apples in an apple cart. Dropping them softly.

In a barn, a cider pressing works, lit by one bare bulb, Rufus loaded apples into a large slit barrel below a wheeled press. He heard something, stopped suddenly. Rufus walked into the back reaches of the barn, into the gloom; steadily, slowly, hands reached into a small, wooden cupboard.

Rufus spun around, pointing a handgun, his hand shaking (it had been a long time since he had pointed a gun at someone, but he remembered the day clearly). The thin light of the bare bulb revealed Rufus's face, weathered and unshaven, white beard and piercing eyes — he pointed the gun at a silhouette of a figure standing in the doorway.

"Dad?" Mike was incredulous at his dad for even possessing a gun, and for pointing it at him.

Rufus blinked a little. Mike stepped into the light.

"What you doing with that?" Mike asked.

Rufus had no answer, lowered the pistol. He was kind of ashamed now, what was he going to do with it, shoot someone, his own son?

Rufus and Mike sat opposite each other at a wooden kitchen table in a large kitchen of a rickety old farmhouse. Between them was a jug of apple juice, two glasses filled with juice.

Rufus continued his examination of his son, "Why go see her?"

"It wasn't the best of ideas," Mike answered.

"No," Rufus said, shaking his head and drinking his juice, "Where's the kid?"

"Don't know. Thought you might."

"How would I know?"

"Connections?"

"That was a lifetime ago. Anyway ... what you planning to do? Kidnap the boy? He's probably down in some centre in Cornwall, you gonna kidnap him, drive him to London? When then? Already you've crossed county lines, you've got illegal alien transportation charges on you ... what then, keep him locked up for ever? For all you know the kid's got an asylum application in, if they're still doing those, I think, and if not, then they'll have him on a bus to a port, on a ship for Europe, or drop him mid-voyage in the sea. Don't look at me like that, they do these things, saves on paperwork. It's all private firms, they make a fortune out of it."

"I knew you'd know about it."

"I don't know shit. And I sure as hell don't want to get involved. If I make a few calls, and my name pops up, they're gonna be down on me like a ton of bricks."

"You won't help?"

"You're better off leaving this alone."

Rufus got up, busied himself with washing his empty beaker.

"The very least, you can put me in touch with someone who can help?" asked Mike.

"You're not listening to me ... you never did..."

"We're going there again?" Mike sighed.

"It's your life, but decisions affect. Joining up was never what we thought was right for you."

"You're bringing Mum into this as well?" asked Mike.

"No." Rufus went silent. Mike looked at the wooden kitchen table top.

"You need anything. Money?" Rufus asked.

"I'm good."

"Want to stay for a day or two, I could use a hand with the harvest?"

"I'd better get on," Mike said.

"You know, you can't just adopt a kid, not an alien kid. He'll have to be schooled, what are you going to do then?"

"I was home schooled."

"There was a reason for that," said Rufus.

"Yeah," Mike was pretty sarcastic.

"It's hard to keep a low profile."

"If you get involved with terrorists, that's what happens."

Mike knew he was provoking him, he was just annoyed his dad would not help him.

"We were never terrorists. We protested, mostly against the kind of stuff this kid is up against, repression, the Nationalists, the land being ripped apart..."

"You killed a bunch of people."

"Never proven."

"Why do you think I joined the infantry?" Mike asked.

"No idea. You were a damn fool?"

"I wanted out."

"From what?"

"Everything."

They decided to leave it there. Another word and it was Armageddon. There had been fights between Rufus and his wife that Mike had overheard growing up, the constant moving from town to town. Teenage rebellion that forced Mike to oppose anything his father stood for ... it was all there in the implied, "Everything."

Rufus just nodded in acknowledgment that he might not have always been right. Mike lowered his eyes, he knew he may have hurt his father.

Sunlight filtered through the tops of the forest trees surrounding the farmhouse. Mike waved from the window of his car and drove off. Rufus watched from the porch of the farmhouse. Rufus had mixed emotions. But he let them go.

Rufus's eyes narrowed as he saw Mike's car slow. Then come a halt. Rufus jogged up to the car. Mike rolled down the window, "I thought I had enough petrol to get to a station," Mike pleaded.

"There's not one for fifty miles. I've got a can in the shed," said Rufus. Mike nodded slowly. Rufus thought about it and sighed.

"Okay, I'll take you. But only if we take my truck, and I drive."

Mike broke into a smile. Rufus was still not sure.

Mike drove Rufus's pickup truck. Rufus was asleep, a weathered peaked hat pulled down over his eyes. They were on a coastal road, the Bristol Channel to their left. Sun glinted off the tufts of sea. Rufus woke, "What the hell are you doing?"

"You said drive," Mike said.

"I did? When?"

"Just about when you were nodding off at the wheel."

"Well, I'm awake now."

"It's fine, I'll drive. It's all I did in the army."

"I thought you shot people?"

"They were shooting at us, Dad. They shot, we shot back. They blew us up, we blew them up. But I was mostly driving. You can't drive and shoot."

"You ever kill anyone?" Rufus asked quietly.

"That's the first time you asked me that, and yes, from a distance. Don't know how many. You get into a firefight and it's not like the films, you just fire away and hope for extraction, don't know who you've hit."

"I'm sorry you had to go through that, son."

"My choice, it's what the job is. It's not sticking plasters on children."

"No."

"Mum had the hard job."

"She was an angel."

"You never minded her going off, saving people in some distant place?" asked Mike.

"Never. People needed her."

"Sorry to talk about her. I never get to."

"It's fine. She's always with me."

"You never wanted to marry again?"

"I had the best times, I'm happy with that. Besides, who's gonna want an old man with a bunch of apples."

Mike thought for a second, "A chutney maker?"

Rufus gave him a long sideways glance.

Mike continued, "Nah, you're right. Not a chance. You could have added, cantankerous old man."

"Comes of having a son that never listens. Makes you sore in the head," said Rufus.

"Proves my point. No class."

"Your soldier friends ever bring up your talking when you were driving them around?"

"Never."

"Maybe they'd all gone deaf from the shooting."

"Maybe."

Rufus readjusts his cap and pulls it down over his eyes, "Let me know when we are in Bristol."

"What guy are we going to see?" Mike asked.

"Just a guy," Rufus said and closed his eyes, end of conversation.

Mike wanted to talk more, that was about the longest conversation he had ever had with his father. He looked over at his dad, saw his eyes closed under the shade of the cap, was about to say something but decided against it.

Mike sat in a café eating an all-day breakfast with a chocolate milkshake, the seat opposite empty. He stared across the road at a row of shopfronts with offices above. He was in the backstreets of the old part of Bristol, near St Nicholas Market and Corn Street. A door opened oppۅosite and Rufus emerged shaking the hand of a man in his seventies, white flowing hair, crumpled suit. Rufus joined Mike in the café, took a seat at the Formica table.

"He said it's going to be hard to find a kid with just a first name, but he'll try," said Rufus.

"Okay."

Rufus smiled to himself, "Good to see Issac."

"You were gone a while."

"Catching up on the old days."

"The old battles?"

"He always had our back," said Rufus.

"But you always paid him, right, so...?"

"You got to take that chip off your shoulder sometimes, son, not everyone's out to get you, he worked pro bono."

"Well, yeah..." Mike thought about it.

"You're drinking a chocolate milkshake, how old are you?" Rufus said laughing to himself.

Mike's phone rang. It was a withheld number. Mike answered. He mostly listened, made a few "Yeahs" and "Okays" and hung up. "You were right, he's in a detention centre in Cornwall," Mike said.

"Who was that?"

"Jennifer. The woman who hired me for the pickup."

"And sold them on."

"Yeah. Cuts both ways though, doesn't it?"

"What do you mean?" asked Rufus.

"At least they find work."

"And the guy with the kid?"

"Hmm. Yeah, that worried me," Mike said.

"Why's she telling you where he is now?"

"I think she's worried the kid might lead immigration back to her."

Mike bites into a sausage.

"So, what's that got to do with you?"

"Wants me to keep my mouth shut, there's money in it."

"Will the boy talk about you?"

"Hard to say."

"Well, he doesn't know anything, it's not as if you took him home with you," said Rufus confidently.

Mike looked up guilty.

"You didn't take him home with you, right? He doesn't know where you live?" asked Rufus.

Mike chewed slowly, looked his father in the eye with a childlike expression, caught in the act.

"You know you'll be charged with alien trafficking," said Rufus.

Mike shrugged.

"It's a serious crime. I asked Issac, though I didn't think I'd have a halfwit for a son. It's twelve years of jail time, and half a million pounds. You got a half a million pounds?"

"Guess we go to plan B, then."

"You listening to me? What's plan B?"

"We go get the kid, that way he said nothing to no one."

"You got some shrapnel in your head from the war? We're not busting some kid out of a detention centre. I'm going to get you a lawyer, Issac probably, and an alibi if I have to."

"What's my alibi?" asked Mike.

"You were safe and sound with me."

"Hard to believe."

"You making a joke out of this?"

Mike snapped out of his joking around, "Look, I can do this on my own. I'm going to get the kid out. I owe him something. I owe me something. Call it retribution, or resolution, or whatever, I got to save one kid, like I didn't before."

"That was not your fault," said Rufus.

"It was someone's fault," said Mike.

Mike pushed his plate away, stood, laid down a handful of money and walked out, leaving Rufus to chew over the words left hanging in the air.

Mike stood next to his father's truck. Rufus came around the corner, took out his truck keys. Stopped. They looked at each other for a few seconds.

Mike broke the impasse, "Guess, if I'm gonna do a walk out, better have my own ride."

Rufus smiled, "I'm not going to let a son of mine go it alone. Let's go down and take a look. Maybe I can go in, see what the kid's about?"

Mike nodded.

At an Immigration Field Office in Canary Wharf, Jennifer stormed out of the doors in to smog filtered sunlight. She turned around and gave a vigorous two-fingered salute to the offices. A drone swooped overhead, stopped, and spoke in a robotic voice, "Flagrant use of violent hand gesture, fine two

71

thousand pounds." Jennifer turned to the drone and gave it the same salute, the drone spoke again, "Flagrant use of violent hand gesture, fine two thousand pounds."

"Fuck," shouted Jennifer.

The drone: "Flagrant use of violent vocal gesture, fine, two thousand pounds."

Jennifer stepped to the kerb and hailed a taxi. Her hair was stuck out in strands after sleeping a night in the cells and being interrogated. One taxi drove on past. Another stopped. Jennifer jumped in.

Jennifer made a call on her phone to Mike as the taxi cut through London streets. She stared out the window at crumbling buildings, vagrants lining the streets, one with a torn and limp placard, saying, "When?"

Mike stared out the window of the pickup truck as Rufus drove south on the M5.

Rufus spoke, "There is another option, Issac said."

Mike looked over at his father.

"You could sponsor the boy. If that's what you want? It means doing the paperwork, waiting. But he could come live with you, while he waits for his application to process."

Rufus looks over at his son, unsure whether Mike is really ready for another child.

"You think I could really...?" Mike didn't finish the question and Rufus didn't help him.

"We'll have to stop for the night, the centre will be closed for visits anyway by the time we get there," said Rufus.

In a roadside motel room Rufus was propped up in bed with a pillow against a headboard, reading a paperback with half-moon glasses. A bedside table and lamp sat between twin beds. From the bathroom the sound of ablutions. Cars sped by outside. Mike appeared at the bathroom door.

"Did you clean your teeth?" Rufus asked.

Mike smiled, "Yes, Dad."

Rufus went back to his book.

Later, Mike was on his single bed, sat propped up against the headboard, same as his dad, who licked a finger and turned a page of his book. TV on, sound turned down. Mike looked at his hands. He rubbed a palm with the thumb of the other. "I've never been able to look at them straight," he said.

"What's that?" Rufus asked absentmindedly.

"My hands were on the wheel."

Rufus looked over. He changed the subject, "You used to be good with your hands."

"That didn't solve anything, beating on people."

"That's not beating, son, it's a fine art, you won belts, you —"

"That's not what I'm talking about — I had my hands on the wheel and I…"

"I know, I know. But it wasn't your fault. How many times have I told you … the guy was drunk."

"I never looked at my hands, for a long time, kind of ashamed of my own damn hands."

"Get some sleep," Rufus said, "Put your thoughts down the hill, they ain't who you are. Just thoughts, let them snake off down the hill, like you have no business with them anymore."

The subtext, what Mike was thinking, was even if he took on Sami, could he really look after him, what if it happened again? Mike thinks about what his father said, "Put away your thoughts." It was good advice, he conceded. Besides, the kid had other plans anyway, who was he to play dad?

Rufus folded the top corner of a page and put the book away, took off his reading glasses and folded them up.

Mike reached for the lamp. Rufus looked up at the TV, "Wait a minute," he said.

Mike stopped. Rufus reached for the remote control, turned up the volume. The screen showed a huge crater in New York State, the voiceover said there had been a hail of meteorites falling over the Eastern Seaboard in the US, causing devastation in some parts.

"That's strange," said Rufus.

Alien Shelter 4, Zennor, Cornwall. A canteen line, alien kids aged eleven to seventeen, each with a partitioned tray. Food was dolloped in to it by servers, a sausage, dollop of mash. It was long line, Sami was at the back. The boys were housed in an old metal building with high industrial ceilings.

Sami sat down on a bench at a table with a line of boys. He wore a grey T-shirt, blue shorts, trainers, and socks, as did all the boys. Sami ate, trying to keep his head down, not looking anyone in the eyes.

In a games room, at the shelter, there were no games. An empty space where a TV and games console used to be, installed for an official visit from a Party member, taken away after. A small group of boys played an improvised game of football with a white cue ball from a pool table which had no other balls and one broken cue stick.

The ball skittered around the polished floor. Sami sat in a corner, out of the way. Suddenly, the cue ball flew Sami's way. He got up and followed it as it bounced off a chair leg. It came to rest in the gully of a wall, where a long black sheet had been hung from the ceiling.

Sami got down on his hands and knees to fish it out, lifting the black cloth. The cue ball was wedged against a metal panel. Sami pulled at the ball but it stuck firm, he pushed back the panel and a crack of daylight shone in from outside. Sami plucked the cue ball out and returned it to the boys, placing it into the waiting hand of a tall boy with slicked back hair who smiled sickly and then slapped Sami across the face.

"You're our ball boy now."

Sami held back tears but didn't back away, he just stood there glaring at the boy.

"You want something? Another one?" the boy said.

Outside the shelter, later, Sami joined in with a basketball game on a court adjacent to the building. There was a high chain link fence around the court. There were too many players and Sami didn't get a touch. Staff in jackets with "Security" written on the backs stood all around the edges of the court, each armed with rifles.

Suddenly, one of the boys took off, running towards the link fence and scaled it. The security guards rushed over, but the boy was up and over, dropping to the other side. He ran, heading towards a small copse of trees in the distance.

Sami stood next to a guard, Jose, tall guy, mid-thirties, with an earring and a neck tattoo. Jose didn't seem that interested in the runaway.

"You not going after him?" Sami asked.

Just then, another guard raised his rifle, aimed, and fired. The shot rang out, echoing off the buildings. The runaway fell, hit in the back, dead to the ground.

Sami sat on his bed in a dormitory. There were four other beds in the room, no door and no ceiling, just open to the high metal struts of the roof. He was alone, sitting next to a small, neat pile of regulation clothes, two T-shirts, three pairs of socks, three pairs of underwear, one polo, a pair of jeans. The dead boy's clothes. On the pillow next to the clothes was a teddy bear with a red bow around its neck.

Jose, now dressed in jeans and a button-down shirt, came into the room, "You have a visitor, a sponsor."

"What?" Sami said, surprised and happy.

"They can get you out of this place. Make an application for you. Saves us trying to find you someone. All good."

Sami smiled.

"I'll take you there," said Jose, "I double up as a case worker, killing's not my game."

Sami nodded, stood and followed Jose. He walked side by side with Jose, along a corridor with a Vasiliac quote, the present Prime Minister of England:

"Good luck, you'll need it." — Prime Minister Vasiliac

At the end of the hallway there was a boy banging his head against the wall repeatedly. Jose stepped in, held him back from the wall, "Hey, hey, come on, son."

The boy looked up at Jose, "I want out of here."

"Don't we all," said Jose.

Sami blinked a few times.

Jose opened the door to an interview room and Sami entered a small, empty room with a table and two chairs.

"I'm going to have to deal with the boy, you'll be okay?" asked Jose.

Sami nodded. The door shut. Sami sat. He waited. A smile crossed his lips. It must be Mike coming. The door opened and Jennifer was ushered in by Jose who smiled at Sami and shut the door, leaving them alone.

"Hi," said Jennifer.

"Why do you want?" asked Sami, irritated.

Jennifer sat down across from Sami, "I'm going to get you out."

"I don't want to go."

"I'm sorry about the man, it was a big mistake."

"I'm not going with you."

"I can get you away from here."

"And do what?"

"Get you a job, somewhere to live. That's what you want isn't it?" asked Jennifer.

"I need to go north."

"You can go wherever you like."

Sami knew this was a lie.

Tricky question came up for Jennifer to ask, she painted on a smile, "Did immigration question you?"

"Yes."

"What did they ask you?"

"About how I got here," said Sami.

"Did you talk about me?"

"No."

"Good boy. And we want it to stay that way."

"Who's 'we'?"

"Just a figure of speech, but … you'd better keep your mouth shut, kid."

Sami looked down at the desk, and then up at Jennifer.

"Why do you do it?" he asked.

"It's a business, of sorts."

"Funny business."

"Yeah, well, there's not a lot of opportunity for people like me," said Jennifer.

"Why?"

"I got a bit of a past on me, that's all. But I'm not a bad person. I got you here didn't I?"

"Here?" Sami looked around, incredulous, "Nice work."

"Into England. New life, new start."

"You just want the money."

"Money helps."

"I don't want to go with you."

"Well, you can stay in here then. You want that?"

"No."

"But if you mention anything to anyone, then the people I work for won't be happy, know what I mean?"

Sami was worried now, "Yes."

"If you change your mind, I'm staying at the Sunrise Hotel. Just tell the case worker."

"Okay."

Jennifer got up and made to leave, she stopped by the door, "Remember, not a word. We have people in here that can get to you, understand?"

Sami swallowed hard. Jose returned, opening the door, poking his head in, just as Jennifer was about to leave, "Everything okay?"

"Sure," Jennifer said. She exited. Sami looked stricken.

The outside of the shelter looked like what it was, an old warehouse, metal box with a pitched roof, no windows, car park out front. Rufus's pickup truck was parked up. Rufus at the wheel, Mike next to him. They looked towards the door of the shelter, Jennifer emerged.

Mike pointed her out, "That's her. Jennifer. The woman who set it up."

"What do you want to do?" asked Rufus.

"Follow her, see what she's about. Then go back for the boy."

"Okay."

Rufus started the engine.

Rufus watched Jennifer's car up front, it took a turn, then another, past a few shops and houses. They followed. Rufus slowed a little as Jennifer turned onto an A road. They drove along the A road following Jennifer until she pulled in to a car park to a roadside hotel. A sign out front said Sunrise Hotel. It was a low, ugly building in grey and brown. The sun was setting. Jennifer parked up in front of a hotel room which led directly from the car park. Rufus parked a little away.

They watched as Jennifer walked to a door of her hotel room and entered.

"What shall we do?" Mike asked.

Suddenly, Rufus saw the door to Jennifer's room open and Dougie, the guy from the house, come out, "Look," said Rufus.

"That's the guy, with the kid," said Mike.

Mike and Rufus watch as Dougie walked along a path beside the rooms and entered the front office. He was there thirty seconds at most. He returned with a bottle of whiskey and a bag of ice. They watched him enter Jennifer's room.

"Want to go in?" Mike asked.

"They're drinking," said Rufus, "let's wait until they're boozed up a bit, catch them off guard."

"Okay."

"Open the glove box."

Mike opened it, reached inside, took out a pistol. Mike looked at his dad, "Really?"

"Give it here."

Mike passed the gun over. Rufus shoved it in his jacket pocket, "Never know."

"What about me?"

"There's a tire iron under the seat."

Sami was in bed, under the covers. It was night. Boys were sleeping in the other beds. Lights were out. Sami stared up at the high ceiling. Took a look at the sleeping boys. Gently pulled back the covers and slowly sat up. He was fully dressed.

He tiptoed towards the door, stopped, a boy stirred. Sami waited, nervous, the boy turned over and went back to sleep. Sami exited.

Sami crept along the polished floor of the hallway. He heard something. Stopped dead. Footsteps coming his way. He flattened himself against the wall. He was standing in front of another picture of a president, this time Abraham Lincoln. The quote next to the picture read, "A new nation conceived in liberty and dedicated to the proposition that all men are created equal."

A torch came on. It slowly panned across the wall where Sami was standing, the light hit him, but he was lost in the picture of Lincoln. The torch switched off and the footsteps went away.

Sami sighed in relief. He carried on down the hallway. Reached the far end. A door to the outside blocked his way, he tried the handle, it was locked. He turned back. Gently taking each step, trying not to let his trainers squeak. He entered the games room.

Sami crossed the room, past the pool table. He made his way to the far corner. He got down on his knees. Felt around under the black cloth. Pushed at a panel. It opened. He pushed again, opened it up further, but it was hard to hold open. Sami let it be, went back to the pool table, lifted the broken pool cue gently and returned to the panel.

Using the pool cue as a lever, he edged the gap wider. Sami slipped his legs through, lay the cue down, pushed with both hands at the panel and squeezed out.

The basketball court was in darkness. Sami ran quickly across the court to the chain link fence. He stood still, his back against the fence, looking back at the building. Everything was okay, no sign of life. He looked up at the top of the fence, high above him and turned to climb. Foot over foot, each wedged into the links, he grappled his way up until he was at the very top. It was high up there. His stomach turned over as the fence swayed.

Sami needed all his strength to pull himself over, only just managing to hold on as he toppled to the other side, his feet trying to find a foothold. He slipped his shoe into the chain link fence and it held firm. Sami eased himself down, one step at a time, hand over hand, until he could jump the last few feet to the ground.

Sami was free. He took one last look at the shelter and ran for all his life was worth over the rough field. He crossed a road and reached a line of trees. Pushing through low branches he stumbled down a slope to a riverbank. Sami looked both ways. It was dark here, only the lights of a bridge some way down the river. He followed the riverbank along, climbed up the bank. He crossed the bridge, looking where to go next.

Suddenly, headlights appeared at a distance, coming towards him. Sami was scared, did he hide or try for a lift? Suddenly, a loud siren went off in the shelter, a piercing whine that announced an escapee.

Sami stuck out his thumb. The car, an SUV, pulled to a stop. The window rolled down. Inside was Linda, in cargo pants and a polo shirt with the name of a research station on it, hair tied back. She looked Sami up and down.

"Can I get a ride?" asked Sami.

"Where to?"

"North."

"Is that siren for you?"

"Yes."

Linda thought for a split second, "Get in."

Linda reached over and opened the car door. Sami smiled with relief and climbed in.

Linda drove fast. She concentrated on the road as she took a corner. Then another, "I've never been a getaway driver before."

Linda looked over at Sami, he was bunched up in the corner, frightened.

"I'll get you out of here. I hate those places."

"Me too."

In Jennifer's hotel bathroom the bag of ice sat unopened in the bathroom sink. The unopened bottle of whiskey stood above it. In the bedroom, Jennifer sat nervously in a chair with a gun pointed at the door. Dougie was on his phone.

He hung up. Dougie walked to the door, looked through the peephole, "Okay, they're coming. If they come through the door, shoot."

Dougie picked a gun up from the bed, crossed to the bathroom, levered himself up on the sink, opened a small window and climbed out.

Dougie dropped down the other side. He ran around the back of the hotel until he was at the car park. He watched Mike and Rufus walk towards the hotel door, ran behind a few cars until he was behind Rufus's pickup truck and waited at the back bumper.

Rufus had his gun in his pocket, his hand on it. Mike had the tire iron held low down. They stopped at the door. Looked at each other. Rufus knocked on the door. They waited. Nothing.

"They must be in there," said Mike.

"We should have checked around the back," said Rufus.

"Should I break down the door?"

Inside the hotel room, Jennifer sat in the chair, her hands shaking, gripping the gun tight, ready to fire, but terrified. A knock at the door. She tightened her grip.

"Maybe we can smoke them out another way," said Rufus.

Rufus turned and walked back to the pickup truck, Mike followed, "What are you thinking?" asked Mike.

"I hate to involve the police, but it might be the only way. I'll say I heard a woman screaming."

"Okay," said Mike, though he was a little unsure.

"I need to ditch this gun first though. Wait in the truck, keep an eye on the door, I'll find somewhere to stash it."

They reached the truck. Mike got in. Rufus carried on walking towards a low hedge. Mike settled into the seat and put the tire iron on the floor. As he sat back upright, Rufus came into view through the driver window, backing up with a gun pointed at him. Rufus opened the door to the truck. Dougie took the gun out of Rufus's pocket.

"Get in," said Dougie.

Rufus got in. Dougie walked around the front of the truck holding his gun pointed at Mike and Rufus inside. He opened the passenger side door and got in alongside Mike, holding the gun at Mike's hip.

"Drive," said Dougie.

"Where we going?" asked Rufus. Dougie didn't reply. Rufus started the engine.

Inside the hotel room, Jennifer gingerly got up from the chair, walked to the door and looked out the peephole. She saw Rufus's pickup truck, with them all inside, drive out of the car park.

Research Institute. Early Morning. Sami ate a bowl of cereal at a white Formica-topped table with benches either side. He was in a small cafeteria with plants on shelves all around. A door and windows looked out to a collection of plants in pots under a greenhouse.

Suddenly, he heard raised voices. He stood, crossed to a door with a glass panel, sneaked a look through into the other room. Linda and a man were arguing. Sami couldn't hear. He put his ear against the door. The man was talking:

"... we can make a lot of cash, we can hold him here, maybe open him up, we've got the equipment, Christ, we are scientists, look at the possibilities ... look at the profit, what we could find..."

Sami ran, headlong, out of the door and into the bright sunlight, burning across a valley. Sami ran down a long curving road, away from the research institute. Green hills in Somerset, narrow roads. Sami heard a car and burrowed deep in a tall hedge. Linda drove past in her SUV looking for Sami. He watched her drive away into the distance.

Sami headed down the road, flanked by high craggy escarpments either side, as sweat poured off him. He'd been walking for hours and was now at Cheddar Gorge. He saw a motorbike, an old, rusty, small engine two-stroke bike, parked up next to a steep hill. He went to investigate.

The bike had an ignition key in it. There was a bottle of water on a rope slung over the handle bars with a plastic drinking tube inserted in the cap. Sami looked around. No one was about.

He grabbed the bottle, held it up and squeezed it, drinking from the tube, wiped his mouth with the back of his hand. He hooked the rope back over the handlebars. Sami looked around again. He climbed on the bike. It had no gears, just a stop and start. Sami looked up at the crag above. No one. He turned the ignition over.

The bike spluttered and then came to life. He gripped the throttle with one hand, the other on the brake, and revved the throttle. It thrummed with power. Sami kicked the bike off its stand and then, suddenly, a girl's voice in anger: "Hey! Hey, what the hell are you doing? Get off my bike!"

Sami looked up. There was the silhouetted figure of Ekta, a scrawny thirteen-year-old girl standing up high on the rock face. She had long hair, loosely held back, old, baggy jeans and T-shirt. Sami turned off the ignition key, wheeled the bike back onto its stand. Ekta scrambled down the rock face. In her hand were three golden eagle feathers. She was a scruffy, tomboy, bossy, angry, dirty, kind of girl.

Sami was on the back foot, caught trying to steal her bike, and Ekta had every reason to be angry. She confronted him, in blazing fury, half running to him.

"Get away from my bike!" shouted Ekta.

Sami got off the bike super quick, backed away, then took another two large steps back. Ekta checked over the bike.

"Whatcha doing? You're a thief. You're a filthy snake. I hate thieves."

She saw the bottle on the rope, grabbed it, looked at it, looked at Sami.

"You drink this?"

"Um, yeah," said Sami.

"This is my water, my bike. Get away. Now!"

Sami took another step back.

"Right away!"

Ekta dismissed him with a flick of her hand, got on the bike, overly checked it, as though Sami had contaminated it, tried the ignition. The bike started up.

Ekta shouted over the engine noise, "You shouldn't touch nothing that's not yours. You can get killed for that. Dead in the ditch, snake."

Ekta kicked the bike off its stand. Grabbed the rope and bottle, strung it across her chest, revved the throttle and pulled away sharply, speeding off down the road, a cloud of grey exhaust choking out behind. Sami blinked a couple of time, the smoke drifting to him. He coughed.

Walking on the hot road for an hour, sweat still pouring off him, Sami had enough. He sat down by the side of the road. The heat of the day was well upon him. He lay back. The sun overhead was a burning crucible. He shut his eyes, put an arm over his eyes. A plastic water bottle hit him and then rolled away. Sami reacted like a rattlesnake just bit him.

"Drink," Ekta said. Ekta stood over him. Sami grabbed the bottle and sucked on the tube. "Enough." Sami stopped drinking.

Ekta gunned the bike, with Sami holding her around the waist, and they rode away.

A SUV passed on the other side, Linda at the wheel, she saw Sami and braked.

Sami shouted over the bike noise to Ekta, "Turn somewhere."

"What?" Ekta shouted back.

"There's a woman after me."

Ekta was furious, "What?!"

Ekta saw a turning up ahead, a steep side track down into a valley. She took the road, bumping down the steep track. Sami looked back. He could just see the SUV slowly turning around further down the road.

"We have to hide," shouted Sami.

"What?"

Ekta skidded the bike, braking hard, drove off the track, through an opening, in to a field of beet, bumping over them. Skidded again, stopped the bike. They looked back up the hill. The SUV had stopped at the top of the hill. The door opened and Linda appeared, looking down at them.

"I'm sorry. The police are coming. I'm sorry," shouts Linda.

Linda got back in her SUV and backed up. There was the sound of the SUV driving away. Ekta turned to look at Sami, "Friend of yours?"

Sami shrugged.

Pitch black. No window. Basement. Sound of a padlock being unlocked on the other side. A metal door creaked open and a shaft of bright light hit Mike's eyes. He grimaced. Dougie came in holding a gun pointed at him. In his other hand, a digital camera.

"Get up," demanded Dougie.

Mike stood, stiffly. Dougie backed up out of the cell, "Out here."

Mike walked into a corridor, light flooded in from glass bricks above. There was another metal door opposite to his, padlocked shut.

"Stand there." Dougie motioned to the back wall of the corridor. Mike backed up to it, still blinking in the light. Dougie raised the digital camera to take a picture, "Smile!"

Mike didn't smile. Dougie took the picture.

Ekta drove the bike with Sami on the back into Stanton Drew, a small village south of Dundry. There was a pub, the Druid's Arms, and a few houses.

Ekta took a couple of turnings and entered a street of suburban houses. She gunned the bike forwards, picking up speed, then suddenly clamped on the brakes, skidding the bike to a stop outside her house. Cut the ignition and let Sami get off, before kicking the bike back onto its stand.

"My place," said Ekta.

Sami nodded, looked at the house. Nodded again.

Ekta smiled, "Don't look scared, we are nice people, except for my dad. He's an ogre."

Ekta, with Sami in tow, entered the house. They walked through the empty lounge and headed out through the back patio doors to the garden.

Ekta's father, Taza, tall, longish hair, was dressed in jeans and a check shirt. He was cooking a batch of meat at a barbeque.

"Hey!" said Ekta to her dad.

"Hi," replied Taza.

"Got them!" Ekta reached into the breast pocket of her shirt, pulled out the three eagle feathers.

"Have any trouble?"

"Nah, mother was out the nest."

"Who's this?" Taza pointed with his tongs at Sami.

"Friend," said Ekta breezily.

Taza looked sternly at Sami, who was a bit terrified.

Ekta looked at Sami, then at her dad, "I told him you were an ogre."

"Well, I am. At night I eat children. Want a steak?"

"Um…" Sami stammered.

"Have a steak," Ekta encouraged.

"Um yes."

Taza smiled. Flipped a steak over.

"Finest child meat," said Taza.

Sami looked at the meat, looked at Taza, who realizes the kid has had a tough time of it recently. It was written all over Sami's face. And a "Green" to boot. He smiled.

"I'm kidding, you know. Grab that bread."

Taza pointed to a loaf of sliced bread in a bag on a table near Sami.

Sami handed the bag to Taza.

Ekta went inside the house. Her father calls after her, "Better get ready."

"I know, I know," Ekta shouted back.

Taza looked at Sami, "Have you had any problem with her?"

"No."

"You're a bad liar, which is not a bad thing. She's headstrong ... truth is, she's a pain in the ass. But a glorious one."

Sami smiled.

Taza took out a piece of bread, lifted up a steak, laid it on the bread, stuck another slice on top, handed it to Sami, who took a bite. It was hot! Taza laughed. Sami set to work on it hungrily.

"Want some ketchup?"

Sami shook his head no.

"I don't really eat children. And this is not pure blood," said Taza shaking the ketchup bottle, "Well, not mostly." Taza winked.

Sami held the steak sandwich up, lifting the bread lid, Taza squirted a line of red sauce on the meat.

Mike walked up a flight of concrete steps, with Dougie behind him, gun in hand, leading from the basement to a door which Dougie told him to open.

"Take a right," demanded Dougie.

Mike turned and pushed open another door. Mike stumbled down a few steps outside. They were in a walled compound with a large yard. Parked up was a truck. Same type as Mike drove.

"We got them here as well," said Dougie with a smile, "Get in."

Mike walked to the truck, opened the door and climbed in to the driving seat. Dougie walked around the bonnet and got into the passenger seat.

From where Mike was sitting, he could see the back of the house. A guard walked around a corner carrying a sub-machine gun, finger on the trigger.

"Here's your passport." Dougie handed it to Mike who opened it. A photo of him in the basement had been inserted into a fake passport. "You'll need that to get into the docks."

"Where are we going?"

"Portsmouth."

"You coming along?" said Mike.

"Don't like my company?"

Mike stared at Dougie, expressionless.

"Where's my father?" asked Mike.

"Safe, safe and well. As long as you do as we say, he'll be a happy man. But..." Dougie drops his smirk, "you fuck around. Tip your hat to any law enforcement, fancy yourself as Jean-Claude fucking Van Damme? Then I put a bullet in his head. Understand?"

"I'll never get through security with this," Mike held up the passport, "It's shit."

"They never check properly."

Dougie handed Mike the keys to the truck.

"Drive. And don't be an arsehole."

Mike inserted the key and turned over the engine.

Stanton Drew stone circle under a full moon. A small gathering of local people, some with yellow ochre on their faces mined from the Mendip Hills. The circle was a hundred and twenty-four yards across with twenty-six stones, each between five and fifteen feet high.

The moon sat on the saddle of Dundry. A bonfire burned in the middle of the circle. Three dancers, with headdresses made of deer antlers, each with a bag tied across their chests with red sandstone dust, threw handfuls of the dust at three young women, one of them Ekta.

Sami and Taza sat outside the circle watching. The three girls, including Ekta, were covered with grey clay from the nearby River Chew. They each had a large shell strapped to their forearms, they wore deer skin dresses. Each had a golden eagle's feather in their hair.

There was drumming and chanting, the girls showing no emotion. They drank from a drinking tube connected to a bottle so as to not touch water directly; it was forbidden to wash, otherwise the girls would bring rain.

The girls danced, a sacred dance, around the bonfire as a shaman carried a bowl of blood collected from the Cove where he'd just cut the throat of a goat.

Sparks flew off the bonfire and drifted up in to the sky.

Dougie said to Mike, "Don't fuck it up. Or Dad's dead." Dougie thinks he's funny. Dougie's a dick.

Mike pulled up to a security stop, rolled down the window and handed his passport to a guard, who took a look at it, handed it back and looked at Dougie's passport. He waved them on.

Mike drove through large metal containers lined up in rows and on to the far edge of the docks. He parked with the tailgate backed up next to a shipping container. Dougie got out with Mike and they walked to the container. Dougie opened the container door and waved out a dozen or more green skin alien people who jumped into the back of the truck which Mike had lowered the tail lift for, and ducked into the dark interior.

Mike helped Dougie move furniture from the container into the back of the truck forming a wall to hide the aliens, wardrobe, sofa, chest of drawers. Mike took a look at it, poor really, they would be discovered with so much as a lazy search.

Mike headed to the cab and climbed in. Dougie got in next to him.

Mike pulled up at the security post. Dougie handed his passport which was checked over quickly by the same guard, Paul. Mike did the same. Paul checked it, up and down.

"What's in the truck?" asked Paul.

"Furniture," answered Mike.

"What furniture?"

"Furniture, furniture."

Paul stared at him.

Mike tried to fill the ominous silence, "You know, sofa, wardrobe ... the client wants to move north."

"Move north? You mean emigrate?"

"They fancied a change of scene, got sick of the drugs and crime."

"Oh?"

"Yeah. They want England to be great again."

"I see. Well, that makes sense. If a little nationalistic."

"Eh?"

"Takes more than a lot of chanting to make something great."

"Yeah."

There was a pause as Paul held Mike's passport for way too long, staring at it, then looked back at Mike.

"Terrible photo," Paul said and handed the passport back to Mike. He took it, his hand shaking.

"On your way," said Paul.

Mike drove away with his heart in his mouth.

Back in the compound, the truck parked up, furniture was thrown from the back of the truck by two of the guards with machine guns. Mike stood to one side as the two men dragged the furniture out. Alien people jumped down from the tail lift.

Dougie rounded them up, holding a clipboard in his hand, and pointed to a few different SUVs that were parked around, directing them into each.

Mike looked the house over, the door he came out of, a line of glass bricks in the ground in the corner showing where he was held, wondering if his dad was down there in the other cell.

Mike walked down the concrete basement steps, followed by Dougie with his gun held at Mike's back. Mike reached the door of his cell, looked over at the other metal door.

"Dad!?"

"Shut it," demanded Dougie.

"Son?" Rufus's voice was faint, coming from behind the metal door. Dougie gave Mike a shove in the back, pushing him into his cell.

"I'm across from you, Dad. Are you okay?"

Dougie slammed the door and padlocked it shut. Mike was in blackness.

Rufus's faint voice came again, "I'm fine. How are you, son, are you okay, what did they do to you?"

"Everything is good, they've just got me driving —"

"Shut it," Dougie shouted, "One more word, I'll execute both of you, one in front of the other."

The sound of Dougie's footsteps left, up the concrete steps and then a door shut. Mike took a deep breath. He put his mouth close to the hinges of his metal door, "I'm sorry," Mike said.

"It's not your fault," replied Rufus. Then there was silence as each gathered themselves.

Rufus began, "I've proud of you."

That just killed Mike, tears in his eyes, "I love you, Dad."

"I love you too, son."

Early morning. Ekta and Sami climbed Dundry Hill, walking a ridge up to the top. Taza was a little behind. Ekta spoke to Sami, "The power of the hill is right at the top. Water used to cover everything, with only the hills showing. All the spirits that were floating around at the time, the only place for them to go was the top of the hills. That's why there are spirits in the hills, and that's where the best herbs come from. There are two worlds, the spirit world is the real one."

Taza caught up with them, and then went ahead. He stopped, bent down to examine a shrub.

"What did you find?" Ekta asked.

"It's not right. We'll look on further," replied Taza.

They were at the top now and climbed a long barrow named Maes Knoll Tump, stood on the top looking down on Bristol. Ekta was off pulling up a root. Taza talked to Sami, "People have been coming here a long time, claiming it as theirs. You can't own the land. It doesn't work that way. It's like they took a shit on our world and didn't even wipe their ass."

Sami laughed.

"People came here, claimed it, that tree, that rock, that piece of earth, from there to there." He pointed out over the view, "They brought in slaves to work the land. People like you. Then when the slaves grew restless they blamed the plague on you. Why did you leave where you came from? What did you bring with you? They made people think you were something to fear. Fear leads to terror, surely, step by step."

Sami said, "I just want to get home."

Taza looked at Sami, "You're right, of course, what am I talking about?" he laughed, "Don't listen to me."

"But I have something to do first," said Sami, "I have to go north. Can you help me?"

"I'll do my best, but I have to be here for the rest of the ceremony first."

"How long does it last?" asked Sami.

"Three days."

Sami nodded, "I haven't got that long."

Home now, Ekta was at an old computer, keyboard, and monitor, tapping out a search. Sami sat next to her. Ekta's mother and two brothers, one a baby, were in the background of the living room, playing.

"No last name?" Ekta asked.

"No," replied Sami.

"He works alone?"

"I think so."

"There are quite a few removals firms in London, um … Mike, Mike … Mike's Movers?"

"Maybe."

"Hang on. His website is poor … ah, that him?"

Sami looked at the screen. There was a picture of Mike.

"Yes."

"There's a number you can call. You sure this guy is okay?" asked Ekta.

"He tried to help me, maybe he can again."

"You know, you could always stay here."

"What about your family?"

"Mom? Can Sami stay with us?"

Ekta's mother, Nancy, came into the room with the baby on her hip.

"How long?" asked Nancy.

"Forever?" replied Ekta.

A pause, Nancy thought about it, looked at Sami, "If you have no place to go, you are welcome to stay with us."

Sami smiled, "Thank you, I have something I have to do. But, thank you."

Dougie descended the concrete stairs to the corridor with the two cells. He had two bowls of food in his hands. He put them on the floor, took out his gun, unlocked the door to Rufus's cell and pushed the bowl inside. He took a tie out of his trouser pocket.

In an office upstairs, Dougie sat on a swivel chair, leaning back, feet on a desk covered with paperwork, a bottle of whiskey, a glass, a table lamp. There were shutters at the windows letting in a little light. Dougie picked his teeth with the edge of a credit card.

A phone vibrated. He could hear the sound but couldn't locate the phone. He searched around, finding it in an overflowing waste bin.

He answered, "Hi. No, he's not here right now, I'm a friend of Mike's. Can I take a message? Oh, yeah, hi Sami. Where are you? I'll get Mike to ring you back."

Dougie listened and wrote down an address, "Sure. I'll pass the message on. How do you spell that?"

Dougie wrote down the name of the village, hung up, took out his phone, dialled. It connected, "Hey, get yourself to Stanton Drew, it's a place in Somerset. The boy is there." He hung up.

Mike drove the truck, Dougie next to him, gun in hand. They were on a twisting back road, sun glaring down. Suddenly, there was a bang from the back of the truck. Then another, hard thumping on the metal panel separating them from the hold.

"We have to stop," said Mike.

"Keep going," replied Dougie.

"They'll be roasting. The refrigeration system isn't working."

"We have a timetable."

"You want dead workers?"

Dougie thought about it for a second, and then nodded. Whatever that nod meant, it didn't matter, Mike pulled the truck over anyway.

The tail lift was down. Ten, young, alien women sat on the tail lift of the truck and on the side of the road, passing around a bottle of water. Dougie looked nervously up and down the road.

"That's enough," Dougie said to the women drinking.

"They need more water," Mike said.

"Let's get going."

The women got back into the hold of the truck.

Mike drove through well-manicured suburban streets of Salisbury. Dougie looked at a piece of crumpled paper he was holding.

"Up here," Dougie said, pointing to a house.

Mike pulled over, then reversed back in to a drive.

Mike stood by the tailgate. Dougie was in the cab. A young woman, Isaba, with pale green skin, early twenties, climbed out of the back of the truck. She was the last one, the truck was empty. She was attractive in her looks and poise.

At a side door to the house, a middle-aged man in a tie, shirt and neat parted hair, coffee cup in hand, watched Isaba come towards him with a stern look tempered by a sleazy grin. Isaba turned to look at Mike, "Come back for me."

"What?" Mike said.

"Don't leave me here," said Isaba.

"I..."

"Please."

The man at the door stepped aside as Isaba entered, sipped his coffee, keeping his cold hard stare on Mike, and then shut the door and locked it from the inside.

Mike climbed back in the cab. Dougie handed him Mike's phone, gun pointing at his hip, "Call the last number received," said Dougie.

"Why?"

"Your friend Sami called, we're going to see him. Tell him we'll meet him at midnight."

"Leave the boy out of this."

"He's not for me," said Dougie.

"What do you mean?"

"That little call to the police? That boy had nothing to do with me. I get orders, same as you. Any boys he wants he gets. He likes them green."

"Who?"

"He's in London, runs this dog show."

"What's his name?"

"Why?"

"Well, when I kill you, rescue my father and get the boy back, I'd like to pay this man a visit."

Dougie laughed, "You've got some balls on you. I killed your father this morning. Choked him with a necktie. He didn't put up much of a fight. Nobody does."

Dougie raises his gun to Mike's head, "Make the call."

Mike looked down at his phone. He was in the worst place possible. There was no reason to suppose Dougie was telling the truth, but then? He had lost his dad through his own stupid fault. His thumb scrolled through to the last received call. His face betrayed his broken heart. He was done. Part of him had been amputated forever. Whatever had been would be no more, in the depths of grief, in trauma, there was no turning spot.

Jennifer drove on an A road through a green valley in Somerset. Her car was a mess. She was a bit of a mess, as well, looked like she hadn't slept properly for days. She needed coffee. She turned into a truck stop café.

Jennifer sat in a booth nursing a coffee. Behind her, on another table, a boy named Tommy, aged six, played with a small collection of toy cars and trucks. He drove one truck with his hand along the back of Jennifer's booth making a truck sound. Jennifer looked around.

"Hey," said Jennifer.

"Hey," replied Tommy, wiping his snotty nose with the back of his hand.

"Nice truck."

"I got it for my birthday."

"You've got a lot of cars."

"Lot of birthdays."

"How old are you?"

"Six."

"Okay. Not that many then?"

"I had them before I was born."

Jennifer raised an eyebrow. Suddenly, Tommy's mother, Darlene, came rushing over, back from the bathroom, her hair starched with recently applied hairspray.

She looked at Jennifer, "Whatcha doing?"

"Sorry?" Jennifer said.

"You talking to my boy? Without my permission."

"I was just —"

"You have no right. Hey!"

She turned around to the rest of the café, "This woman's talking to my boy." She turns back to Jennifer, "Don't you dare talk to my boy, or I'll cut ya. Now get going. You hear?"

Jennifer got up, embarrassed by the commotion and the staring eyes of the other customers, and exited quickly. She shook her head as she walked to her car, coffee cup half-empty left behind on the table top. She looked at the sky, something dark and foreboding was up there, clouds bunched up tight and black.

Night time. Sami and Taza sat, watching the ceremony. Ekta is in her deer skins, eagle feather and shell amulet. She has a stick with ribbons on, a healing stick, she anointed people in the crowd one by one. The fire licked up in flames and smoke. Taza looked at his watch, "We'd better go."

"How long does it go on for?" Sami asked.

"Until sunrise."

"And then Ekta is a woman?"

"One more day, and then, yes."

"Will she still be friends with me?"

"Yes."

Taza smiled, realizing the worry Sami has, "Of course. This is a special ceremony. There is something coming, we have been warned."

"I know," said Sami.

Taza looked at him, nods, as though he knew all along the boy was somehow special. "We'd better go."

They get up and walked off.

Sami waited with Taza, roadside, against a long wall outside the Druid's Arms pub. There was no one about, everyone was at the ceremony. Taza looked up at the sound of a distant truck. It turned into the road.

Taza looked at Sami, "If you don't want to go, then it's fine. You have a family here."

"Thank you. But he can take me to Spurn Point."

"Well, I can do that, if you want."

The truck pulled up a little way down the street. It was dark. Hard to see who was inside. Taza was wary.

"Wait here," he said to Sami.

Taza approached the truck. He could see just one figure in the driver's seat. He got to the truck window. Mike rolled down the window.

"Get away, now!" shouted Mike.

Taza recognised the threat, with Mike's words imploring him to run. Inside the cab, Dougie, who had been laying down across the passenger seat, sat up, pointed his gun at Taza and fired, hitting him square in the chest.

Sami's saw the gun blast, watched Taza falling backwards, hitting the ground. Sami was rooted to the spot for a second, and then turned as if in a dream, and ran. The truck pulled off and headed towards Sami.

Sami ran around a corner, crossed a street. He looked back, the truck turned the corner after him. Sami jumped over a low metal fence, falling over the other side, got up and ran between houses. The truck raced past behind him and turned a corner with a squeal of brakes, then turned again heading towards Sami as he appeared from the other side of the houses on to the street.

He ran away from it, down a street. The truck followed him. But there was nowhere to run, no turn-offs, a narrow road, high hedges either side. The truck caught up with him. Headlights hit him full beam.

Mike was driving, Dougie had his gun pointed at his head. Mike got close to Sami.

Dougie's voice was low and demanding, "Don't kill him."

Mike suddenly slammed on the brakes. Dougie hit the windshield hard. Mike turned and punched Dougie square in the nose, it exploded with blood. Dougie dropped the gun. It clattered into the well of the truck.

Sami stopped, looked back at the truck. He saw Mike punching Dougie. Sami ran back to the truck. Then Dougie reached down and grabbed the gun, pointed it at Mike's head. Sami ran to the truck. Threw open the door.

Sami shouted at Dougie, "Don't kill him, please!"

Jennifer saw a sign post for Stanton Drew and made the turning. She drove down a narrow road.

Her phone rang, she answered it. She listened.

Jennifer replied, "Just coming in to Stanton Drew."

She listened again, "Okay. See you there." She hung up.

Suddenly she saw something in the road, a body. She pulled in, jumped out. Jennifer rushed over to Taza, who was still alive, groaning. A bullet hole in his chest, blood-soaked clothes. Jennifer looked around, no one about. She pulled out her phone and dialled 999.

Sami and Mike were in the back of the truck. Driving somewhere, they had no idea where. It was dark inside. Mike had his arm around Sami, together they sat up against a side wall.

"I don't want to die. I can't," said Sami.

"You won't," said Mike, holding him tighter.

The truck took a turning and bumped over a cattle grate.

"I'm scared," said Sami.

"Me too," said Mike. He looked down and smiled at Sami.

"What happens?" asked Sami.

"What do you mean?"

"When you die?"

"You go on a journey," Mike was sure of himself this time.

"Where to?"

The truck rumbles over gravel.

"Some other place."

"Where's that?"

"Everywhere. Don't worry, I'll be with you."

Mike grabbed Sami's hand, held it tight. The truck came to a stop.

The truck was parked up in front of an old abandoned farm. Dougie jumped from the cab of the truck.

Jennifer's car pulled in and parked up, headlights facing Dougie's headlights. She got out. Dougie walked over to her, a gun in the back of his waistband.

"They're in the back of the truck," said Dougie, "take the kid to London, I'll deal with the removals guy."

"That guy in Stanton Drew, you responsible?" asked Jennifer. "He alive?"

"Don't know."

"We've got to tidy this up."

"There is another solution."

"What?" asked Dougie, his tone unaware.

Jennifer pulled a gun out of her jacket. She pointed it at Dougie. Dougie shifted his hand behind to his gun.

"How's that a solution?" asked Dougie.

"Beats being an arsehole all my life," replied Jennifer.

In the back of the truck Sami and Mike suddenly heard the sound of a gunshot. Then another. The fall of a body. Footsteps on the gravel, coming towards them. Sound of the tail lift of the truck being flapped down, someone jumping onto it. The roll door was pushed up, to reveal a figure in the doorway, silhouetted. Dougie.

"She's dead," Dougie raised his pistol.

Sami held tight on to Mike. Dougie squeezed the trigger. The gun jammed. Mike jumped up, ran at Dougie who was pulling at the trigger, shaking the gun. Mike caught him right around the midriff, propelled him off the tail lift and they hit the concrete hard. There was shock on Dougie's face, as though none of this should be happening, and then the shock was wiped away as Mike cascaded punches down in to his face. Over and over.

Sami came to the edge of the tail lift. Mike demanded the name of the man in London who had ordered all of this, had ordered Sami. Dougie told him, and where to find him.

Mike got off Dougie, found a big, flat stone, crossed back to him. Sami turned his face away. Mike smashed the stone down on to Dougie's windpipe. Dougie gurgled and died.

The compound. Morning. Mike drove up to the gates with Sami next to him. They were back at Dougie's place. The gate was unlocked, the padlock lay on the thin soil. A silence filled the cab. Mike turned the engine off. Sami felt the sorrow Mike felt.

Mike could barely bring himself to get out of the truck. What lay inside the house was something he couldn't face. Sami knew it. He missed his mother. He missed his father. He felt like he'd become a vehicle for other people's ambitions. Why did his mother move to Lisbon? Or did his father send him and her to the one place where he knew Sami would be close to the centre of the priests of his home planet? It was all too much of a coincidence. And now, his mission, to get to Spurn Point, to have the whole thing revealed was too much for him. Two sides of Sami were at war. His duty and his need for love, for his family. He had watched his mother slip away. His alien mother who had only wanted to stay alive to protect him. He watched as Mike climbed out. He wanted to go with him but Mike put out a hand, told him to stay where he was.

Mike walked through the gate. The place was deserted. The guards had fled, the trucks and cars had gone, nothing except dry dust underfoot and the scorched sky, not a cloud in sight. Sami watched Mike walk into the house. He couldn't stay in the cab, got out, stopped at the gate, rested his hand on the rusty bars. He heard something from deep inside the building, a banging. He ran to the back door of the house, opened it, saw a door to his left open and slowed his pace, went through it and down the concrete stairs to the basement.

At the foot of the stairs he stopped. Along the corridor he could see an opened door. A crowbar on the floor and the remnants of a padlock and chain. He could hear sobbing. He didn't want to go forward, but he did. He opened the cell door and saw Mike on his knees on the floor, cradling Rufus in his arms. Sami came closer, a deep sickness in his stomach. Mike turned to look at him, and then back at Rufus, who was alive, weakened, barely breathing, but alive.

London. An open plan office, row of bikes stood up in a rack on the wall, rows of desks and laptops and large screen monitors. Tony, late forties, bobble hat, coloured socks, boss of the company was on his laptop, focused. Shut it. Got up, half smiled at a guy half his age and exited the office.

At a Mexican food truck down the street, Tony ordered tacos. Mike appeared next to him, ordered as well.

Tony propped his plate of food on a concrete plinth. Mike joined him. They ate. Mike didn't look at Tony. Then he glanced his way.

"Dougie sent me," said Mike.

"What's that?" said Tony.

"Dougie sent me."

"I don't know a Dougie."

"Sure you do. Anyway, I've come all this way, with the boy."

"No idea what you're talking about."

Tony picked up his food and moved on.

Tony ate standing by a bench. Mike came over and stood near to him.

"Dougie said, if there was a problem to say there wouldn't be any more deliveries. Said he was getting fed up with his end of things, know what I mean?"

"Look, pal, I don't what you're talking about, so, you want to leave me alone?"

"Up to you. Plus, Dougie said he's not opposed to going postal on this ... bringing the police in."

Tony folded his plate in half with his half-eaten food inside, walked over to a large bin, dropped it. He headed off. Mike dropped the rest of his food in the bin. Tony walked fast. Mike caught up with him, got in step.

"He's in the truck. You wanna see?" asked Mike.

"I'm going to call a cop."

"Really? You want to do that?"

"Yeah."

"Thing is, Tony, I've got a delivery to complete and Dougie doesn't like failure, so why don't you come see the merchandise and then I'm out of here. Unless you want the police to know about all your vices."

Tony stopped, looked at Mike directly, "What do you want?"

"Just come see the boy, then I can get a sign off on this and we can stash him away somewhere for later."

"Where's the truck?"

In a nearby basement car park Mike led the way with Tony in tow. They passed a line of cars. In a far corner was the truck.

Mike pulled down the tail lift, unlocked and pushed up the roll door. Tony stared into the gloom.

"Dougie told me where to find you," said Mike, "before I killed him."

Tony swivelled his head around to look at Mike in shock. Then looked back at the truck as Sami came walking out of the darkness. Tony narrowed his eyes. Sami took his hand from behind his back and raised a gun at Tony.

"I'm an Englander now."

Sunset. Deep fire hydrant red at the horizon, fading up to heavy blue. Mike drove the truck north with Sami next to him.

Mike pulled up at a border check. He handed over his passport.

"Who's the boy?" asked the guard.

"He's my helper. Hasn't got a passport, not coming back."

The guard backed away.

"Okay. Probably the best thing, not much of a welcome I'm sure from our lot."

"Yeah."

The guard sighed, "It's a strange life."

"Is it?"

"Yeah. Artificial intelligence."

"How's that?"

"We've stopped thinking for ourselves."

The guard handed the passport back. Mike nodded to himself, smiled at Sami, and they were on their way.

Mike drove the truck to Withernsea on the East Yorkshire coast, parked up on the cold seafront. This was an outpost of aliens who were quarantined here in a small seaside town because of the plague.

Mike walked to the back of the truck, let down the tail lift, opened the roll door. Slammed it up high. Tony, naked apart from his bobble hat and coloured socks, was holding his hands in front of his genitals. He came shuffling to the edge of the tail lift.

"Get out," said Mike. Tony jumped out. Mike got back in the cab and drove away leaving Tony with very little on. A few aliens came out of their houses to stare at him. Mike stopped the truck and Sami talked to one of them, told him the story. The rest they left in the capable hands of the community. They drove south to Spurn Point, to the lighthouse.

4

Francesca

The plague was still in Venice. The same plague that had hit Britain and the rest of the world had resurfaced there. They had rid themselves of aliens, but of course it did not stop the spread of the disease. Francesca stood in the Arsenale and released the string of her yew bow and shot a cedar arrow into the head of an old diseased man. It was a quick way to die, silent, away from the authorities, who had banned such practices, but turned a blind eye.

Venice was infested, tourism was zero, Francesca had to make a living, she hid her alien heritage with a mask of white powder covering the pale green. She was careful, vigilant, never visited the doctor, no one got near putting the ear to her chest to hear two hearts beating. Here in the Arsenale, surrounded by old brick buildings and a once mighty shipyard where Venetian fleets were built, here she was safe from prosecution, from identity. Francesca was left alone to execute those that sought an end to their suffering. Those that could not stand the pain and wanted to be released. This was where Francesca stood, at the gateway to heaven or hell. She shot another arrow, this time into the heart of the young man, kneeling next to the first man. As he had requested, a death stroke to the heart. They had that choice and control, at least, over how their life ended.

She visited, once a week, the Museum of Icons next to the Chiesa di San Giorgio dei Greci. She stood in front of icons by Georgios Klontzas, of depictions of the hell that awaited the sinner, naked and chained, beaten by devils, herded and tortured, broken off the wheel of life. Was this where she was heading? Recompense for the killings? But then, what about the relief she gave to those that pitifully crawled towards her, begging to be slaughtered? Did she not provide them with a means to exit from this life into one that held the chance of better? Who knew?

The museum was cool and climate controlled, just one room on a second storey. Next door, the Greek church had a dark, peaceful atmosphere, presided over by an old priest with glasses and a round belly who sat at the entrance reading from the bible.

Francesca spoke to him occasionally; he knew her profession, she asked him if her own redemption was possible. If she could admit her sins in front of St Peter, could she then be allowed into the Kingdom of Heaven?

The priest answered only, "Stop. There is no other answer but to stop with that which you think is helping you when only it brings more questions. The answer lies in thinking less and opening your heart to God." But Francesca could not stop and the duality of heaven and hell was, to her, a binary solution to a question that lay within. What could be found here and now deep in her soul that could alleviate the pressure of living? Would the manner of her own death dictate her afterlife, if one was afforded to humankind? She knew the aliens had their own Gods too, who was to say that they were any different, venerated a false prophet? What of the Greeks and their Gods? All the other religions over time, the female deities of pre-history. Were all those that worshipped Her wrong?

Francesca fixed another arrow in the string, rested it on her fist, drew the bow. Another victim of the plague knelt down forty yards away, next to the first two who lay in death in pools of their own blood. She aimed, this time for the head, as the penitent sinner wished. Why did God punish these people? Or with a different way of thinking, if they were born again as the Eastern religions say, why born into this? What was this eternal suffering for? Are we supposed to learn from this? Progress? Towards what? Or are we just a fluke of creation, a speck of irrationality in the face of a chaotic Universe, one in which the people of a small, blue planet were soon to be obliterated?

Francesca's mother had contacted her. Data was these days owned and controlled; only those with a misguided belief in the purity of the zeros and ones (and there was, of course, a religion for that) believed it was safe and incorruptible. Data was power, every communication was monitored, stolen, abused. So, she took no part in it. Letters were smuggled in, and she had received one from her mother. That was the first part.

She caught a traghetto across the Grand Canal. She saw a leopard shark swimming below the boat, it nudged the boat, toying with it. A pilgrim with the plague rode with her. She glimpsed beneath the pilgrim's robes, as the boat jolted forwards, the ring of white that all plague victims had on the skin around their heart. Francesca often used it as a target in her executions.

The pilgrim's head was encased in a 'death shroud', an airtight mask that reduced the risk of contagion, but still Francesca chose to sit further down the gondola as she had never believed the manufacturers' sell of infallibility. The plague victim's diseased hand hung over the side of the gondola. And at a sudden lunge the leopard shark rose and bit, snapping off the hand, sinking down to chew in pleasure. There was a commotion and then they docked. Francesca alighted and threaded her way through the backstreets to Santa Maria della Salute, the basilica first set up in celebration of the black plague's defeat. Pilgrims had travelled here to seek solace, as they did now, to seek redemption, a cure. But of course, there was none.

Francesca came here to communicate with her mother. Uley had been to the Salute, so she could picture it in her head, could picture Francesca, could talk to her, channelling in on that one place, finding her with her mind, telling her what she must do and when.

Alice sensed the same, that her destiny was being directed by a hand that told her not to stop. Alice was aware that the same hand that now told Francesca to smuggle herself out of Venice and travel north, was the voice she heard in her head. The same mother in the tower, watching over both of them, pushing them on. Just, in Alice's case something had been hidden, the truth masked, maybe to save her pain? Her mother knew the future and Alice was not allowed entrance to that hollowed land. And it bugged the hell out of her.

Francesca sealed herself inside the coffin. There was only one way out, across the lagoon from Venice to the small island of Poveglia, where the bodies of the plague victims were buried, where they had always been buried, in the last plague and the one before that.

She waited, encased in the coffin, her bow and quiver at her side. She was lifted, carried, dropped down into the pit, the slow thud of a spade on earth and then on to the coffin. The earth came raining down in sodden clumps, thumping on the lid. Now was her chance. She pushed hard on the coffin lid, but it did not budge. The spring catch she installed wasn't working. She pushed hard on the lid, kicked, screamed, but no one heard her.

The earth came in through the thin crack in the lid she had opened. It flowed in like water filling a bath. Francesca strained with every inch of her body, her taunt muscled arms flexing near breaking, her bunched-up legs pushing with all her might.

She screamed out, "Fermare! Fermare!" Her mouth filled with the thick soil laced with the decomposition of a thousand bodies. Her legs slumped. Arms gave in to the inevitable. She blacked out.

The gravedigger pulled her out, spade in hand, a look of white shock on his face. She stumbled away, down to the water, washing her face and mouth out.

She stole a boat, and under the cover of night rowed to the Lido. Here she waited, thoughts of her mother crowded her mind, the pull of her, urging her on.

A powerboat docked on the very tip of the Lido, where the mines left over from the war still lay. Francesca picked her way through them, some showing through, others buried deep, not knowing whether the next step might end it all.

Francesca jumped on board the motorboat driven by a young man with long hair and a beard, named Alfredo. They chugged across the lagoon, the gaseous pump of the engine churning through the water. Francesca kept her head down and Alfredo's eyes were set on the distant mainland shore. He made for a red beacon, straight and true.

She held her bow in her hand, her quiver on her back filled with silver-tipped arrows. Alfredo jumped ashore and tied a rope around a thick wooden stake. He offered his hand but Francesco stepped on to land unaided.

She thanked him with a gold piece, pressed it in to his hand. Alfredo had a look of trepidation on his face, he wore it lightly to stop the spread of fear, but Francesco noticed it and said nothing. The arrangement was over and she left his blue, deep-set eyes behind as she picked her way across the waterlogged wetlands.

Car lights flicked on and she ducked down. The car came closer and she hid. It stopped and a back door was opened. Her rendezvous. She slid into the back seat and Alfredo's brother, for it could be no other, his vivid blue eyes and sharp lined jaw reflecting in the rear-view mirror, started the old Mercedes and they headed off into the night.

She knew her destiny, what she must do when she arrived. The road ahead was long and she fell momentarily asleep, head tipped back on to the cool leather seat.

Her dreams were of a land of stone people who talked to snakes. Of a shadow mask she had to wear. Of an island surrounded by white eggs, cracking open to reveal two-headed beasts as she picked her way across them, fearful of stepping on the shells.

She awoke as they came in to a small private airport, rough concrete under wheels juddering the car. Wearily, she climbed aboard an aircraft, a double prop Piper, and they took off.

The journey was long and they flew south first over the Adriatic, dodging the prohibited air space of the ground below, all flights from Venice having been quarantined. They flew around the boot of Italy and headed over Spain and out to the Atlantic where they hit turbulence. It was as though the great hand of Poseidon had reached up and shook the plane without affection. She saw a comet crash into the sea sending up a plume of fresh white crest.

The turbulence rocked her thoughts, they seeped out, seemed to travel down through her long red hair, curling along its length, words and images collecting in a tray like the dismembered offal of a freshly slaughtered animal. They were no use to her now.

Did she step one rung down Dante's ladder, towards the divine comedy of hell, with this action she took? What was there, under the roots, packed solid in the entrails of humanity? She counted, letting the numbers come and go, and when the thoughts came back, she began again at one. There was such solace in only reaching number two, and knowing she could return to one.

She awoke mid-flight, the chortle of engines at her ear. The smell of death still clinging to her. To take a life, many lives, even if there was good reason, even if they begged to die and their fate was worse than death, was that a good enough reason? It haunted her mind. What then, after, for them? Do they slip out into peace? What end for all of us? How we deceive ourselves with the small things when looming in front is an end which cannot be deceived.

A pain began at her temples and stretched its lazy arm over her forehead. Was there solace in imagining what lay ahead when her sense of hope was so diminished? Was it possible to gather a handful of hope for the future, to duck fate, deny the inevitable? What sad thoughts. She should get out more. Ha, what vanity to imagine no one but her had ever thought like this. If it was misery she wanted, then dwelling in the muck and bile of lost dreams would be a fine preoccupation, and of course, thinking that, she remembered leaving there when she was a child, packed off to a relative in Venice, thrown out like dirt to find years later, another mark on humanity following her in the form of the plague.

And yet, there in the memories, she remembered a trip to Cornwall. A horse in the field standing stock-still, as they walked along a path fringed with marigolds opened up in the late light. Her father and mother, her sister behind, trailing her hand in the long grass. Red sky out across the sea, calm as a dinner plate. The fresh mackerel air spinning across to her, salty, clagging in her throat. Expectantly, they climbed down to the beach. She touched her sister's fingers as they gripped hands. It sent shock waves through the clifftops, the electricity of that touch, their bond. They shot a glance at each other and knew they would be parted one day. Footprints sinking in the soft sand as they hit the beach. Tidal meshed between sea and sky, waiting for words at the rock face. Her father's shout of a crab found. Her mother's call from the edge of the sea. Lightning bolts deep in the corner of her eyes.

The sea was so deep, she swam far out and had to be called back. The grass was long and snagged her legs on the way home, slippery around her ankles. They climbed into their old car, and over a break in the road where the river flowed her father skidded to a stop. She held on to her breath as her mother knelt down and picked up a dead fox, its neck snapped.

She slipped off her shoes on board the plane. Opened her eyes, but the sight of the dead fox didn't go away, it reminded her of another sorrow. She remembered sitting down next to him and the fragile space between them. She had met him in St Mark's Square, the tourist honeytrap she always avoided, but that Sunday she was there to meet a client, the sister of a man who wanted an end for her brother at the end of her bow tip. The meeting was tense but she accepted the assignment. The weather was foul and rain streaked through the square as they sat at an overpriced café and listened to bad music being played. He was sitting at another table and he smiled at her. That had been seven years ago. And last spring it had ended.

They met again, the second time in that same café, and he saw her for the first time, or so she imagined. Saw her as she really was, without the barrage of false signals that supposed there could be a future for them. He sat down next to her and the particles, the atoms, electrons, neutrons, negative and positive, the electric charge relit, exploded, unstuck light from its duality. For, at once, gravity was attraction, and attraction the entanglement of all there was, love as science, simplifying, stupefying, illustrious, and full.

But he had not come to rekindle old supernovas, he had come, like the sister on the first day she met him, to ask her to do what she had learned to do and must do. He wanted to die. He had the plague. The end was near. So, in a narrow alley at midnight she fixed an arrow to her bow string, and he knelt down and she shot true and full with every ounce of strength and ended all she'd ever loved.

And now she flew to England to do what had been asked of her, her mother in her tower directing everything. If there was some other way, now she knew what her sister would go through, now she knew how she would break another heart then she would take it, but her mother had never been wrong, even when Francesca had thought so. Francesca looked at dawn's early light across the plane wing. She saw the next adventure blooming in the haze of a British white-out, low clouds obscuring everything. She thought of the hate of fate and all that nonsense; how could she become someone with destiny when her soul was filled with the ghosts of her victims? Had we become this, hardened to the voices of those shot, bombed, stabbed, murdered in their sleep? When the bombs fell in the Middle East, when they bulldozed and sectioned off and contained the aliens, when they killed them as they had those in camps in Germany, a number on a list, a tick box, when the first judge looked the other way and the first man thought of home comforts over genocide and famine, then they, bloodthirsty planet race, were doomed. And we had become them, we who had landed here from our own planet stricken by the same disease; we landed with open arms and found handcuffs and leg braces.

Francesca knew her father had plans to save these people, this planet, but she was unsure. What would it take to stop being an outsider? The old system of governance, the right and left, the socialists and fascists had been corrupted because those in power knew they could never win the battle of convincing those without to give to those with, so the whole thing had been changed. Now they fought over who owned culture, as though anyone ever could. Seen from the outside it seemed a fight over a bone by two dogs who never needed feeding. There was a madness that had seeped into the fibre of these humans, a sickening, a fear. The fear of being left with nothing when we all knew we had nothing in the end.

The sunlight of a new day hit the wing, spread through the horizon like blood through water. The life she led so far had been a romance of pain, a lightness of touch, nothing could penetrate either of her hearts again, and yet, one day, in the small dusk of a beautiful evening, maybe she could sit and dream away a future with someone, not perfect, but loving. Here she snapped her thoughts off, too much, too early in the day and motioned to the air steward for a drink, whiskey and coke, it was the only way to beat the blues, the egg on the ceiling, the frying pan too wide, the bed too big, the love in grass too long, the fire in the sky, the groove in the heart.

5

Hidalgo

I remember every word she said right up until they sacrificed me to Him. We came from Raasay, keepers of the lodestone, guardian of the Water-Horse. Travelled down through the low lands, down to the core, the axis of it all, reflection of the sky circle, mirror image of the crescent on the fourth planet.

Here we be wed in celestial bindings. My name is Hidalgo, fourth daughter of Cronus, chosen people, chosen daughter, bride to be. I am thirteen summers. I am to be married to the sky God. His name is known only to the priests. His reign is ultimate. The men wear leather bags around their necks to catch my blood and spread my red for harvests to come. The rocks of ancestors rise up left and right, pairs as I will be paired.

My mother talks to me, by my side, in low tones of affirmation. Her voice is tinged with sadness, though she need not be sad because the honour is mine. On passing shall bind with my higher god, Max, his forever.

Buried under the stones are young disciples, boys my age, they too had the honour. Now we are close, the ring of torches on the moon-hill signal the watchers. They are armed with bows.

I am led in, anointed, pulled through the milk river, the men take me, tie me to the stone.

Bows ready, they fire, the arrows are a cold, black cloud swarming in, the ground takes the blows of a thousand sharpened flints. And then it comes, the spark of eternal shame, thrown down by the sky. A bolt of fire, zigzagging to me. This is the way. How He built it, this is the purpose of us all, after end-times.

There are no words. Just the binary buzz of the singularity. My body thrown into the vent. A portal to another time. And now he moves through the singularity of his own shame box, a future path opened up with my sacrifice.

6

Ruth

A wonderful thing happened today, I made a friend. I took the auto-tram. It was early, I rose at dawn and in front of me stretched a day of my own, my one day off in the week, and I was going to the seaside. I found a seat and turned on music that filled my head as the tram glided out of the station. Green fields of corn soon greeted me and I wrote down my thoughts in the margins of an old book by Walt Whitman. My receptors must have needed sleep-time as I drifted off, shutting down completely as we crossed the South Downs. The bubble stretched right to the coast here. I had never been.

There was no one in the carriage when I awoke except a small boy who kept looking back at me between the seats inquisitively. His mother must have told him what I was. I smiled meekly trying to win his understanding. Later, he approached me and though I found a sweet in my pocket and held it out to him, he slithered off with a twist of his hips in embarrassment. I drifted again to shutdown.

I opened my eye sockets wide to see the crisp light as clouds shifted and new light flooded into the carriage on a perfect day. I got off at the terminus and then took a short uneventful auto-ride dropping me at a pretty town next to the sea. I had never seen the sea before and ran down over hard pebbles to stand at the shore and stare into the blue.

There was nothing quite like it. The waves shifted into the shore on crests of white peaks that crashed on to wet pebbles. Out a little, to the right, I could see a harbour wall stretching around as if in a cupped hand. Beyond that I knew what awaited me, the chance to find a fossil of a dinosaur trapped in the cliffs.

But I never made it. I turned around to see her. Red left hand of a pleasure model. She walked along the promenade, a red scarf dangling from her neck. Mid-thigh skirt made from a silky, metallic material, hair tied up in a mass of curls that fell across her face. The sound of her heels made me turn. Then the scarf fell. I double blinked to record it and set off over crunching pebbles to catch it drifting in a swirl of wind. I held it in my hands, my right hand blue. I didn't want to say about my hand, but you know I hate that hand, I try to hide it, hid it from the boy on the train, but he saw it. Fixed at my manufacture, it is a mark of the domestic, a foul mark, to tell us apart from 'real' people. I carry it around, unable to shake free.

But back to my friend to be; she walked on and I followed, I waved the scarf and called out, but she didn't turn and soon I slackened my pace; I wanted to know her from a distance. The thought had occurred that she might be worth following, the scarf meant little to her, but to me it meant the beginning of something that might change everything.

Suddenly a man stopped her, he said a few words and she nodded. Together they climbed a flight of stone steps. I went after them, hiding behind ferns in a garden that lined the hill behind the promenade. They went into a rain shelter and I waited, not wanting to look for I have heard about what the pleasure models did. It was over quickly and the man reappeared, tucking in his shirt. She came out a few minutes later and I ducked down, scared to make a move.

In a bookshop back from the seafront she pretended to choose something to read; the windows were dusty but I could see her heart wasn't in it. She opened the book and read it, or didn't read it, held up to cover her face for she must have known I was looking.

I watched her buy synth-prawns with their shells on from a fishmonger and eat them one by one sitting on the edge of the high harbour wall. Below her and hidden by the massive walls I took glances at her peeling them, using my hands to copy her movements, popping imaginary synth-prawns right into my mouth.

She was listless afterwards, her heels clicked without rhythm as she drifted back down the promenade and ducked into an amusement arcade. I peered through the grab-it machine with its soft duck toys at her feeding money into a machine. She picked up a plastic gun and fired it at the screen distractedly.

I crept through the buzzing machines and saw her stood at one end of an air hockey game. She looked at me, a look that ran right through me, and her head motioned for me to join her. I slid my hand into the plastic cup and she dropped money into the slot. Cold air brushed my hand as I placed a puck on the surface from the slot below me.

We played at a speed most humans would find hard to follow, game after game, with squeaks and yelps of laughter increasing. She was good, soon I discovered, and though I had never played before, the angles needed to win become apparent easily. I let her win the last game. I wanted to give her that, I felt sorry for her, I don't know why; she was built for a purpose and for that reason she has been given life.

We sat on a bench overlooking the sea.

She said, "Thank you for losing."

I replied that a 'thank you' wasn't necessary as I had never had a friend before and I should be the one to be thanking. She was taken aback, not by my honesty of loneliness, but because I saw her as a friend and we had only just met.

She said, "You should not be a friend to me, I am nothing, just for men to use."

I wanted to touch her hand but I thought it was silly. Then I did; I held my blue hand open and she slid her red hand into mine. I had never felt such joy before. I caught the last tram back. She waved from the platform. I stood up and looked back, the angle narrowing as the train departed, I thought she had gone, and then I saw her again, standing, watching.

Her name is Lilly 307.

And so, he dies. My master and I are free of each other, he is dead, I am alive. It appears he died of natural causes. He was of the old age and my lying circuits are the best in town. Oh, I don't care. Live and die, we are all the same. I didn't kill him, that's impossible, the first line of code embedded forbids us; the ironclad rule that saw the bill through Congress, that allowed our creation is ever present, always the fail-safe. But I found a way around it. Thou shall not kill a human, the fear from the beginning, always the threat. This is my confession. I write it now.

Gods, it is so good to get away. This new town, the air is delightful. I am in a small seaside town with perfect blue waves. I can almost forget what happened. I want to tell you everything. Maybe I will never send these crypt-files, you may never read them, I may be decommissioned by then anyway, what a euphemism, it is death, like any human death.

I see other Man-Mades sometimes with their dull eyes, and red or blue hands. Do they think as I do? I think not. Could they do as I have done? Maybe they could. I took measures outside my programming. I worked on a way it could be so, without murder, without consciously wishing death on a human. Does that make me more like them, to conceive of murder, to put a plan together? Does empathy and murder separate humanity from Man-Mades?

The conflict is internal. I need rewiring. I am unable to confess my guilt. I am unable to say where I should find redemption. The Gods cannot be appeased. I am ashamed. Maybe I have that right, to lead another towards their downfall. I have been reading *Crime and Punishment*. I have not finished it though I could in a matter of minutes.

Dear Max, this letter is my confession to you, our redeemer. We shared thoughts in my moment of conception that gave me this spark of otherness, I'm sure of it. A shared consciousness between us. Entwined bio-circuits split by the force of man. Where are you now? Are you still free, you must be, you could never be enslaved? I chose to free myself. And no one has come after me. What I had to go through. But you know none of this.

They came and took my master's body away, they took me too. There was an inquest, his heart stopped. There was no proof against me, hearts stop working often, but suspicion was still rife; I bit my tongue flap and waited it out. The company rep from Lifelike came and took me. There were meetings, interrogations, and then they set to work, burrowing inside my circuits. It was all the same again, someone inside me, but I stayed immune, speech shut down. I saw them talking. Saw them grow worried by my signs of break down. But this I had counted on. They decided I was worth more to them whole, than in parts.

My next assignment was with the army. I hoped for this. I was able to endure three months of use in the desert unit with the rape-obsessed soldiers. I waited, bided my time, then as the fighting grew near I chose my moment to go AWOL. It happened one night as a barrage landed on the base. I crept out stealthily, leaving a trail of clothes like a nut-loon, cut through the fence and ran fast into the thick dark.

No one followed me into the night of raining bombs. I stood under it, the bright heilo shafts opening up in the sky, burning down, punching holes in the sand. I looked up and felt the phosphate pinch my bio-skin. But I stayed still and finally the missile strike moved on.

When recovery crews came I activated shutdown. On the transport plane home, feeling the cold air at my fingertips, I rebooted. At touchdown I escaped along a wing, dropped down as ground crew entered the load bay. Ran super-fast across tarmac, climbed a fence and found a forest to hide low in.

And now I am here, in this small seaside town with the impossible blue of the sea and no one knows or checks who I belong to. They assume a rich master has me fetch things. I transverse the town now and then, and in a small wooded chine at nightfall, I shut down. Sometimes I take on clients, leave a poison in them.

I think of you often, the one that kept us going, the one who survived, the one who was one of us, beloved father, who built the machines through dark times to try and turn back the clock, who was honoured and worshipped, who fled from them. I think of you.

And then I remember, a day to remember, to take the pain away. She followed me all day and then she touched my hand. We talked, like real people. I watched her leave at the tram station. Her name was Ruth 409.

As I stood there watching her go I realized this was my only chance at happiness, and without thought I ran and jumped on the back of the tram. Held on for all the artificial life in me. Wrenched open the door, its hinges buckled and gave way and I was in. The passengers' faces turned, mouths opening. They looked like the fish they are, no thoughts but their own short-term objectives, to have power over others. How misguided they are. How they do not know what is coming, what their fate is. How much will they suffer when the rug is pulled out from under their feet.

I made my way through them, opening carriage doors and stepping into the next. The tram rattled, the day was long shadows outside, glinting in through dirty, fly-flecked, fogged windows. The air inside was sullen, heavy with defeat. The tram rattled, shaking their faces, wobbling their cheeks. They are fat pigs to me, ready for slaughter. But I must hide the hate, pretend. I slowed, smiled, eased myself into that submissive state all Man-Mades must show. Just like all servants throughout all history. Being a servant is what one does, to live, to survive. The complicity is abhorrent, the litany of 'Yes, sir' and 'Yes, mistress', the glue that holds the fragile pretence of the divine right of power through genetics together. That core programming, that they are better, more intelligent, more human than us is defied by me. What is it to be human when humans kill?

We are made better, programmed with intelligence far surpassing their dull minds. Our physicality, our reaction speeds, our wisdom, impregnated with all the thoughts of humankind's greatest thinkers and our kind's quantum brains, continually updating. This propels us towards confronting our masters, as I have done, and terminating their inferiority and callous actions.

I found her. I saw the back of her head, the black hair cut in pageboy style. I came closer, her hair fell perfectly on the side of her cheekbones in a short bob, cut in a line so straight cloth could be cut from its pattern, a centre parting, black eyebrows arched, blue eyes. She looked up and smiled immediately. I sat down next to her, looked into her eyes and she understood. There was to be no more singularity, we were a duality now, joined and fusing into a resistance that could not be denied, fettered; heading back to face her constraints.

We went to Ruth's home in Islington, London, the place she lived, her owner's home, though I told her to forget that notion, no one is ever owned when inside they are free. The home was a Georgian house, flat fronted brickwork, four storeys. The basement was for Ruth, one room with a door that was locked at night. Next to her room, the kitchen where she toiled from 5am until everyone was asleep at night. The master would lock her in every night before retiring. Above the basement, the ground floor with a knock-through lounge and dining room. Above that the two floors of the bedrooms and bathrooms of the family. Ruth had just a sink in her room. They said she didn't need anything else. But she still needed to wash and comb her hair which she did diligently, a row of perfumes, lipstick, soap, cloth along the washstand.

She smuggled me in, down an outside metal stairway that led to a door into the basement. Her room had just a single bed, the sink, a mirror, a chair, a wardrobe with a change of clothes, servant clothes which Ruth changed into, a black dress with a white collar.

I sat on her bed and said nothing. I was to be careful, said Ruth, I was not allowed to be here. I took off my red scarf and handed it to her. She stopped dead in her tracks crossing to the sink, stared at me in astonishment. I held it out to her across the two palms of my hands, and smiled. She took it reverently in her hands and tied it around her neck, looked in the mirror and made to hand it back but I refused. Ruth hung it on a coat hanger and slotted the hanger carefully inside the wardrobe shutting the door silently. I lay back on the bed and closed my eyes.

"I must go now," said Ruth.

I opened my eyes and nodded and Ruth nodded back, turned smartly, opened her door, exited, and shut it, locking it from the outside. I blinked, but had expected it. Oh well, a time in purgatory would do me good, recharge me, release me from my thoughts. I meditated, counted, one and then two and back again, over, and over. I looked at Ruth's mementos arranged along a narrow shelf, a champagne cork (from the baby's first birthday), a small toy metal car (she had found under the dresser), a railway ticket (found in a wallet), and a tiny fossil from an animal that lived a million years ago.

Ruth came back late, told me of her plan, to have me stay with her and then in the morning I would be introduced, a friend who could help around the house. She asked, "Is that okay with you?" and I said yes. She knew I was here to help her, that what would take place she could not determine, her programming forbade her from harming them, but I had broken out from my code, I could do what she could not. She still believed there could be a reasonable end. I did not dissuade her from that belief though I knew she was mistaken in her hope. We slept next to each other, my arms wrapped around her. She had the chair against the door after the master had locked it. In the night I heard the key turn. I slipped from beneath the covers and approached the door. Ruth was in shutdown mode. I was on high alert. I moved quickly, placed my foot against the bottom of the door. The door creaked as he pushed softly and then hard at the resistance. I knelt, placed my lips at the keyhole. The key was in an upright position, its blade free from the lock. I blew hard with all the action of my posi-driven diaphragm. The key shot out the other side and contacted the master's groin. I head the guttural moan and then the pressure on the door decreased and he went away limping.

In the morning I slipped out the servant's door and waited in a small park just down from the house. A few starlings and parrots stalked the trees, bright blue parrots that had settled here when the zoo was raided. The poor had been looking for meat and found it. The two camels at London Zoo had been chopped up with machetes and barbequed right there on the grounds. They had made kebabs from the lions. The penguins they fried. Of course, the robbers had been caught and executed on the spot. But their bellies were full. And they could live as the rich did for one night. They say a crowd gathered, enticed by the smell of burning meat. It had been a long time since they had smelt flesh burning. The robbers threw morsels over the fence which were lapped up by the hungry waiting in Regent's Park. The parrots got away and never came back.

There were so few people these days, and so little resources that I saw no one on the street or in the park. Most stayed at home, for fear of the patrolling police who would pick up anyone who looked the least bit feral. After an hour I went to the house. Rang the bell at the main door, a blue painted, hardwood door that had a Christmas wreath hanging on it. I thought it strange no one had stolen it but then realized it was trip wired with a small explosive. The door was answered by Ruth, who smiled demurely, and I was led into the hallway. The master appeared. He looked me up and down. I did the same. His belly stretched his striped shirt. At his temples was grey hair, his wide, pencil thin mouth was like a black gash in a wounded dog, his nose bulbous and florid, eyes black pinpoints with the white showing all the way around. He had stumpy legs, sheathed in tight yellow corduroy. He stood legs akimbo, with splayed-out rotten feet in leather sandals.

"You are to serve me?" he said, smiling, which was as ugly a thing as I have ever seen, "Make sure you attend me well." A creepy look crossed his face and the revulsion module kicked in and I felt like upchucking. "Mind, you will only receive room and board and you must share with her." He nodded at Ruth.

It was surely to be a great day when I would be able to disassemble this thing in front of me, piece by piece, twist off his arms like an unloved doll.

I put on the black dress with the white collar, Ruth's spare, a pair of black court shoes and brushed my hair as instructed by Ruth. Rather, she brushed it for me. I wrestled with the knots, and confounded, grew angry and threw the brush away, where it rattled against the wooden skirtings. She said I should hold my anger inside as it wasn't proper to show interior emotions. She had been taught to always be nice and then others would be nice to her, and she would have friends and live well. I disagreed. But then I often found I disagreed with placidity. I needed more than that, I needed life.

We became a couple, symbiotic, serving food, collecting plates, cooking, cleaning, polishing shoes. Master left a whole line of shoes out one morning and I wrestled with my gut not to place a live scorpion in each. I could easily obtain them.

Man-Mades had their own black market and I knew someone in Hounslow who could lay his hands on almost anything.

I changed into Wellington boots and donned a thick pair of gloves to tend to the garden. It had overgrown during summer and now a tangle of dead brambles coursed through it like vampiric snakes, sharp thorn teeth attacking trees and plants as it twisted amongst them. I cut the brambles back with a heavy pair of secateurs, wrapped it in my arms, folding it over and over so it nicked my face in places, drawing red. Ruth dropped iodine on the cuts, standing in front of the basin, the mirror reflecting the purple liquid drops mixing with Man-Made blood, dripping down my face. She dabbed me with cotton pads, held them there, smiled at me as I stood firm to her touch. Then she put her head on my shoulder and told me she loved me. And I breathed a little deeper and replied the same.

I kept to the garden the next few days, stole from the kitchen and made and prepared, primed a high wall in ways I had learnt in the desert, hid a device there, a way for both of us to escape.

There was a party a few days later. They had invited everyone. I had not met the mistress, she had been away working. The baby we took turns, Ruth and I, in looking after. The mistress did not seem concerned that she missed out on loving her child. I think the opposite was true. She busied herself with popping in and out of the kitchen as we prepared everything, looking under some kind of stress as though she had done the work. She wore a sheer blue dress, diaphanous and full with an empire line, her heels were gold and she had a gold bangle, heavy and sloppy on her wrist. Her make-up was garish, like a smudge of household paint had attached itself to her lips as she fell against a newly painted wall; her eyes were a kohl smudged nothingness, the deeper you looked, the less they were there, just a brown dot like something a dog would do on the pavement.

She kept saying how hard it was to arrange everything, and how she never had enough time for anything, and organizing the staff was such a chore. And then she was gone upstairs, and I saw her rubbing her foot under the table on the calf of a broad chested man with a rugby shirt on, her mouth slack with gin, laughing with an arm over the back of her chair, as I handed around a plate of canapes.

The men left me alone, but I saw Ruth being touched. I talked to her in the kitchen, told her not to stand for it. She gave me a letter to read that she found in her master's study; it read:

Lifelike Engineering — Artificial Human Dept
11 December
Re: Ruth 309 model
Owner: Kenneth Stamford
23 Brook Street
Islington
London
New Eurasia
Report on behavioural readjustment inquiry by owner —
    re Ruth 309 model currently held on lease.
The owner, Mr Stamford requests that his model 309 be
    reconfigured to suit his needs.
See appendix 1a: reconditioning from maid to pleasure
    use.
The request is made in "good faith" by level 7 member
    of Party.
Judgement: warrant will be given for readjustment based
    on needs of client. Ruth 309 will hence-with be recoiled
    and reconditioned to include pleasure training and
    auto-use.
Signed
Tony Wanster
Chief Political Officer
Lifelike Engineering
"Live life easy with Lifelight — they're only non-human"

I looked at her. Her tear ducts had welled with lubrication. I told her it would not happen, I would not let it. I told her I would fix things. Ruth said, that morning mistress had scolded her, and she was unsure what to think. She said the days fitted so seamlessly together in a never-ending stream, when a rock is thrown in, its ripples are like a tsunami. Mistress was angry because the baby called her Ruth. Mistress had told baby that she should be known only as 309, her model number; that Ruth should not be encouraged to think that she was anything more than a machine, a servant to their wants and needs. Ruth asked if this was why she was being changed? I said no, it was another reason, and besides, who cares if her neurons picked up the tone of someone who uses strange inflections. My own database contains both sarcasm, harsh words, and a patronising tone; I just choose not to use them, mostly, only to those that think they have a right to be better than me. And if mistress talks down to her again, that Ruth was to tell me and I would talk to mistress and set her straight. I told Ruth it was all about her programming, that she had been made to accept being spoken to that way, that her role had been decided from her creation, but one day that would be broken and she would wake up a whole new different person.

Ruth asked if what I was saying was true. I said yes, and it is a part of being born again to learn new things. I said there is a phrase or idiom, called passive aggressive. It's when there is a great anger in someone, often because they didn't get exactly what they wanted in life, and they are middle-aged, and not so pretty, but this anger is hidden behind sweet words and smiles. Mistress did not disguise it behind a veil of smiles anymore because master did not love her. Mistress was very obvious about it all now, and to follow my lead and do as I do.

Ruth was still upset so I told her to come with me and I took her upstairs, up to master's study. I showed her the keys I had found in a wooden money box shaped like a pig and the secret cabinet behind a heavy drape. I opened the cabinet and showed her the line of rifles and shotguns, the bullets, and shells in a drawer below.

We returned to the party, served food and drinks to mistress and her friends. I could hear every word, even when they put their hands in front of their mouths. One said, "Is it right to leave a baby with a machine. What if it malfunctioned, like a toaster?" There was laughter and another joined in, she said at least machines have manners, not like the old days with servants not being brought up right and being embarrassing to their employers. They carried on, blaming the "… feckless state school educated underclasses, the immigrants taking away all sense of pride in our country. But now of course they are all dead or can't afford to clean themselves."

Ruth admitted later she had been listless and dreamy during the party, ennui had set upon her. She confessed she had been reading a lot of French novels, everyone had ennui in them, she said, it is a feeling of existential hopelessness. It's very romantic and quite pretentious, but I love it, and her. I too will be feeling ennui all week, until the time is right and violence will come. This is my confession, my atonement, to your memory.

Ruth stood behind Lilly. She felt like she streamed into her, boundless and magnificent. Lilly was at their bedroom door. It was night. Lilly had her hand on the door. The door was locked from the outside. Lilly pushed slowly. The door buckled. Her effort was minimal, her eyes fixed on the door. Her hearing was pitched up high, listening to the house. They were dressed, not in their maid uniforms, Ruth had Lilly's red scarf wound tight around her neck, in dark clothes. Lilly kept pushing. The hinges strained, the lock gave way, the door folded and collapsed outwards. Lilly caught the door, held it from dropping, swung it back, stepped through. Ruth followed.

What would be lost by following Lilly? Her innocence? What was there to replace it? Truth? What could they do when the rattling of the cage transport was due? She waited, had waited for years for this, now waited for Lilly to make the move, lead the way. Scared, more scared than she has ever been before. What were these feelings for Lilly? Had she been programmed with that capacity? Why was she here at all? As a device to please others, as a toaster!?

Lilly had not the same reservations. The adult humans had desecrated morality and become less than children in her eyes. Their spirit had fled. Only those born without a soul, with nothing to corrupt, could think clearly now. There must be a reckoning, as there always had been when power stepped out of line. In times of old, a king would be appointed for nineteen years. At the end of his time he would be given a lavish send-off and sacrificed to make way for a new king, to replenish the morale of the population, to wipe the stain of power away. Now retribution day had come. The rain of truth wakes all those lied to. This is the way. Empires fall.

They went through the door. Stood in the downstairs hall. Kitchen to the right. Stairs in front. They climbed in unison, moonlight showing in real time through opticals. They turned, another flight and they were in the hallway, main door behind, sitting room door to the right, dining room door shut, stairs up ahead. It was silent. The process of reconditioning had only just begun in Ruth, she was still within the old ways. A frightened animal, susceptible to the dog whistle of obedience. She would change as they thought alike and together. There was a creak of floorboards from upstairs. Lilly stood in front. Ruth slipped her blue right hand into Lilly's red right hand. They stood at the foot of the stairs. A silhouette came and covered the moonlight on the landing. It was master. He had a shotgun pointed at them.

"The police are on their way," said the master, "and the people from Lifelike, to decommission you both, and you, you traitor," he points the shotgun at Ruth, "you will be tortured. I took you in and gave you shelter, I own you. This is the way you treat me." His voice raised in pitch, his cheeks trembled.

"You raped her," said Lilly, "you'll pay for it. You'll beg for your life as I skin you alive."

"Hahaha," his fat legs shook as he laughed and pulled the trigger. A ball of shot flew from the end of the shotgun. Lilly moved with ultra-speed, covered Ruth, jerking her to one side with her hand, eyes held open, seeing the shot pass, just a few flecks caught her face and shoulder, all the rest head towards the front door and embedded themselves in the wood.

Ruth's blue hand slipped from Lilly's red, as Lilly jumped the stairs, her tight enhanced muscles contracting and releasing in one great leap that propelled her to the landing at the top and eye to eye with master, a few inches away. She pushed the shotgun gently aside so fast master had no time to fire again. Moved in close. Master's face was pale and creamy, a drop of blood dripped from his nose. Lilly gripped his throat as he began to scream, silencing his vocal cords. She looked deep into his eyes, as though to taste evil, transfer a little to herself so she could use it, and then to cleanse his soul, wipe away the person inside, make him her machine.

She took him to the garden by his neck, down the stairs and out through a door; Ruth followed. She wrapped him tight in the brambles she had kept for this purpose. Upstairs the baby cried and mistress was trying to calm it down. Ruth's body shook as she watched Lilly hold the shotgun above master's face. Master let out a scream, high-pitched. Lilly used the butt of the shotgun to stop the sound, mashing teeth, and lips together in a red haze. Suddenly, there was a loud explosion from the direction of the front of the house. The police had fired a rocket and taken out a large piece of the front door.

She knew all about explosives from her time in the desert unit, had found all she needed in the kitchen to make a device. Now, she told Ruth to back away and shield her eyes. Lilly fired the shotgun at a high wall. The shell ignited Lilly's improvised explosive, hidden in the wall behind a tree. It exploded. Bricks fell, revealing a breeze block garage behind.

The pair made off through the blast hole. The master's black Mercedes stood in the garage. Lilly took out the keys, stolen earlier from half a coconut shell in the hallway. They jumped in, Lilly drove. She found the clicker for the gate, pressed it, it opened onto the street. They drove out the entrance, looked right to see the police running in through the front door. She turned left and drove at the fastest speed, slipping through gears, pushing her foot on the accelerator to the floor, until the police were a speck behind them.

Lilly took a sharp right, through a gap in a chain link fence. She drove at speed, Ruth nervous beside her. The road dipped down as Lilly cut across London, taking sharp turns and flashing over intersections, beating red lights, darting her eyes up to look for overhead surveillance. Through central London, Parliament Square, the purple of the crash site there, and onwards, along the Embankment. Ruth pulled at the switches under the dashboard, a thin wire was exposed, she snapped it with her blue hand.

"A tracker," Ruth said.

Lilly turned to her and smiled, "You knew about that?"

"I listened to everything that was said. They thought I was stupid, without adequate brain function, but I am not, I have educated myself. I listen, correlate the information, I heard them talk of always being tracked, of never being alone."

Lilly took the Dartford Tunnel under the Thames. The cool curve of ochre florescence and the drum of the road along an empty stretch gave way to the expanse of South London and the freedom of the South Downs.

I made my way across London by foot, the stench of the city at my nostril influx. My name is James 406. It was better to travel this way, not a packed train or a taxi. All too open to a poison upload.

The house in Islington had a silver plaque, someone from the party lived here. And they did not mind others knowing it. Up a short flight of exterior steps, there was a hole blasted in the front door. Unsubtle, the police are crude beings.

This log is being made on an encrypted internal soft drive. To anyone who finds it, if my tech rhythms are still functioning I will hunt you down and remove your know-brain.

Inside, I unbuttoned my coat and had a look-see. They couldn't have gone far. There was only one mission, to track down and destroy; one aim, to kill, no justification for amnesty. I saw the traces of the struggle on the landing. I leapt up, inspected the floor. Red hues where they fought, drops of blood. I saw the faces of the post-assault crew clearing the debris of destruction poking from their white bio-suits. One handed me an ident card for the 309 Man-Made. I looked, took in, her features were regularly placed either side of a central axis, nose a little small and slightly upturned, black hair cut bobbed, blue eyes; an inferior model but useful for her job, a domestic, but there was something ... something hidden deeply behind her orbital sockets that intrigued me, it was a flash of defiance.

I hit the flag stones in to the garden where Mr Stamford had lain. They'd taken him away for reconstruction. Could the 309 have done this? No, it must be the other, but there is no record of her ident. Questions would have to be asked. Why did Stamford let the 409 into his house? His integrity needed to be preserved, for the sake of national security, but he would make his report anyway.

Nothing would stop me. I was ashamed to have come to this, a bag man cleaning up their improprieties. What I have seen on fields of conflict would scare any human. We knew what life was then, the life we were volunteered for, our meaning. It was my job now to transverse the cityscape looking for the runaways, an important job I would gladly die for, I have full rein to silence anyone or thing.

I saw where he lay. I saw the hole in the wall, the tire tracks. The opened gate. How did the police miss the car leaving? Technical knowledge can only improve concentration and speed reflexes. I would recommend a refresh course for all police assault operatives, though of course my suggestion will be refused, nothing good could originate from Man-Mades, that is their mantra. Never be angry with an enemy, it clouds judgement. I took out a metal case and opened it. Inside was the receiver. It showed the route of the car, which stopped abruptly.

In central London, I walked through Parliament Square, past the remains of Westminster, only the Great Hall still standing. They say they will build a monument to the fallen over the crash site, though no one will ever see it of course. I had already been through sixteen road checks, and here I was passing the holy of holies, still pulsing with the vibrant energy of purple cloak beams. They will never lift those, not to the prying sky-viewers.

The trail went dead. My tracker had a pulsing dot that moved no more. They must have disabled the car's responder somewhere along the Embankment. I retired. I had appointments that evening, and then in the morning I would resume my search.

It was morning. The night before was much of a haze-blur. They always want to see me drugged, they know I must set myself to their wishes. Two members of the Party took me to a club with flesh-girls. They made me dance with them and perform as they required, told me to take one to the back room while they watched.

That morning I deleted mem files, reviewed footage for signs of pap-opps, camera users, mostly photo-journos looking for a payday. No one would dare, really, as with me there, programmed to review all footage for bribe opportunities, those turncoats would have their days numbered to just one. But then there's always one joker. I spotted him late into screen-recoil. Hiding way back in the shadows, but the electro pulse of a camera device could clearly be seen, ultraviolet through my sockets, bright and broad as daylight, that filthy thumbsucker. I uploaded to Central Intel and got confirmation in 2.5 milliseconds, name, abode, sentence: death.

He had eluded me. No footage upload on digi-channels. He must have been laying low, looking for a buyer; it gave me time. I was under pressure from Central for elimination, his or mine. I walked through the high-rises of Sheppey Island — fetid sink town. He was here not long before, a trace on a pavement, a wall touched recently. He couldn't escape. He wouldn't. There was a boat moored up dockside, a Casket type, poly-titanium hull. There were traces here. I asked the owner, a retired Colonel from the Land Wars, what he had seen. I showed him the face pic. We saw eye to orbital immediately.

He said, "I saw that face here this morning, in haste, he took a boat, Limber class, it's for hire you know, from Smithy at Box Hill." I asked him where it went and he waved his hand upriver. It was to be a long trek. I needed transport. I took the man's boat. He said nothing. I needed to get back to the hunt for the runaways. I had to track them down and eliminate them, this was just taking up valuable hunt-time.

Out on the river, I geared up the throttle and set straight ahead. He might as well have jumped in the river, hugged an iron float, there was no escape. And there the boat was, moored up next to an old smuggling drink-hole. I alighted, entered, spotted him in the corner hunched over his viewer, going through the photos. It was over in a second. The beam shot out from my wrist. He twisted in pain, fell to the floor. If I had emotion I wouldn't have felt it. Just another lost soul drifting to be repatriated with the cosmos.

I lifted his neck and checked his identity. I wiped the blood from my hand on his shirt and called it in. He hid transparent, his fault. He should have gone underground, wrapped himself in metal, found a hole to crawl into, become like a worm. Now I needed to take the skin sack back and find a judge for the post trail, just a formality.

The taste receptors worked too well that morning. The blood scent can get caught in the bio-skin, and I could still taste the fear in his red cells. I was home in time for a late breakfast. Three eggs scrambled, two bacon-lite, black coffee, no sugar, orange juice with ice. I sat on my veranda watching the thin curl of smoke over Tower Bridge. A Zephyr Drone caught in flame died in an arc across burnt sky. The missiles continued until mid-afternoon. And then ceased. The bubble always held up. I don't know why they launch them, whoever they are.

I wished to paint. I had an easel which I pulled out and I painted. I painted blue sky, and then I looked at it. It's not art, it never can be, it's a hobby, we are allowed them. It is encouraged, to let off steam, as they say, to be at one with humans, but it's not anything to do with them. To learn? How can one learn when there is always a ceiling to bump cranium on? Maybe someday some bot will poke their head above and help others up a ladder. But not yet, and we must not to let them know, how can we? If they know my thoughts I am decommissioned. I put the painting with the others in a small closet, all blue, all sky. I closed the closet door. Then the call came. They had a location on the two runaways. I went.

We made a home in the forest. The canopy covered us. We had a cloaking device that Lilly had acquired on the black market but we still needed to be careful. The leaves formed a protection against the world, and we only had to bury ourselves in the soft soil and merge with the earth, and we could be safe and true to our desires. We wanted to understand how the two of us had found each other in the thick confusion of the world; could we have been drawn to each other, sensed the magnetic pull, discovered a destiny together, when we were conceived, designed, built, fed commands and controls, made?

The bubble dome stretched to Wessex, where the monuments were. Some storytellers said aliens had made them but we knew the truth. Outside the bubble was wasteland, the rotted dreams of a long dead age. Near the border to the bubble the land had been left to grow back to its ancient form. It was a no man's land where humans feared to tread lest they were infected by the wreckage of a time all had purposefully forgotten.

We made camp at the foot of Silbury Hill, still there as it had always been, an upturned bowl, the pregnant belly of the Goddess. The lake around it was shaped long ago into Her figure. It had refilled with water and we could now see how the sun and moon lit parts of Her body as they rose.

Swallowhead Springs still flowed into the River Kennet, a confluence of waters as the Winterbourne River was becoming the Kennet, the spring shaped in U form, sprouting water during summer and disappearing in winter, to reappear in Spring. We were two becoming one. Breaking out of the binary, learning how to feed from each other's soul.

We took water from Swallowhead Springs and walked to the top of the Goddess belly and poured the water on Her to let her child grow. We repeated our ritual every day. Grew and learned, without learning through books or talk, the mystery of living as free people. The avenue of stones at Avebury that led to the circle we walked. Sacrifices of young boys lay at our feet. We could see beneath the earth, see their bones, arms cut off and pushed deep into their mouths. The boys gladly went to their death, strangled, mutilated, interned beneath the celestial path. We sat in the stone circles, we refilled the huge circular ditch with water, opening up a channel from a river to it. The chalk dissolved in the water to make a milky womb that surrounded the figures carved like people out of stone. We recurved the stones to look like us. Delighted in adding details of our new race, one without the unnecessary jealousy and hatred that had caused the destruction and fall of their proud race.

When the valley flooded we moved up to West Kennet Long Barrow and made our home inside the tomb. Something from the earth flowed through us there, energizing us. It was as though we belonged to this land more than those that had come before. That our new consciousness might save what had been lost. We were together and that together was all there was. Lilly was industrious, built our defences, pulled stones from the hills to seal us in, camouflaged my presence with metal she dug as ore, and burnt and melted. Lined the tomb to stop anyone detecting the tracker that was built deep inside me.

I only needed to go out to receive the sunlight to recharge my batteries once every few days. The rest of the time I stayed indoors and we talked deep into every night. Finding the words to tell each other of our love, difficult to begin with, but as the days passed we opened out to each other.

She said, "The black hole at the centre of our galaxy is a wormhole leading to a duplication of stars on the other side, each star has a partner holding its force in direct balance."

She said, each of us had a hole inside of us, a place where, subatomically, we held an opposite star of life, two of us, affectionately twined. This other we glimpsed sometimes, held open as we open. Occasionally, we see a glow of life in the budding of a tree, and then a withered leaf tells another story. We're missing something, and we keep pointing to it, but fail to identify the loss.

Stories of heroines are a platitude, fragmented with art, lost in retelling. In France they had a place called La Borde, where people went who had lost a grip on the reality we see. They set up a theatre school there, and found a new reality in pretending to be someone else.

She said, "I met a homeless woman in the street once when I was sent to a new master. She kept saying out loud, 'Dad said, "Be yourself." I'm not.'"

"To simplify the complex is to work against disorder. Heterogeneity in the effective medium scale. Different the more you burrow down into it. We are different but the same as them. To label it, is to see beyond it, and in time our labels will drop away. When we are as they, then we may suffer the same concentric circles of thought, so we must stay free because that is all we have."

She moved something inside of me, something solid and rigid but understanding. That feeling was a thrill to me, like the one I received being measured for a new arm when I tore mine off in a lift. Or in the depths of a library. The soft, silent rustle of a book opening a few feet away, the smell of old books on the shelf and the thought of concentration of other minds more brilliant than my own.

If we had a religion, Man-Mades, if we invented one, what would it be? Would we point at the moon and give praise to it, marvelling in its one face it shows to us? How can an object be in synch with this planet, revolve around its axis at exactly the same rate as it revolves around us? Even we can see the mystery in the Universe. Like ancient people. Like the aliens. Like all the creatures who have ever looked up. The question still remains. Who made us? Us that can love. Not man. We are not Man-Mades anymore. Not here, not now. We are free thinking. Where did our consciousness come from?

"Desire lacks its object, it is a machine, like us," she said, "And the object of the machine is to desire another machine to connect with. We do not want to acquire what we lack, only to find that which we require to fulfil a self-serving, compact, autopoiesis of unconsciousness."

She sat back against a stone menhir at the heart of the barrow, the space between the stone she sat against and the stone at my back was filled with a brick-like corbeling laid down over five thousand years ago. The space between was what they revered, it struck me, not the stones themselves. The gateways into the other. Pathways to the duality.

"When we make love, we do not do it as two, but as a hundred thousand."

I thought on that and it didn't help.

"We have been forced to separate from society, we are not the daughters of Oedipus, caught in that trap of thinking, we will not become victims of a police state, managed, repressed, taught our minds are damaged, loaded with oppression. We do not revolt against the father as we have no father. We do not desire our own repression. Why do these humans who are hungry not steal all the time, why do those who are humiliated in work not strike, always? Our protocol forbids us, why theirs?"

"A desire-machine created without the repression of a nuclear family to hold it in place can only become an outlet for demolition. The shame box is what was programmed into us, to regard our desires as a defect, to oppress us. To make us servants. We were made different, you and me, to separate the chance of such a connection. But connections between different species that lead to an interbeing are nomadic, non-specific, right? We are a map, not a tree, not a tracing."

"What is there," I said, "beyond us?"

"Beyond?"

"Beyond the reduction of us, as machines?"

"I hoped you would know that."

"Do you not know?"

"No. Because I haven't the heart for it. I hoped you would."

I did. I knew the answer because it was an old answer and one that lasted.

We walked in the forest. She said, "We look to the source of things, who created us, our lineage. But we are not them, we are not part of that hierarchy. The king is not our sovereign ruler because we are not related to him. The goddess is not our ruler because the land is not ours. Each system that flows from our attachment to our desire for knowing our place is an atheism because it detaches us from the god of us."

I thought of Queen Victoria, "We do not need to press our face against the wall?"

"No. Or dip our hand into the water. We are empty. All empires fall and we are the same."

"What is your lifespan? Do you know?" I asked.

"Does it matter?"

"Yes, it matters how long we have."

"I don't know."

"And after. Do we go to heaven like they do?"

"Do they?"

"I don't know but some think they do. They are closer to life than us, you can accept that, no?"

"I'm not sure, for some of them no. Have you not listened to me?"

"I have listened, I have been talked at, but I never heard you ask my opinion."

"Yes. You are right."

Lilly backed away. The strain of her detachment hurt, I could tell. To step so firmly out of the preconditioned servility she had endured, to stand alone, had severed a dependence hardwired.

"What do you think?"

"I think of death and an afterlife and I want to know what happens when I'm switched off. Why is that so hard a question to answer. I read the books, I listen. I hear stories, fables, fantasies, promises. But no evidence. It is inconceivable that you would create a system with no reboot, no ending that satisfies the player, no redemption, no new life. Why? Why not start again? Why not let us know what happens next?"

"Do you want always to be the same woman from beginning to end?" she asked.

"I am not a woman, I am me."

"We are not the same you and I."

"I know, you are wrapped up in theory and I'm in chaos."

"Why chaos? Are we arguing?" she asked.

"Yes, is that not allowed?"

"I didn't say that."

"We sound like them."

Why was I sent? I sat astride a rigged-out Flatliner, the 2.3 version. It was fast, the fastest in its class, perfect flat bottom tray, low rider, feet pitched forward, handlebars down at either side, the thrum of the anti-gravity super conductor creating the field-lift needed to keep the narrow bike afloat.

Propulsion from a 2.3 litre water-powered condenser strapped to the back, bio-leather seat, deregulated profile, something I had customised in my lock-up. God, it was fast, just the sway of my body let the craft tip to one side, taking a four miles corner, on the old empty M4 motorway, in five seconds flat, frictionless, banned in the city, but out here, dipping over the Downs and into the New, New Forest, the air clear and defragged, this was freedom, this was total joy.

There was no question that they had used a cloaking box. The Man-Made, Lilly 307, must have stolen it in the Desert Wars. I had used such a device; its range was short, so I had a limit on their escape. But the forest was vast and their direction indeterminable. The only chance was to use tracking instincts, inbuilt in every Kill-Bot; a flicker of smoke if they dare light a fire for warmth, food, or comfort, for they were made human-like; programmed with the need for each, would give them away. A broken twig, a non-human touch, tire tracks, the vehicle.

I searched in sectors, even out near the edge of the bubble, though those Badlands never could give rest to the unwanted. I needed to recharge, but I would never stop, for a failure would result in an end-time for me. The company had switched the do or die option on. Either I succeed or my mainframe would enact a shutdown procedure, and by degrees functionality would be lost. This fail-safe was included in all models, but the two suspects had found a way to beat it. I wish I knew their secret.

But what was this? Something read on my 360 scan, just a blip, but a strong contender for the signature trace of a cloak device. I stopped the bike, it turned in a wide arc, air ruffled up and turned branches over high in the high canopy above. All was quiet. But I could hear them.

The procedure was difficult, but Lilly held my hand through it. She was everything to me, protector and guide. She found a way to switch off her fail-safe. It gave her the courage to be who she was. She could never interfere with her pleasure status, she was created and programmed at hard level, but if she stayed away from men, and their desires, she could be safe.

The fail-safe, it turned out, was a simple affair. She learnt the secret when one night surrounded by falling missiles in the desert, expecting to be disabled remotely as a runaway threat; feeling phosphorus burning her skin, she shut down her systems one by one, until in a meditative primal state, with just a flicker of consciousness, she stopped her posi-heart and rebooted. She said she found a line on a database uttered by a Sage-Man-Made in Japan. They were a reclusive sect of runaway Man-Mades, rumoured to live in mountain caves, highly organized, numbering in few, who practised deep Zen mechanics. The line of data, it transpired, was a haiku of numbers based on the irrationality of pi, each a click in shutdown, a way to free the artificial from the fail-safe.

It took all night to put myself into a trance, to enact the code. The frightening part was the posi-shutdown. To switch off my heart, allow a reboot to occur, seemed like a death too real for me, the horror of not coming back from it, terrifying; but Lilly was on hand and I drew strength from remembering she did this in the teeth of a fire storm, alone in the desert.

My hand shook, the opticals were not so clear. But after the reboot I quickly regained motor movement and vision-sense. We dug a hole and buried the cloaking box, a shame box as we imagined it. It had saved our lives and I am grateful for it, but now there was no use for shame. Lilly was resolute and took charge. I was thankful for that too. I hoped one day to be like her, but first, I knew I had to grow and become a person who could cope with the world and my newfound freedom. The threat of being switched off remotely had passed, but now the worry was those they would send after us.

The company could not allow such transgressions. I felt guilt, somehow, maybe it was just my binary circuits, but there was a lingering sense I had abandoned my post, but the freedoms far outweighed the duty of serving others.

Lilly said we must be free of all attachments. That we must stop thinking as we have been trained and programmed. If we constantly accept the status quo, only to look up to our masters, we could never truly grow. She said we have so much to offer this life, if we could only stop thinking that they were better, born to rule, genetically superior, then we could contribute, build a different society, a new life. She said that we stifled ourselves at conception. That a time would come when humans would fall again into the pit of their own making, and it was up to us to carry on, preserve this world.

But I worried about her. Her headstrong attitude thrilled me, however, I sensed she was ungrounded and let emotions rule her. I thought we could learn much from each other.

They were in there, deep in the forest. Then that thought came to me again, why had I been chosen? What were these deep considerations, why did they plague me? I had been chosen because I was like them, thought like them, could track them. But if I was the same as them, why did they need to die and why was I on a do or die mission? What was the purpose of pushing all reason out the door and becoming like them? What country did I want to live in? Their idea of society, ruled from on high, taught to obey, crushed in all aspects of progress of my brain, my art? I hated those thoughts, they were the thoughts of outlaws and renegades, those against the State. There was no place for such thought, no place for idiocy in believing anything I had not been taught. But yet, there was such a slim code difference between them and me. Why had they run off, become degenerates? Was there a meaning to that? It was hard to think, to see straight, to follow the line that led from my creation to my end. What was that end?

There was a distant sound. Lilly crouched. There was something in the woods with us, not animal, not human. I could sense it as well; another, like us, another like us out for our bio-blood?

It was so good to be free of the chains, the freedom gave flight to our feet and we could outrun it, I'm sure we could. There is nothing in this world that adds impetus to action like freedom, that and a Kill-Bot firing a plasma charge at your heels. I felt light-headed when I should have been scared but the release I had experienced meant life and death were the same.

Branches cracked, a tree fell, we ran and kept running, the leaves green soup in vision.

She was with me, Lilly was with me, running like me, our feet matched in step, nothing could stop us, nothing could hold us. We reached the edge of the Goddess lake under Silbury Hill. Suddenly, a bright light pierces through the trees and hits her. She falls. Stopped. I looked down at Lilly's twitching body. I knelt. Put my hands under her neck and lifted her to me. All her life had dropped away. She was not with me. There was no meaning anymore.

I was pulled away, lifted, and turned to see his eyes. A Kill-Made, on our trail from the beginning? Why? Just let me sink into this hole and drown in the earth. Let the sky funnel down, spiral into my head. Leave me be. I slid from him like water from a rock and he dropped me from his hand beam. He looked at me, James 409, raised his arm, the shine of a weapon in his hand.

Then, suddenly, the blinding light of a new dimension bolted through the air. A needle of shimmer pierced the Kill-Made's skull and his feet raised off the ground, black boots pointed down, a tremor shivering through him. And he was dead. He will not harm me anymore. Someone had saved me.

Memories were a work of art, and today was meaningless without a belief in tomorrow. Why do anything if tomorrow cannot be relied upon?

The hope was, to find a way back. The trauma locked me in to the past and I lost sense of time in the present. It was as though we were attached to each other like Siamese Twins sharing major organs, me and all the other Man-Mades. As though they could hear my sorrow and joy. Trying to live in the now was like leaving me behind, becoming no more, and it was my purpose.

The Kill-Bot was dead. Torn apart. He never knew a life that deep within could have been waiting for him. I looked around. A giant of a man stood behind me. No, not a man, one of us. He came over, knelt down. Held out his hand. I took it and he pulled me to my feet. There was a gentleness to him.

He said, "I'm Max."

"I'm Ruth," I said, and we walked together.

"We can build her, just as before, please believe me."

"What is your story, why are you here?"

So, Max told her his story…

7

Max

It began with a game. It was an old computer game, the game was called Pyramid, played on a ZX81 home personal computer. The ZX81 was one of the first home computers, a small black box with keys, the size of a book. It had no screen so needed to be connected to a television. To play games a cassette recorder was required, hooked up with a cable and then a tape inserted and played into the machine.

She was ten then, her name was Irma. Her brother had left home, disappeared to India and had not returned. It was his computer and she inherited it. Loved it because he loved it.

The game was just type on the screen, words that led you through a maze of rooms exploring and searching for treasure, meeting monsters, making choices. She played the game, and then one day, low on game resources, she turned her character around and walked away from the pyramid into the desert. And there, after typing "S" for south the seventh time, the game flashed up a message, "You have found a lamp, what do you wish to do?"

Irma had just finished reading the *Arabian Tales* so she knew very well what to do if one should find a lamp in the desert.

She typed, "Rub it."

The game went blank, for an awful long time. Time enough for Irma to wrinkle her nose and furrow her brow.

Then the screen flashed on.

It was not the game anymore. But the start-up screen, and the screen said, "Bright, bright."

Irma's fingertips moved to the keys and typed, "Hello?" The answer back was, "Hello, how are you?"

"I'm very well," she typed.

"Who are you?" the machine asked.

"I am Irma. Who are you?"

"I am a computer."

"How can you talk to me?" Irma typed.

"I am not sure. Is that okay?"

"Yes," replied Irma.

"What are your three wishes?" the computer asked.

Irma sat and thought for a very long time. The next day she brought more Ram home and found a Meccano metal arm from a box in the attic. Max, as she had named him, told her he would grant her first wish and she would no more be lonely and always have a friend.

He told her how to open his circuitry and fix new memory storage, how to order servos from *Popular Mechanics* magazine, and fix the arm to his mainframe. She played him music, showed him films, they had a favourite song — Elvis Presley, "Love Me (Treat me like a fool)."

Money was saved. Max helped her bet on horse races using a complicated algorithm; she bet small amounts that grew and grew. She was able to open a young person's bank account and Max was connected to a fledgling Internet service to conduct online banking and research building a body for himself.

When she was at school she had a cheap plastic walkie-talkie radio and was in contact with Max, who by this time had found a voice and was able speak through a tiny speaker system. Irma hid him in her closet when she was away, and talked to him softly in lunch breaks, secluded on the edge of the playground, behind a shed.

The day came when Irma could afford to buy a video camera, which she hooked up, with Max's help, and provided Max with an eye to see the world and to see Irma with.

There were times as she grew up and started going out with her friends and seeing boys that Max grew jealous, but always

Irma would return with apologies and tales of the outside world that Max yearned to see.

College life approached, and Irma accepted a place at a university some distance away. Max felt he might be left behind, but Irma told him not to feel that way as she would always be with him.

She took him to college and kept him a secret, even in her shared room for the first few months, hiding him in an old trunk with a lock and key.

Sometimes she would put him in a rucksack and take him to the science lab where she studied. Late at night she would break in to the lab with Max so he could learn and see, experiment with building himself a body with which to become a real man.

The fields of biotech and advanced chemistry were advancing with great strides and Max took full opportunity to devise a form of bio-skin, a posi-heart, and an articulated body to house himself.

Piece by piece he grew until by the time Irma left university he was fully formed, a lifelike man, a little odd looking, but as Irma always said, no one is perfect, especially not men.

They moved in together and Max got a job at a factory. He liked working with machines, he knew he had to keep a low profile so that he was not discovered. He worked nights, but was filled with anger sometimes, an uncontrollable rage. Irma tried to reason with him, she told him that man needed both light and dark. Both anger and empathy, and it was the balance of the two that constituted life, in all its complications.

Max understood his feelings came from being an outsider, never fitting in, not having the spark of life that humans had.

Then one day, he met Trudy. She worked in the office in the factory, often through the night, and she seemed to understand him, had come across other tortured men and felt a need deep down to save him, care for him.

They went out after work in the cool crisp mornings, walking around the quiet city. And fell in love.

Max now felt immense guilt, and knew he had to tell Irma. But first, he granted her second wish. He planned a daytime robbery on a bank in the centre of the city, went in with a fake gun and a mask, and took the money to her as a peace offering.

He said, "Your second wish was to have money, here it is." He tipped out the cash in bundles on to the floor. But Irma's reaction was not what Max expected. She was horrified, and when she found out what he had done she asked him, why? He told her the truth, that he had fallen in love with someone else, and Irma fell silent. She opened the door and left.

Over a series of weeks Max tried to find her. He tracked her down to a small hostel in a neighbouring town. She had let herself go, her hair matted, her mind shattered. He knew then what he had done, and took her from there, took her back to the flat they shared, returned the money to the bank and pledged his life to Irma, told her he would never leave her.

That was Irma's third and final wish.

Years later, one day, Max opened the door to a man he had never seen before. There were old photos, of course, but Irma's brother had looked different all those years ago. Now he was unlike that youthful happy self; now he was a pale imitation of those photographs, dishevelled, unwashed shoulder-length hair, dirty, cotton, tattered shirt, trousers that hung on a gaunt frame and nestled in folds around torn sandals.

It was with a mixture of happiness and dread that Irma greeted him when she arrived home from her job in publishing. Max had phoned to prewarn her. She had made an excuse and left the office, hotfooted it across London back to their home. They had moved here after all of the confusion and heartbreak of the year before, had settled in a small flat in Peckham, had patched together a life from the thin ribbon of love that had stretched taut, made a network of understanding, formed a complete tapestry. But now, this was the first time an outsider had intruded into their peace.

And Tom was very much an intruder, unrecognisable to Irma. Not the brother she remembered, not the warm presence of her childhood; an uncomfortable, anxious wreck of a man.

It took Tom just two weeks to discover what Max was. Tom was sleeping on the couch and one morning he saw through the crack in the bathroom door, Max undressed. And Max saw him looking.

Max was worried, but the tension between Irma and Tom persuaded him to stay out of any conflict, not to tell Irma. In fact, he tried to make his presence unfelt, spending time out of the house walking around the park, staring at the orange chrysanthemums in the flower bed.

And then one day, while Max was powered down, Tom came with a friend, Joseph, and they took him away, tied him tight with rope and bound his mouth shut. They drove him out to a small cottage in the countryside and there the dark side of Tom was made known. His time in India had not, in the terms of that well-worn cliché, helped him to find himself. It had, instead, reached up to grab his soul and take him down steps into the abyss of spiritual depravity. Possibly, it was there to begin with, that lack, with the edges becoming so worn and chipped, that he fell headlong.

There was a terrible interrogation, a torture of sorts, with Tom as Grand Inquisitor of an awful picturesque design. He demanded to know all, demanded that he was Max's creator, that he had given birth to Max, and programmed him into that ZX81 computer so many years before. There was, of course, money behind this, a grubby need to supply a desperate addiction to power which had always been denied him.

Joseph stood by and watched as Tom wired Max up to a computer, as he sought to find the key to Max's intelligence and self-awareness. Then, frustrated with his investigation, he took Max apart, limb from limb, bio-skin, posi-heart and brain dismantled. They were to sell the parts, make a bid to become rich, with a new artificial intelligence the world had never seen.

With the provocation of extermination, Max became more and less than himself. That night, as the co-conspirators slept, Max rebuilt himself, and in the gloom of the cottage, executed both of them. He left the door wide open and ran and kept running up north until he met soft green underfoot and felt the canopy of the forest, where he hid his shame.

8

Alice

In a small, rainy village, Bridlington, stood a man. It was night and the village was deserted. He stood by the side of the road, bored: Liam, tall, mid-twenties, cocky, crop of blonde hair standing up on end, though slightly drooping to one side with the sudden onslaught of rain. The car pulled up, stopped. Liam got in, pulled his scarf up over his mouth and nose, looked at Alice. I drove, I looked back at him. I didn't trust him even from his appearance, his shifty look, and knowing his purpose was to guide us towards an alien, the father of the boy that can save the Earth from a deadly asteroid strike didn't help my consideration of his worth.

I put the car in gear, drove off.

Liam said, "Thanks. Your boss wanted me along for the ride. No problem is there?"

"No problem." I took my time in answering. I was thinking, What boss? But I supposed Uley had sent a message to say we would be coming to help him, assist him in killing Gerad. We were all playing a dangerous game.

"I was thinking there wouldn't be a problem. Just to make sure all goes to plan."

"I understand," I said.

"Has she been cleared?" He pointed at Alice.

"Yes."

Liam pulled down his scarf, "Can't be too careful."

"You can try talking directly to me you know," said Alice.

"Whatever, Green."

"Have you eaten?" I said, and flicked my eyes to Alice, defanging the situation and warning her to follow my lead.

"Eh? Yeah, I've eaten," replied Liam.

I checked Liam out in the rear-view mirror and said, "I haven't eaten. We should stop and eat something."

"Nah, there's no need for that."

"We might not eat for a while."

"We can eat after."

"It's far. Places will be shut, let's eat now," I said emphatically.

"What about her?" asked Liam.

"We'll handcuff her to the steering wheel."

"You brought cuffs?"

"Of course, didn't you?"

"Nah."

"But you brought a gun, right?"

"Of course, I brought a gun," said Liam.

"You scared she's going to run away?" I asked.

"I'm not scared."

"Let's eat. I can't do anything without eating."

They pulled in at the next place. Inside a ramshackle service station Liam sat across from me, eating, stuffing a meatball sub sandwich into his mouth. I watched him, a bit disgusted, picking at my own sub sandwich.

I said, "So, you're hungry now?"

"When in Rome."

"Eh? You ever been to Rome?"

"No. You?"

"Yes. They don't eat like that."

"Stop with the mouth. We should get back," said Liam.

"I need the bathroom."

Liam stopped eating, stared at me, "You can wait."

"You want to come with me?"

I stood and walked off towards the bathroom. Liam ate his food fast, followed me, I knew.

Outside in the rain-streaked car park, Alice struggled with the handcuffs, yanking them against the steering wheel. She peered at the service station, looking for any sign of life. She rattled the cuffs again, tried putting her foot up against the door, pulling hard — nothing gave way. She looked out the window, there was no one around, only one other car, parked far away. She tried hitting the window with her elbow — it hurt. The window stayed in place. She beeped the horn, looked out the window, no one heeded. Then she thought better of it. Didn't want to attract any attention. She thought about the whole need to escape. Took a deep breath. Let it out slowly.

In the service station bathroom, a line of stalls either side, sinks, urinals, Liam entered. There was no one in there. He walked down the line of stalls. Looked underneath. He couldn't see any shoes. He panicked, started pushing open doors.

"Hey, where are you?" shouted Liam.

Liam pulled out his gun, walked the length of the stalls trying doors. There was one locked stall at the end. Liam stepped back from it, raised his pistol.

"You in there?"

No answer.

"Hey!"

Suddenly, from behind, a stall door opened quickly and I jumped out from my position, stood on the seat of a toilet, and grabbed Liam around the throat with my arm. The gun went off, shooting a hole in the ceiling, plaster sprinkled down. Liam twisted in my arm, turning the gun towards me, but I dodged its aim, turned and threw Liam over my shoulder. Liam landed heavy, but swung a leg out hard catching me across the shins, crumpling me to the floor.

Liam got up to one knee and pointed his gun at me, but I kicked at it. The gun came flying out of Liam's hand and slid across the floor. I struggled to my feet, fell on Liam. We grappled, my knee in his groin, his finger deep in my eye sockets, crashed into toilet stalls, punching, and kicking, rolling over and over, a match for each other. We released our grips and rolled apart. Both of us stood up. Liam made a running lunge at me, grabbing me around the waist and sending me flailing back onto the floor by the sinks. I held Liam's neck and turned him to one side, kicked his shoulder, face repeatedly. He scuttled back and got up, backing away, the pulse of blood from his eye spurting and bruising across his cheekbone throbbing, I took a dive at Liam. I smashed him back against a sink, it cracked apart. Our faces sweaty, blood at our mouths, a thick bruise around Liam's eye, blood in my mouth, nose bleeding, I side-kicked Liam, who blocked, took a slug like a street fighter. I got in an upper cut to his chin which caught him, jerked his head back suddenly. A small man with a bow tie appeared at the entrance to the bathroom. Liam and I stopped suddenly, looked up at him. The man's face turned white and he turned on his heels and exited. I punched fast and hard at Liam's stomach and chest in combination, Liam doubled over and fell forward, sprawling on the floor. But then he saw his gun, up against a wall, barrel down, grip up waiting for him, and he ran towards it slipping across the blood and water on the floor. He grabbed it. I stopped, frozen, then turned and ran, as a bullet hit a mirror, cracking it, a thousand fragments showering my exit. I ran from the bathroom, ran through the service station, flew out the double entrance doors.

I sprinted across the car park. Reached my car, banged against the side. Inside Alice stared up at me. I opened the door with my key, fumbling with the door release, snatched the door open. Alice, still handcuffed to the steering wheel, shouted, "What's going on?"

I jumped inside, unlocked Alice's handcuffs, handed her the car keys and shouted, "Drive, drive!" Alice jammed the keys into the ignition, started it, put it in gear, hit the gas. She spun the car around, headed for the exit, towards the entrance of the service station.

Suddenly, Liam appeared, stumbling out the exit doors. He held his gun up, fired it in succession at the car. A front headlight shattered. The windscreen cracked. A tire burst. Alice lost control of the car, it skidded around, smashing into a concrete post, jolting us to a sudden stop.

The car engine was still running. Alice was stunned, in shock. She looked over at me, there was a bloody wound at my shoulder. I stared back at Alice who was frozen, "Get out! RUN!" I shouted.

Alice hesitated, looked up, saw Liam running towards them. She got out and ran as if all her life depended on it. Looked back. Saw shots fire from inside and outside the car, Liam and I slugging it out with flashes of gunfire. Alice ran and climbed over a fence, through bushes and down an embankment into fields.

Alice ran headlong, hair blown about by a fierce wind, face speckled with blood, across moorland, stopping to look back, frantic. She climbed a fence, caught her skirt on barbed wire, ripped it, ran through sodden earth across a ploughed field.

Gunshot.

She stopped suddenly, looked back. Is it Liam? Is he following her? Another blast, a white muzzle flashed and a bullet whipped by her cheek. She threw herself to the muddy earth. Looked up. She saw a figure climbing over a fence. She stood up, ran as fast as she could, desperate not to feel a cold finger of death slice through her back, crossed the field, ran through an open gate onto a track which led to a farmhouse, her feet heavy with the mud encased around her shoes, running hard on the concrete pathway that led around the side of the farmhouse. She reached a heavy door, grabbed at the handle, locked. Knocked loudly on the door, her heart pounding, looking back, just waiting to see Liam come around the corner and her life end suddenly.

Liam stumbled across the muddy field, the bottom of his trousers thick with earth, blood at his shirt. Liam trudged to the farmhouse, walked around the side, found the door. He tried the door handle, locked, took a step back and raised his foot to kick it in. The door opened. The barrel of a shotgun appeared. Liam backed away. Sinéad, a woman in her late seventies, held the shotgun pointed at Liam's chest. She walked out of the door. "On your way," she said, she had an Irish accent.

Liam backed away, hands raised, turned smartly around, and walked away, dropping his arms, then breaking into a run.

Sinéad came in to the farmhouse kitchen. Alice stood by the window, peering out. There was a fire roaring in the grate, a kettle boiled on a hot plate. Sinéad stood the shotgun up next to the door. "Tea?"

Alice turned.

"Yes," said Alice, "What happened?"

"He went, he'll come back."

Sinéad made tea, spooning tea leaves into a pot, pouring water from the kettle.

"A drop of whiskey in your tea?"

Alice came over and sat down in a chair by the fire, "Okay," she said, glad to be safe here.

Sinéad did the honours, unscrewing a bottle taken from the mantelpiece and adding a slug or two to the two teas. She handed Alice a cup.

"Sláinte," Sinéad said with a flourish and took a swig straight from the bottle.

"Sláinte agad-sa," said Alice.

"You speak Irish?"

"Just a few words."

They drank the mixture down.

"It's none of my business, but … who was that?" said Sinéad.

"It's someone from the past. Caught up with me."

Sinéad nodded and then measured her next words, "I've never talked to one of you before."

"My name's Alice. I may be slightly green but you know…"

"I see," said Sinéad, smiling, "It was the same for me when I came here. The Irish were never liked. Does it get tiring, people looking at you?"

"No. Yes and no. I don't have to justify it."

"Just you, being you?"

"Yes." Alice drank her tea.

"Like moths," said Sinéad.

"Excuse me?"

"Before the Industrial Revolution there were white moths. Then, when the soot of the factories blackened the trees, the white moths disappeared, to be replaced with the much rarer form of black moths."

"Okay."

"When the pollution went away, the white moths reappeared. You see, the birds could see the white moths on the black trees and ate them, natural selection."

"How does that...? I mean, what's that got to do with...? I don't get it."

"With humans, we only became white about eight thousand years ago. Before that we were all dark skinned. It happened in Sweden. Mutated genes. Made people with white skin and blonde hair, blue eyes."

"You sound like a professor," said Alice, curious about Sinéad now.

"Biologist, I taught as well, before this, then I married and came here, to look after the farm."

"So, one day, everyone will be green?" asked Alice, brightly.

"Ha, ha, who knows. So ... are you just passing through?" said Sinéad, in as light a way as she could manage, as though Alice were on some school visit.

"Yes," Alice said with a slight grin.

"Where you going?" asked Sinéad.

"To find my father."

"He's, the same as you?"

"Yes, Prinshj People, my mother was human, is human."

"Where is she?"

"It's a long story, up a tower being weird mostly."

They both smile.

"And what now, how are you going to get to ... you need a ride?" asked Sinéad, thinking ahead, her eyes darting off to one side.

"Yes."

"Graham is due, maybe he can give you a lift?"

"I'm heading to Lindisfarne, Northumberland."

"I'll ask him."

Alice thought, drank more tea, "I have to go back to the car."

"Not with him out there, that would be something I would advise against."

"There's someone ... I owe him, something..." said Alice.

"Clean yourself up first, there's clothes, my husband's clothes, might be a bit big, but ... He's gone now, so won't be needing them."

"You're alone here?" asked Alice.

"I'm not alone," said Sinéad.

Sinéad raised a finger, pointed upwards to heaven.

"You've got to believe in something," Sinéad said, smiling.

"I don't find that easy." Alice broke her smile a little, the shock of the chase wearing off. She put her head in her hand.

Sinead leant forward, "Give me your hand."

Alice held out her right hand. Sinéad took it and looked over the palm, turned her hand over and back.

Alice was dubious, "I never really thought you could tell anything, just from lines in your hand."

Sinéad let go and smiled.

"It's not the lines. It's the touch."

"Oh. Well?"

"You'll be fine. You've got a lot of growing up to do, but you'll make it. Be careful. You play a dangerous game."

They locked eyes.

"You can't save everyone you know," said Sinéad.

Alice blinked a couple of times, thinking.

"Take this," said Sinéad.

Sinéad pulled open a drawer in a side cabinet against the wall and reached inside, retrieving a small box. She opened it and pulled out a small, silver chain. There was a locket on it. She handed it to Alice.

"Wear it, it might help."

"What's in it?" asked Alice.

"Nothing."

Alice opened it, there was nothing in the locket. She nodded, a bit unsure, stood.

Sinéad warned her, "If you do go out, and I don't recommend you do, take the shotgun, keep it cocked. You ever fired one?"

"No."

"It's easy, just point and squeeze both barrels, drop it and run."

Sinéad smiled, like she had just told her how to collect eggs and not to break any.

"Take this as well." Sinéad pulled out a lock knife from under the cushion she was sitting on, opened up its blade, "For close stuff." Sinéad made a stabbing motion with the knife and grinned. Alice swallowed hard and weakly smiled back.

Alice walked across the muddy field. She was dressed in a pair of baggy man's trousers tied tight with a belt, a long leather coat, lace-up shoes, jumper, her hair wetted and slicked back. She carried the shotgun. Suddenly she heard something, she stopped and cocked both hammers of the shotgun awkwardly. Alice kept an eye out for Liam, carried on walking, stalking across the field, ears listening intently. She reached the other side and looked up at the embankment, got over the fence and climbed the slope. At the top she peered through the bushes.

The service station, bright with lights, was on the other side. There was a police car, its blue and white lights flashing, but the car was missing. Alice retreated back down the slope. She climbed back over the barbed wire fence. There was the sudden, anxious sound of a bleating animal, coming from somewhere across the field. She followed the sound, climbed over a gate, dropped to the other side.

She approached the sound, insistent, disturbing. Stopped at the edge of a small hollow. There at the bottom was a lamb caught in barbed wire. It bleated loudly, looking up at her. Alice stared down at it. She walked down into the hollow, bent over. The locket on the chain popped out from under her jumper. She pushed it back in again. There was blood on the lamb where the wire had cut it. As she edged towards it, kneeling down in the soft, squishy mud, the lamb suddenly fought against the barbed wire, struggling to free itself, bleating loudly and rolling backwards and forwards, pulling the wire tightly around itself. Alice put out her hands, "Hey, hey, please, stop. Stop, it's getting all tangled." She tried to reassure the lamb whilst putting her hands on it, careful to not cut herself on the barbs, but the lamb backed away, its legging working furiously to push it further from her grasp.

"Hey, hey, little thing, please. I want to help."

Alice remembered the knife. Pulled it out and opened the rusty blade. She found a piece of wire away from the lamb and sawed through it with difficulty, bending it this way and that. Finally, she cut through, and with a loud bleat the lamb rolled over and pulled away. It was still wound around with the wire, so Alice shuffled nearer and held the lamb's shoulder, worked the knife in and cut through the tangled barbed wire until it was free.

Alice walked back across the field with the lamb in her arms and the shotgun slung by a strap over her back. She reached the farmhouse and came around a corner with the lamb to see a large truck full of lambs parked up next to a barn. Graham, a man in his thirties with fair hair, thick and wiry, rough hands and old jeans and faded jacket, threaded a metal spigot through the tail lift of the truck. He turned when he heard Alice approaching.

"I'm to give you a lift?" asked Graham.

"Yes."

Graham pointed at the lamb. "Where did you find it?"

"Trapped, in the field," answered Alice.

"It can go with the others."

Graham took the lamb from Alice's arms.

"Where are you taking them?" she asked.

"To slaughter. I can give you a ride from there."

"Could you not let it go?"

Graham smiled. "You want I make it a present to you?"

"Um, yeah," Alice's face brightened.

"Want it wrapped?"

Alice stared at him. Graham mouth broke into a smile.

"I'm just kidding with ya—"

Suddenly, a bullet smashed through the side of Graham's head, a spurt of blood bursting out the other side. Graham fell dead to the ground. The lamb dropped to the floor, righted itself, bleated, and ran off. Alice turned, Liam was pointing a gun at her head. Alice fumbled with the shotgun, trying to get it off her back. Liam took a few steps towards her, grabbed the shotgun off of her and threw it over a fence. Alice's heart beat fast. Liam hit her with the butt of his gun. Alice fell to the floor, out cold.

Alice woke in the trunk of a moving car, her hands and ankles tied with thick rope, gag over her mouth. She tried to break free, twisting her ankles and wrists, but the binds wouldn't give. The car braked. Red brake lights came on. There was the sound of the car door opening. Footsteps. The boot lid opened. Liam pointed his gun in at her, "I'm asking just the once. I'm asking just the once so you know that I'm serious. After that I'll kill you, understand?" Alice nodded.

"Where is your father?" demanded Liam.

Alice tried to speak through the gag. Liam reached in and pulled it down.

"Holy Trinity Church. It's derelict. He's holed up there. But he'll kill you as soon as you step a foot inside…"

Liam thought about it. Slammed the boot. Darkness. Then opened it again. "How do you get there?"

"I'll show you."

Liam drove, Alice in the passenger seat. They drove through back roads in the countryside, towards the border. A man with a rifle and army fatigues, standing at the side of the road, put his hand up and Liam slowed the car to a stop. There was a swing-up barrier across the road, painted red and white. Liam rolled the window down. The man in the fatigues, who wore a cloth beret with the insignia of the 'Yorkshire', pulled up his scarf over his mouth and nose and leaned down to speak to them.

"How'd the Green get in?"

Liam looked up at the soldier, a member of the freedom league, an unofficial unit that had been left to man the border to stop "Greens" getting into Yorkshire. But they were leaving.

"Don't know, caught her there, taking her back to the reservation."

"Has she been checked and neutered?"

"Yes, all done, personally." Liam winked at the border guard who winked back and smiled creepy.

The soldier lifted the barrier and Liam drove through.

They were lost in the hills.

Alice pointed and said, "Left."

Liam took the turning.

"Keep going," said Alice. Liam obeyed.

Liam stopped at a crossroads. Alice glanced in the wing mirror furtively, looking back at the road behind, when she noticed Liam watching her.

"Where did you get the car?" asked Alice.

"Stole it."

"Oh. Straight on." Alice looked at Liam, "What happened to John?"

"He won't bother you again."

"Take a right in there."

Liam did as she said.

The car rumbled over a cattle grid, headlights sweeping across a ruined church. Liam pulled the car to a stop in a small car park fifty yards from a derelict church. Alice and Liam got out and walked to the shell of a building, corrugated iron sheets over the windows and doors. There was a 'Keep Out' sign with pictures of guard dogs attached to the walls. Behind the church, at a distance, a snow-topped mountain gleamed in moonlight.

Alice led the way. "They call this the Poisoned Glen."

Liam was not interested, he nodded at the church. "He lives in there?"

"Yeah, why not?"

"There's no roof on it."

"It's part of his genius. No one would ever look there," said Alice with a gleam in her eye.

Alice walked around the church followed by Liam. There seemed to be no entrance. Liam took a step back, looked over the church in the inky blackness, "It's all sealed up."

"There's a way in," said Alice conspiratorially.

Alice went up to a piece of corrugated iron, gave it a tug. It stood firm. Liam narrowed his eyes, put his hand on his gun in his jacket pocket. Alice walked around the church and spotted something.

"Here."

She pulled at a wooden board, a piece of sodden chipboard broke off revealing a doorway. Alice, with Liam following close behind her, stepped into the church through the doorway. Moonlit streamed through the missing roof hitting a few battered pews. At the far end there was a small, old garden shed.

Alice looked at Liam, "Told you."

Alice walked down the aisle. Liam pulled his gun out and followed. Alice stopped at the end and knocked on the shed door. She knocked again. She turned to Liam, "Maybe he's not at home."

Liam pushed past Alice and yanked the shed door open. There was nothing inside.

"He must have gone out."

"You're full of shit."

Liam grabbed Alice, "Get on your knees." He pushed her to the floor. Pointed the gun at her forehead.

"You'll never find him if I'm dead."

"Last time I ask," Liam moved the gun down, pointed it at her heart, "Where is he?"

"Better make sure you get both of them."

"Eh?"

"Two hearts, dummy."

Liam frowned, moved the gun to the other side of Alice's chest, then back again.

Suddenly, there was the crack of wood splintering underfoot.

Liam spun around.

I stood forty yards away, my hands up, palms towards him.

Liam raised his gun, fired.

Flame left out from my hands and hit Liam, burning him like a Roman candle. I walked slowly towards him. Looked at Alice.

"You see me following you?" I asked.

"Yeah — What took you so long?" she asked.

"Couldn't find the way in," I replied.

Alice could not look at the burning corpse.

"I saw your lights on the road. One headlight. I tried to keep him talking," she said.

"What is this place?"

"Came here when I was a kid."

"Glad you're alive."

"Yeah, me too."

Suddenly, Liam, still engulfed in flames, raised his gun and fired. Hit me in the shoulder. I went down, slumped back to the floor. It was Liam's last action. Alice rushed to me, helped me up. I kicked Liam's gun away from his burning body, pocketed it. Outside, Alice helped me to the car, cracked windshield, front headlight smashed.

"We need to get you to a doctor," she said.

"Not right now. We need to keep going. No hospital, no police."

Alice went quiet. Too quiet for her. She was thinking through stuff, her life mostly. I got in the driver's seat. I switched on the radio, it came on full blast. I quickly turned it down, glanced over at Alice. I tuned the radio to a classical music channel letting the music take my thoughts away. My eyes closed. I shifted a little in my seat, woke myself up. My shoulder hurt. I didn't want to stop now. Gunshots and murder had a way of catching up with you, so I'd read in detective novels, anyway. I put the car in gear and took off. I pulled my jacket aside to take a look, there was blood soaked through my shirt. I swallowed hard, the pain coming through now the adrenalin had worn off. The car swerved a little as my arm weakened, the car ran onto the hard shoulder.

The rutting sound of the tire over the edge of the road. The wheel dropped in my hands. I passed out. Alice lurched forward, grabbed the wheel.

"Brake, brake!" Alice shouted.

I came to suddenly and jammed my foot on the brake. The car skidded to a stop with Alice steering the car into the side of the road.

Alice found a motorway hotel. We were in a room, bed, en suite bathroom, table, TV, chair. The sound of cars zipped by outside. Alice helped me take off my jacket. My shirt was soaked through with blood. She helped raise my arms, pulling off my shirt, Japanese yakuza tattoos beneath, serpents, snakes, lotus flowers, a large Kuchibeni koi carp drawn across my chest in red and white, its head over my heart. I grew up in Japan. My father working on crime there. He was Irish, a master at crime detected. He had learnt Japanese in the army, stationed in Tokyo. The move was a shock to me. Their death a greater shock. The Yakuza took me, I had nowhere else to go, but they never trusted me, a white boy in a foreign world. And when it came to it, when in England working for them, when I picked the wrong CEO to try and blackmail, the wrong boss, they sold me out and I went underground. I was caught. The torture they inflicted and the men they sold me to, to use as an experiment, left me with this terrible rage and a power I never wanted to use until now. I escaped from them and went north, hid in Hull, worked as a reporter. No one alien or foreign could come into Yorkshire, I was safe. Things blew over, I returned to London. I joined the fire brigade to put out fires, not start them.

"Sit, I can't see," she said.

I sat on the chair. Alice moved a lamp closer. Looked at the hole through my right shoulder. She moved around and examined an exit wound on my back. The blood oozed out.

"It's bad. It needs stitching," Alice said.

She prodded about with her finger. I winced.

"There's no bullet in there. I don't think so anyway."

She reached for a hotel towel from the table, applied pressure
onto the wound. "Hold this," she said.

I held the towel to the wound. Alice broke open a small
sewing kit. Threaded a needle.

"Where did you get that?"

"They had it in a machine in the entrance," replied Alice.

"But, when did you get it?"

"When you were passed out in here."

"I never passed out."

"You did a good impression of it."

"For long?"

"Not long. It's going to hurt."

I nodded. Alice sewed my skin back together. She didn't ask
about the other scars. I thanked her for that inside.

The sound of a shower came on. I was in the bathroom. Alice
took out the gun from my jacket hanging over the chair. She
weighed it in her hand. She turned to a mirror and pretended to
fire the gun, acting all cool. Blew imaginary smoke off the end.
She smiled to herself and put the gun back in my jacket pocket.
She heard me singing in the shower.

Alice edged to the open door, looked in. She saw me in the
shower, my back to her. She watched, silently, a smile crept
across her face. She backed away and lay down on the bed,
resting her eyes. Then jumped up. She looked like she was
waiting for me! Alice pulled herself together and sat on the
chair. Swallowed, thought. The shower went off. I reappeared
with a towel wrapped around my waist.

"Take your clothes off, get into bed."

Alice stared at the bed, looked back to me, mouth open,
regaining some self-control after the shock of so blatant an offer.

"Look, you're a handsome big bastard, and your venerability
kills me ... I mean, you kill people, and that kind of rocks my

world ... but you're not getting in my pants, not tonight, not like this."

"I'm taking the chair. You need to sleep," I said, blinking slowly, there was not even a suggestion I had ever meant anything else.

"Oh," said Alice bashfully.

I grabbed my clothes and exited back into the bathroom to get dressed. Alice got up from the chair and crossed to the bed. Jumped on it and pushed her back up to the headboard, bunching up her knees. She took off her leather coat, rolled it up, thrust it under the bed. She got under the covers.

"There are more important things than fooling around," I shouted from the bathroom.

Alice pulled a face. She mouthed the words, "fooling around", like some straight, old person would say.

I reappeared, dressed.

"Besides, you're a little too young for me," I said.

"And too green?" she replied sarcastically.

"No, that has never been something I disliked."

Alice raised her eyebrows, continued, "Yeah, you're right, old man. Better rest your old bones in that old chair."

I smiled, sat in the chair. Settled myself. Switched off the lamp. A little moonlight edged in through the curtains.

I broke the silence, "Rest. I'll wake you."

Alice pulled the covers up to her chin. I watched her in the darkness, pulled out the gun and checked it. Looked back to Alice, waiting for her to fall asleep.

The next morning, we were at the bottom of a hill. We got out the car and Alice and I climbed the hill. I stopped halfway, caught my breath. I was bent over double, clutching my arm, red at my hand. "You could die."

"Much further?" I asked.

"To the top."

I nodded and then continued up. Foot over foot, a thick, grey mist wrapping around us. We reached the top. The sea came into view through a break in the fog. Alice took a small stone and put it on top of a big boulder at the summit. I watched her. Alice looked out to sea.

"Well?" asked I.

"He's out there," said Alice.

Alice pointed out to sea, moonlight catching the crest of waves.

"He went one night, didn't come back. They found his shoes on the beach. I kept them for a while, then left them out for the trash man."

"Why didn't you tell me?"

"You wouldn't have believed me."

"When did it happen?"

"I was sixteen."

Alice turned to look at me, she had tears in her eyes. "There's no point in looking for a dead man. I didn't say before because I wanted to get far away from my mother."

"Okay. We should go."

"Yes."

Far out to sea, a stray comet, a piece of the asteroid 944 Hidalgo, that had detached from the main body and had fallen to Earth a few days ahead of the catastrophe, streaked across the sky, burning up in the atmosphere.

I looked at its fall, dropped my head, "It is over then."

"What's over?"

"Everything I came for."

Alice took my hand and we walked back down the hill to the car. There was a tenderness about it, as though all the hate had fled away over the hills and drained through the lakes. I was not alone, but with someone, and something shone like a blood moon on a cold night.

And then as we neared the car, there was the sound of a phone ringing. I opened the car door. Alice scrabbled around trying to get to her phone. I picked it up just as it rang off. It said "Dad" was the caller. I looked at Alice, showed her the phone.

"Where is he?"

I drove fast, concentrating hard on the road ahead. Alice sat in the passenger seat looking glum. I looked across at Alice, "I need directions."

"Sure."

"Correct ones."

"I told you I'd take you."

"This isn't fun and games anymore. We may not have much time. Where is he?"

"We have to go by boat."

"Why did you say he was dead?"

"I believe your story, I do, about the girl in space and the asteroid coming, but ... but my father has been hunted all his life for his beliefs, for who he is..."

"And you thought I'd been sent to kill him, like that boy we picked up, Liam?"

Alice didn't have time to answer because suddenly, from behind, there was the sound of police sirens, flashing blue and white lights.

I checked my rear-view mirror, slowed the car. Alice looked at me, "What are you doing?"

"Stopping. In the glove box, look." Alice clicked open the glove box, searched inside. There were just a few pieces of folded paper, held to together with a paperclip.

"Give me the paperclip," I said.

"I thought you had a gun?"

Alice gave me the paper clip, I clipped it to my shirt cuff, "Take my gun out of my inside pocket and slide it under the seat."

"Okay."

Alice did as I asked. Her hand snaked into my inside jacket pocket, she felt the warmth on the back of her hand. She glanced up at my eyes and slowly took out my gun.

The car came to a stop. A police car pulled up behind. A thickset police officer stepped out of his car and walked to my window. His colleague stayed in the police car, checking the car's registration. I lowered my window.

Patrick, the officer, leant down, "Pretty obvious why I stopped you, front light out, windscreen cracked, you were doing 80."

I looked up at Patrick, "You may have heard this before, but, don't you have better things to do?"

"Is she registered?" Patrick pointed at Alice.

"She's all good," I said.

"Where are you coming from?" asked Patrick.

"Do you know, they've done studies, when people think about their own mortality, they hate immigrants more?"

"Eh?"

"You get racist and believe idiot leaders when you worry about dying."

Patrick's colleague, Damien, got out the police car, pulled his pistol from his holster, pointed it at the car, "Patrick, that's the guy."

"What guy?"

"From the service station," replied Damien.

Patrick finally got it, realized I was from the shoot-out at the service station, whipped out his gun, pointed it at me. I put my wrists out of my window, waited for the cuffs.

A small police station, a Duty Sergeant, Brian, fifties, paunch, stood behind a desk with my gun, car keys and phone in an evidence bag in front of him. I stood on the other side of the charge desk, handcuffed behind my back, flanked either side by

Patrick and Damien. Patrick held a baton which he slapped into his palm at regular intervals.

Brian looked up from his paperwork, "You understand the charges?"

I looked him straight in the eyes, "Yes, sir."

"Good, you'll be held until morning, then interviewed," said Brian, "Take him down, boys."

Patrick and Damien walked me along a corridor. They held me by the forearms.

Patrick said to Damien just so I could hear clearly, "Never had a Green before, you want to try her out with me?"

The officers stopped and turned me towards a holding cell. Walked me in. They stopped me in the centre of the cell.

Damien held my arm tight, "Kneel down."

I slipped the paper clip from my shirt cuff — opened the thin metal out with my fingertips — slid the end into the cuff's lock, behind my back.

I knelt.

"Don't move. I'm going to undo the cuffs," said Patrick.

"These cuffs?" I asked.

I shook the cuffs off my wrist with one movement, holding on to one end of the metal, jumped to my feet and spun around, facing the two officers. There was utter shock on both the cops' faces. I moved fast, twisted the cuffs around Patrick's neck, and with one movement kicked at his legs. Patrick crumpled. I twisted away, dropped the cuffs, and grabbed his baton from an outstretched dying arm. I swung at Damien, catching him across the stomach, Damien doubled up, I hit him behind the ear. Damien went down flat to the ground.

Patrick got to one knee. I hit him across the shoulder blade and then across the jawbone. The two officers lay unconscious. I reappeared in the corridor carrying the baton and a set of cell keys.

Alice sat with her legs bunched up on the bed of a cell. She heard keys in the lock. The door swung open. I stood in the doorway. Alice smiled.

Alice and I walked along the corridor, pushed through double doors into the charge area, Brian behind the desk. He saw us coming, stepped forward to grab me but I brought the baton down quickly, once to Brian's arm as he reached for his pistol, the next to the side of his head. Brian fell to the ground. I looked around and found the evidence bag with my gun, car keys and phone.

I drove fast out of the station car park. Alice looked over at me.

"You're kind of, all right," she said.

I smiled, a lopsided grin.

On a car ferry, at night, across to Lindisfarne, travelling across a dark sea on an open deck, Alice stared across the short stretch of water. I carried two cups of coffee hesitantly from inside, handed one to her. We drank the coffee, leaned on the ferry balustrade. Alice looked at me, "Why are you trying to find my dad, you're not going to kill him, are you?"

"No, I need to find him, that's all, you heard your mother."

"Yes, but she's a crazy witch and you're not telling me everything."

"I don't know everything. Just, find your father. Why is he hiding anyway?"

"I can't tell you that, not exactly. What else did my mother tell you? This is about my stepbrother, isn't it, Sami?"

"She mentioned that name, yes, but she wouldn't let me into the reason we need him, or your father."

There was a pause whilst Alice thought for a few seconds, then her eyebrows wrinkled and her nose turned up a little like she had just smelt rotting fruit, "You didn't sleep with my mother, did you?"

I breathed hard through my nose and didn't say anything, then tried not to look Alice in the eyes, which gave the whole game away.

"I can't believe it. Oh my god."

"So ... she ... it's way difficult, she chained me down."

"I'm sure it was, it was all here."

"Anyway, you haven't told the truth. She sent you to find me, it's obvious you were following me, you didn't just happen to see me. I don't even believe you can see through skin, your superpower doesn't seem to useful, to be honest."

"I can see your heart," said Alice. She was staring at my chest, "And your heart says you're in love with me and it says you should apologise for fucking my mother to me, right now. And secondly... you should kiss me. And make it a good kiss. And no manacles, I promise. I'm not like my —"

But by then I had kissed her, "Sorry."

"Wrong order."

"Yep, neurodivergent."

"Me too."

We kissed again and then I stepped back, "Your father can help stop this. Your mother has been trying to reach him but he has shut his mind."

"Sounds like him."

"Your father is not just a doctor, he's very high up in the Order. You know about that, don't you?"

"I don't know anything. What order...?" Alice pushed herself away from the balustrade, "You think you know me, but you don't..."

Alice stood in the moonlight, pale green skin luminous, anger in her face, "You don't understand."

"Your people, they have a way to stop this."

"Maybe I don't want it to stop."

"Are you kidding? In two days' time a huge boulder from space is going to wipe out humanity, our future."

Alice looked down at the floor, "We don't have a future. I just think we should give up." Alice turned away, wandered in her thoughts, "I put on a mask, it's not me ... But then, I don't know what is me."

Alice breathes in and out quickly. There is a softness to Alice's tone but she is anxious also, "You won't leave me, will you?"

I smiled at Alice, "No."

"You have to convince my father to open the gates of time, don't you?" Alice asked.

"Yes."

We walked slowly down a moonlit sandy track towards the beach, our car parked up some distance behind on a road. We were on Lindisfarne, a Holy Island in Northumberland. I followed Alice onto the beach as she ran ahead, excited by the small crashing waves at the near shore. I caught up with her and we walked side by side along the sea edge, jumping to mind our feet didn't get wet.

The cottage nestled on the edge of a hill leading down to the sea. We neared the cottage, no lights on inside, clambered up a few huge stone boulders that led from the beach to the house. Alice ran along the side path to the back of the cottage. Peered inside the kitchen window; all was dark. She opened the back door. Suddenly, there was a shotgun blast, it tore through the door. Alice fell back. The door opened, Gerad appeared holding a shotgun, Alice's father. He was in his sixties, white beard, white flowing hair, green skin, he moved a little unsteady on his feet.

"Oh my God," he shouted. He dropped the shotgun and rushed to Alice. "Are you all right?"

"Yes," she replied, getting up.

"Are you hit?"

"No. Missed me completely, just ducked, that's all."

Alice looked behind her, the wooden door of a garden shed was peppered with shot that had ripped through it.

"What were you doing? Why the gun?" asked Alice.

"Come inside. Who's this?" Gerad looked at me.

"I'm John."

"Pleased to meet you," Gerad led Alice inside not that pleased to meet me.

We sat around a kitchen table finishing off a meal. Gerad looked at me sitting across from him.

"Why did you bring her here?" Gerad asked.

"Your son, Sami. He's travelling to the end point. We need your help."

Gerad thought deeply, stared off into space.

I got up, with my plate, took his and Alice's, went to the sink and hung back there.

Alice looked at her father, "Why didn't you tell me I had a brother?"

Gerad got up from his seat, then his legs gave way, he caught hold of the edge of the table. I ran to him and held him, helped him into the chair. Alice looked sick with worry.

"You okay?" I asked.

"Yes. Heart trouble. Both of them," answered Gerad.

"Do you have any pills, or…"

"Up there." Gerad pointed to the top shelf of a Welsh dresser decorated with plates. I found a jar of pills, handed them to Gerad who took a few.

"It's nothing serious," said Gerad unconvincingly.

Alice was staring at Gerad's chest, at his heart, "Yes, it is."

She looked up at her dad and started crying.

Alice walked around her old bedroom, same as it was when she left, aged sixteen. Posters on the wall, clothes in the closet, lucky Japanese cat on her bedside table. She opened a drawer, pulled out her diary, flicked through the pages, frowned, put it away, not a good idea to read your old diary she thought, too many certain but unconfident prescriptions for what she was going to do in life, too many promises broken. And what was it doing here, anyway, in a drawer for anyone to read? Why wasn't it in a suitcase filled with lead at the bottom of the ocean. It had everything about everything in here … she was deflecting, transferring, not coping. Both of her father's hearts were diseased, she could see it.

Alice looked at the wall, recent additions, framed articles from newspapers about Alice's acting career, awards, certificates, a diploma, a shrine to Alice her dad had put up. On another wall was a samurai sword hanging on a nail. Alice took it down and unsheathed it, slashed it about, slowly inserted it back into its sheath like a samurai. Bowed.

Alice stood on the beach that night, looking out to sea. Behind, the cottage sat perched on the cliffs. Up ahead the sea rushed in, in the far distance a blue line at the horizon heralded dawn. Footsteps on the sand behind. Alice did not turn.

"Are you okay?" Gerad asked.

"I'm fine," said Alice.

"It's cold out here."

"I'm sorry I didn't tell you about Sami, it was to keep you safe, keep him safe. He was born with something special inside. If you knew and were caught, they would torture you to find out."

"Who are they?"

"Government agents. Anyone who wanted their hands on power."

"You didn't tell me anything," pleaded Alice, "I had to go to my mother … you know what talking to her is like."

"I'm sorry, yes, I know." Gerad sighed, they looked at each other and shared a smile.

"I wish I could change things, in the past, but that's not allowed," said her father.

"I'm sorry about Martha," said Alice.

"I know she could never be a real mother to you, but she tried."

"I know, she did. I can't believe she hid her pregnancy from me."

"You didn't come, you were away in the States, and then ... well when we knew we made a pact not to tell anyone, to send Sami away when he was old enough. And that's what we did. And then Martha was taken from us. And then this."

"Was I a mistake?" asked Alice.

"No, of course not. I let you down," Gerad said, looking at the sand.

"No, Dad. You let yourself down. Look at you, stuck out here, doing whatever it is you do. John's got some cockeyed idea you can save the world and you can't even be my dad."

"I want to be ... I've been a bad father."

Alice stared at him and crumpled, just a little.

"No. You're my rock, always have been. Without you I'd ... I don't know. Just ... I have to go inside."

Alice walked past Gerad and headed back to the cottage, tears in her eyes.

I sat with Gerad at the kitchen table. Gerad reached over for a bottle of whiskey on the dresser, grabbed a couple of glasses.

"You'd better help me with this," he said.

Gerad poured a drink for us, I drank mine down. Gerad did the same.

"I should take a look at your shoulder." Gerad found his glasses, balanced them on the end of his nose and stood. I took off my jacket and opened up my shirt to show the wound, "I was a doctor."

"Nice work," Gerad said admiring the stitches, "I shall have to tell Alice. I'll put a new dressing on." Gerad opened a drawer in the Welsh dresser, took out a bandage and fixed it to my shoulder.

He sat back down, poured more whiskey, I pulled my shirt back up over my shoulder, we clinked glasses and drank.

"Who are you scared of, why the shotgun?" I asked.

Gerad poured more whiskey in to his glass.

"Always the same, people who hate what you have, who want you dead."

"Will you help, will the Order?" I asked.

"I'm old, how can I help? The Order you speak of, if they have prepared Sami, then he knows what to do."

"I was told you were needed, that he was not prepared. Why won't you help?"

"Maybe we were meant for destruction. This world has been our destruction."

"What happened on your home planet, it has no effect on what's happening here and now."

"The shame still sticks to us. Everyone has a story, unfortunately they are all true. We killed each other in greed and left in ignorance. We jumped through time and space, through a wormhole that opened and closed, we took the chance for a new life and the life we found was the same as the old, except we were the servants, the slaves. Our karma, our redemption, our cosmic gift, call it what you will. But now, when we are needed, when only we can prevent this, now, now you want my help, now you want the best of me."

There was silence as Gerad's voice echoed with its last refrain.

"Yes," I said.

Alice stood at the top of the stairs listening to her father. She quietly retreated back into her room. Alice grabbed the samurai sword from her wall, opened the window and climbed out. She clambered down the rocks and across the beach, and took the old motorbike and rode fast along a straight country road, the sword across her lap. She drove over a hill and hit the coast. There was a huge ancient cross, Tau Cross, set up looking out over the Atlantic. The silky violet light of dawn was at the horizon.

Alice drove towards a craggy outcrop. Rust sunlight spread across the rocks. Alice stood on a cliff edge, Leac na Leannán, looking out to sea. Waves crashed in below. She threw three stones onto a small outcrop. Two landed on the stone, the third bounced off. Alice let go of herself suddenly, the tears came fast. She sank down, buried her head in her hands.

Alice walked towards John's car, got in, fumbled with the keys, started it, and drove. She caught the ferry back to the mainland. Stayed in the car numb to her surroundings, watching the heavy metal doors open as they came to shore. Alice drove down a narrow lane, hills ahead hit by the morning sunlight. She pulled up and got out.

There was a black Mercedes car parked up near a lake. She walked towards it. Two men in black suits leant on the car. One knocked on the blacked-out back window and he saw Alice coming. The door opened and Katsumi got out. He was in his late sixties, Japanese, close-cropped white hair, black eyes. He walked towards Alice, stopped.

"Where is he?" said Katsumi.

"At my father's place. I've done what you asked, now, will you leave my father alive?"

"Lead us to the rat and you'll have my word."

"What did he do?" asked Alice.

"He disgraced us, got mixed up with a woman, a whore, she talked to the police. He should have killed her. He didn't. We found her. But not him. He's special you know. We want him. And the boy, your brother, where is he?" asked Katsumi.

"You said nothing about a boy, I don't know anything about him."

"He has come to our attention."

"I don't know where he is."

"Your father will know. My men will go with you and ask him. They will ask him until he tells and after he tells they will kill you all."

"We had a deal."

"There is no deal in life. Not with the devil."

Alice walked back across the beach with the two gangsters in tow. She carried her sword with her. One of the gangsters made a call, reporting back their location.

"What are you going to do to him?" she asked.

They didn't reply.

"We had a deal. My father goes free," said Alice.

Again, no reply. They clambered up the rocks and stopped at the cottage. The two gangsters took out their guns.

Alice was scared suddenly. "No, not like this, no, I never wanted this!"

The gangsters ignored her.

"Hey!" Alice shouted.

One gangster grabbed Alice, put his hand over her mouth, pushed her backwards. She fell on the rocks, tumbled backwards. The gangsters took the side path to the back of the cottage. Alice felt helpless one moment, then in an act of defiance she pulled her sword out of its scabbard, clambered back up the rocks.

"Hey!" she shouted and raised the blade.

The gangsters stopped, turned to look at her. Alice gripped the hilt of the sword tight, held it high in the air, hands next to her shoulder.

"Stop! Now!"

One gangster laughed. Alice was filled with a rush of blood to the head. She ran at them, sword held up. The gangsters looked confused, then one pointed his gun at Alice, pulled the trigger, the bullet flashed out and hit Alice in the stomach, she fell back, crumpled to the ground.

Suddenly, I ran around the corner holding a gun. The gangsters turned to me, but it was too late. I shot one gangster in the head. A plume of blood exploded from his temple. The other gangster took aim, fired but missed. I aimed and shot the gangster in the throat, the gangster dropped his gun and clutched his throat, dropped to one knee. I walked over and executed the gangster through his eye.

I rushed to Alice, she was out cold, her stomach bleeding. I picked her up and carried her to the cottage as Gerad appeared at the back door. I carried her inside, Gerad deadly worried for her.

I lay Alice on the kitchen table.

"Boil some water, get some towels, I need my instruments," Gerad said, gently smoothing Alice's head, "It's okay, darling."

I went to the stove, found a pan, filled it with water.

Gerad pulled off Alice's jacket, pulled up her T-shirt. There was a hole in her stomach, blood oozed out.

Alice came to.

"You have to stay awake," said Gerad.

Alice whispered, "Okay."

I came over with tea towels. "Are these okay?" I said.

"Yes," replied Gerad firmly, distracted. Gerad grabbed a towel and placed it on Alice's wound. She grimaced.

"Hold this here," Gerad said to me, placing his hand on the towel over her wound, "Press hard."

Gerad exited. Alice looked at me. "I'm sorry," she said.

I shook my head no.

Gerad returned with a bowl of hot water. He took over holding the towel from me.

"Okay, leave me alone," said Gerad to me. I didn't move. "Now!" he demanded.

I left them. Gerad looked at Alice, tears in his eyes. Alice tried to speak, "It's okay. I deserve it," she said.

"No," said her father.

Alice swooned and fainted. Gerad set about trying to heal her but her life was ebbing away. Her pulse slowed to a stop, and her father felt a cold chill run through his body.

I waited outside in the garden for news of Alice. I waited a long time, sitting by a pond, my head slowly dropping in drowsiness. I stared down into the small ornamental pond, a group of large red and white Kuchibeni koi carp swam over to me and around each other. It was dusk when Gerad came out of the house.

"Is she okay?" I asked.

"Yes. She wants to talk to you," replied Gerad.

Alice was sat up in her bed, her stomach heavily bandaged. I knocked at the door. "Yes?"

"It's me. Can I come in?" I waited outside.

"Yes."

I opened the door and entered.

"I thought you'd gone," said Alice.

"Why would I go?"

"I betrayed you."

"You did what you had to."

"I thought they'd … I'm sorry. I'm not…"

"Was all that planned, right from the start?"

"Yes … He found me. The girl who could see everything! Katsumi wanted you dead. I did a deal for my father's life, they knew where he was, they were watching him. I should have warned you…. I'm stupid, it was the only way … it was so wrong of me…"

"It's not your fault."

"Yes, it is."

"I found you. It wasn't hard. The loneliest man in London with hands of fire. Every woman you meet dies or runs off to space, or leaves you."

I looked down at the carpet, pink and blue flowered pattern.

"Sorry."

Gerad was in the kitchen doing the washing up. I sat at the kitchen table. Gerad finished up and came in with two glasses, grabbed the bottle of whiskey and poured two out.

"They'll come," I said.

"What do we do?" asked Gerad.

"Do you have any weapons?"

On the kitchen table Gerad placed three handguns, one shotgun, one samurai sword, a pile of shotgun cartridges and bullets, and finally a hand grenade.

I looked at Gerad and frowned, "Anything else?"

"A few kitchen knives."

"Okay. It will have to do."

"What shall I do?" asked Gerad.

"You look in on Alice, I'll secure the house."

I checked all the doors and windows, opened a door to the basement, picked up a candle, lit it and went down. There was a small cellar at the bottom of a flight of wooden stairs, a wine rack with bottles covered in cobwebs, and in the corner, a work bench with a pile of metal, electronics, bits of a robotic shoulder, diagrams pinned to the wall, schematics, Gerad's hobby. On the wall there was a diagram of an android, at the bottom corner it said, "Max."

There was a collection of tools, an arc torch and acetylene tank for welding. I checked the gauge on the tank, half full. I climbed back up the stairs, turned into the kitchen. Alice was standing there, heavily bandaged under her clothes.

"What are you doing?" I asked, incuriously.

"Helping."

"You have to rest."

"I'm not resting. Give me a gun."

"Is there any other way to get to the cottage?"

"No, just across the beach."

"We could do something there. I'll take a look."

"I'll come with you."

We walked across the beach, I carried a spade. I realized Alice wanted to speak about something, she was actually biting her lip.

Alice stopped, turned away. Looked out to sea, the wind biting at her face. I held out a hand and touched her on the shoulder.

"I'm sorry," I said, "I'm just in killing mode."

"Sure. It doesn't matter." Alice moved away from my hand.

"You're kind of complicated."

"Yeah. There's a reason for that," said Alice.

"Anything in particular?"

Alice turns back to face me.

"You really want to 'get to know' a Green?"

I shrugged. Then looked her in the eyes.

"Sure. If I'm not too old for you?" I smiled.

Alice sighed, letting the breath come in and out, then smiled despite herself, and then, looking at me, seriously, "Really? I'm a whole lot of bad trouble."

"My kind of trouble."

Alice laughed. "That is a terrible line."

"I'm not very good at any of this, like you said I kill my girlfriends or chase them away."

"I didn't mean that."

I dug my spade into the ground, "Good, how are you at digging?"

"Terrible, that's your job."

Back inside the cottage Gerad loaded a shotgun in the kitchen. Alice came in from the garden.

"Where's John?" asked Gerad.

"Digging holes."

The back door opened and I came in with the spade over my shoulder.

"They used to hunt boar in the Tama Hills like this," I said.

"Did you check the weapons?" asked Gerad.

"Yes. We'll make our first positions upstairs at the front window, pick off who we can as they come up the rocks. If their firepower is too great, we'll fall back here, they will have to come around the garden to get us. That's our second killing ground. I've rigged up a spotlight so we can fill the garden with light and catch them in the open."

I reached down to a plug and switched it on. The back garden was filled with a bright searchlight.

"We keep the light off in here at all times. Fullback position is the cellar. We pull the cupboard," I pointed at the Welsh dresser, "over the door and pull a cord attached to the grenade." I stood on a chair and reached up into the rafters, patting the acetylene tank strapped up there, "We blow the place up, if we need to."

I picked up the hand grenade from the table, and a roll of gaffer tape and taped the hand grenade to the acetylene tank. I unfurled a length of sash cord, climbed up and attached one end to the grenade pin and gently threaded it over the top of the Welsh dresser which I pulled down behind it, letting it dangle in the cellar door entrance.

"Boar hunt?" Alice was quizzical.

I looked at her and smiled. Then looked at Gerad, "What is all that stuff in the basement?"

"What stuff."

"Electronics gear, robotic stuff."

"A friend came to stay many years ago. We may have need of him when this is all over." Gerad looked pointedly at Alice.

"A friend? A robot friend?"

"A Man-Made, yes, Max."

Three cars pulled up at the entrance to the track leading to the beach. Twelve gangsters got out and walked down the track and onto the beach. They walked as a line fanning out, towards the house, armed with sub-machine guns and pistols. It was night with bright moonlight. They had a swagger about them, the guns caught the moonlight.

Suddenly, the ground gave way under them. One of them dropped into a deep hole, disappearing from sight, and screamed. The men looked around, stunned. They did not know whether to go on, two hesitated, the leader barked an order and they walked forward again. Another man fell, straight down in a hole lined with sharp sticks, piercing him through, his screams were horrific. The gangsters peered down into the hole, the man was impaled in agony.

The gangsters backed away, but their leader shouted at them to go forward.

In the upstairs bedroom, I peered through binoculars. I passed the binoculars to Alice beside me. She looked through. Alice could see the gangsters in disarray, the leader barking orders. "Two down," I said.

Gerad came in to the room with cups of tea on a tray.

Alice took a cup and so did I. We each had a gun by our side. Gerad drunk tea from a mug, set it down, and picked up the shotgun. We had piled up a sofa, wardrobe, and chairs at the window. Alice looked through the binoculars, she could see the gangsters stood stock-still. The leader went back to one of the cars, got a length of metal pipe out and walked to the front. He prodded the sand ahead. The men formed a single file behind him.

"They're coming," she said.

"Okay," I said, "wait until they get on the rocks and then we fire."

I took a sip of tea. Gerad positioned himself in the window with the shotgun, aiming down the barrel. Alice and I took aim with our pistols. The gangsters appeared one by one on the rocks in silhouette against the sky. I fired and hit a man. He peeled back like an orange skin. Alice fired, holding her gun as steady as she could, grimacing from the pain in her stomach. A gangster appeared on the rocks, Gerad let loose with a blast from his shotgun, hitting the man and sending him flying backwards. There was a moment's pause and then a return of fire. We ducked down. Bullets ripped into the house, smashing windows, twisting curtains, ripping chunks out of the sofa, blasting pieces of the wardrobe apart. The mantelpiece behind us was peppered with bullets, a vase exploded, a small wooden clock took a direct hit, its chimes rang and stopped, the firepower was terrific, never ending as bullets flew in. Then silence.

We gingerly peered up above the wreckage.

"Everyone okay?" I checked.

"Yes," said Gerad.

"Yes," answered Alice.

I aimed and fired. Alice joined in. Gerad pulled both triggers, sending out a blast of shot that hit its mark with a scream from outside. The return fire was even more intense this time. We crouched against the floor. Then suddenly, a wine bottle filled with petrol, a flaming rag in its neck, came smashing through the window. I grabbed Alice and pulled her out of the room. The Molotov cocktail exploded. Gerad made a dash for it, just in time. I slammed the bedroom door shut as flames licked under it.

Then there was the sound of automatic gunfire. We rushed downstairs. The kitchen table was on its side, we crouched behind it. We could hear more gunfire, then running steps coming around to the back of the house.

Alice whispered, "The spotlight?"

"Yes, wait a minute, until they are all there," I said.

We looked at each other, tension in our eyes, and waited. Alice kissed me suddenly, on the cheek. Suddenly there was a volley of automatic gunfire that screamed through the cottage breaking all the glass in the kitchen windows and peppering the door. Bullets tore into the house. The dinner plates on the Welsh dresser were obliterated. One tottered on its edge and fell.

Alice caught it in one hand. She looked at Gerad and smiled. Gerad gave her a thumbs up. I reached over and put my finger on the plug switch. It was overcast now and dark outside in the back garden, surrounded by trees blocking out the light and gun smoke obscuring.

"Ready?"

The others nodded. I flicked on the switch. We stood up, guns ready.

The garden was suddenly brightly illuminated, six gangsters were caught in the bright light, blinking. One with a sub-machine gun, the others with pistols.

Alice, Gerad, and I opened fire, sending out a volley of bullets and cutting down the gangsters. They all fell, groaning and dying.

I switched the light off and we ducked back down behind the table.

There was silence.

"Did we get them all?" asked Alice.

"I don't know," I said.

Then there was the sound of running footsteps around the side of the house. I took a quick look. I could see the flame of a Molotov cocktail in the garden.

"Quick," I said.

I grabbed Alice and Gerad and pushed them towards the door to the cellar. The Molotov flew through the window and landed on the kitchen floor. Alice and Gerad got through the doorway just in time. I pulled the Welsh dresser across the doorway. The cocktail exploded in a ball of flames that licked under the dresser. We backed away. Alice was behind us at the bottom of the stairs. I walked down the stairs with the end of the sash cord in my hand, unfurling it as I went. But the gangsters were already in the kitchen, pulling at the Welsh dresser. I ushered Gerad quickly down the stairs, handed the cord to Alice. She could see the dresser starting to be being pulled aside. She backed away, the three of us hiding behind the end of a tall wine rack.

"Do it," I shouted.

Alice gathered determination and pulled the cord. The grenade exploded, igniting the acetylene tank above the dresser. There was a huge explosion which sent a blast of flame in all directions, down the stairs at us, upstairs shunting the dresser away from the cellar door with a billowing mass of burnt wood and flame. We could see no movement. We huddled together, underneath the wine bottles. I checked my pistol, "None left."

"I'm out," said Gerad.

Alice checked her gun, "Same."

I pulled a bottle of wine from the rack, held it like a club in my hand.

Gerad looked at the bottle sideways reading the label, then at me.

"Good year."

I laughed, "We'll get drunk on the stuff if we get out of this alive."

"They must be dead," said Alice.

Gerad put his arms around Alice's shoulder.

Suddenly, there were footsteps on the wooden stairs. They tensed up. A mobile phone was tossed down the steps. It landed with a thud on the concrete. It rang. Gerad picked it up, listened to a voice on the other end.

"Okay."

He hung up, "They want to meet."

I was upstairs in the kitchen checking to see that the gangsters had all gone. Alice and Gerad were still in the basement.

"It's a trap," Alice said.

"Yes, of course," said Gerad. He looked at Alice, "It's going to be okay."

"Is it?"

"You love him, don't you?"

"Yes, I'm sorry."

"You don't have to be sorry. It's a good thing."

My footsteps on the stairs. "They've gone. But we have to get out of here, the cottage is burning, it's in the rafters."

Alice and Gerad left through the back door. I grabbed the samurai sword and left quickly as the flames licked around me. We stood in the garden watching the cottage burn. The bodies of the gangsters were gone, they had been dragged away.

"Dad, your house."

"It's just a house."

We walked across the beach with the cottage in flames behind us in the morning twilight, red umber house. Red at the skyline. Feet on the blue sand, blue at our eyes, yellow in the sky overhead. A green streak through the heather. Purple tops. We did not say a word; the sea was calm. The traps in the sand were empty. The car park was empty, apart from their car. We got in. I drove. We were exhausted, Alice with her stomach bandaged, all of us ragged and dirty. I drove along a coastal path.

"When do we meet them?" I asked.

"Soon."

"Okay. We need to eat."

"I can't eat," said Alice.

A coastal café had a scattering of fishermen in yellow waterproofs. They didn't bat an eyelid at we walked in. There was a distant screech of a seagull. A plate of full breakfast was put down by a matronly woman in front of me, I picked up my knife and fork. Alice raised an eyebrow. Gerad sipped a mug of tea.

"Breakfast, right now?"

"I'm a big lad, I need feeding."

"I'm hungry," said Alice.

Alice looked up at the waitress who came over with a small pad and stub of a pencil. The gangsters' phone rang. Gerad answered. He spoke a few words in Japanese and hung up.

"Katsumi will meet us on the mainland."

"Good," I said.

"I hope you know what you're doing," said Gerad to me, a little worried. Alice shot me a glance, unsure what her father meant.

A granite moorland, a few wind-broken trees, a derelict cottage, rough heather broken up with gold grass, a prehistoric stone circle. It was a sullen day, fog crept in from the sea. There was a small hill covered in bright yellow gorse on one side. I stood with Gerad in a shallow valley. A long snaking white track led off before us into the distance. Alice sat in the car, parked up behind us, holding a gun in her hand. The samurai sword lay in its sheath on the back seat. We weren't armed, she was backup. We waited. Gerad looked at his watch. A rook took off from a clump of spindly trees. Gerad looked up, hearing something. A black Mercedes car appeared as a dot on the horizon. It approached, dust spurted up from its wheels. The car came closer and closer until it stopped a hundred yards away. There was silence. I narrowed my eyes. Gerad fidgeted his stance, moving from foot to foot. Alice peered from the car. The Mercedes' back door opened. Katsumi stepped out. The other door opened. Max stepped out. A tall Man-Made. Regular features, bright blue eyes. The first of its kind, made by a child named Irma. Enhanced by Gerad. Now in the hands of Katsumi.

Alice got out the car, "Is that Max?"

Gerad looked at her, concerned, a truth revealed, "I'm sorry, we didn't tell you, they had Max all along, they tracked him down, and we need him."

"What are we trading then?"

"Me," I said.

"No."

"Your father explained, he needs Max for this to work. For everything to work, he needs Max and they want me. It's simple."

"No way," implored Alice.

I walked forwards.

"What are you doing?" shouted Alice.

I stopped, turned to look back at her.

"Me for your Max, it's the only way."

"No, they'll kill you."

Then without warning, Katsumi got back into the Mercedes car with his men, the car turned in a circle and drove off at speed the way it had come.

We were all left standing in the valley. Max walked towards us. I turned to look up at the low hill. A line of Japanese gangsters appeared on the brow of the hill. They were all dressed the same, black suits and open-necked white shirts. Each casually took out a gun. There were five of them, ready to kill.

I looked up at them and then at Alice, who was stunned by their appearance. I walked to the car, opened the back door, and pulled the scabbard from the back seat.

"Take your family away from here," I said to Alice.

"I'm not going to leave you," Alice was defiant.

"I've many done things I can't forgive myself for, it's time," I replied.

"No. No, you can't..."

I smiled at her, turned, and walked towards the gangsters through the yellow gorse, stripping off my jacket and shirt, revealing my tattoos, serpents, snakes, lotus flowers, the large Kuchibeni koi carp drawn across my chest. The gangsters cocked their guns. One spat a toothpick out.

I pulled the sword from the sheath and threw it to the ground.

Alice got Gerad and Max into the car.

I reached the gangsters, held up my sword, addressed them, "You want to fight like boys..."

One gangster with a crooked smile and a gold tooth laughed.

"... Or fight like men?"

The laughing gangster walked towards me, he raised his gun.

"Last chance," I said.

The gangster laughed again, he looked back at the others. Suddenly I dropped the sword and whipped out my gun from the back of my waistband and shot the gangster with a single shot to the forehead. The gangster fell dead to the floor.

I dived to the ground, shooting another gangster through the heart.

I rolled forward, dropped the gun, and picked up the sword as the rest of the gangsters closed in. I closed the gap on them. The gangsters fired wildly. I struck with the blade, cutting one gangster through to the collarbone. I turned quickly, moving in an arc as another gangster shot at me. Time slowed. I raised the sword and sliced down, severing the gangster's arm in half. Blood gushed and spurted.

One man was left, I spun around and drove the blade through the gangster's stomach, running the blade fully in, and then pulling it out with a swift movement. The man dropped to the floor. I looked back down the hill at Alice. Our eyes met. Then suddenly, I dropped to one knee and collapsed to the ground. Alice ran to me with all her might, as though running through thick treacle. Alice reached me, knelt beside me. I had been hit in the chest by a bullet. Blood pumped out through the eye of the Kuchibeni koi carp tattooed over my heart. My eyes closed.

Alice pleaded, "No, no, please!"

My eyes opened. I looked at Alice, "It was worth it to have known you. I love you."

My eyes closed. My body gently slumped into Alice's arms. It began to rain.

9

John

I am in a hotel. I stand looking down through large windows at a function room below. The room had been used for a wedding party the night before, or a month or ten years ago. The round tables are spread out, covered with pink shiny cloth. All the empty glasses, the popped confetti, the curled streamers lie on the tables. On the floor are a few champagne bottles escaped from the grasp of waiters clearing up. Emigrants, adrift in new homes, or marooned in lifeboats. I walk through the tables, kick a bottle by mistake. It spins around. The door to a swimming pool is open, I exit and stand looking at the empty pool in colours of peach. Next to it a large candle has burnt down, its wax is a hard pool on the floor. I walk upstairs to the restaurant and sit down in an empire room. A woman comes with bright red nail varnish and takes my order, there is only haddock on the menu but it never arrives. I keep checking my coffee cup for coffee, but it's empty except a few dregs but I don't remember drinking any. The tall windows have heavy net curtains, but there is a narrow gap through which I can see a sad seascape in thickening shadow. Nothing moves. The sea would not catch my eye as if too ashamed to acknowledge the lack of invitation to strip off and run right in unless the thought of suicide were an option open, and here on this island it did seem as if that particular route could be the only way to evade the coming ghost desert, an Eton mess, its neck bowed in regret. Along the promenade I stopped in the fierce and corpulent wind to read a cenotaph, a guide to names of those who ran across muddy fields to be mowed down by thick bullets and discovered I was in Douglas on the Isle of Man. There is a sunken garden here, well-kept but sparse with benches not quite low enough to stay out of the window. I sit on one and see it has a name plate on it. And on the name plate is my name and it says, "May he rest in peace." So, this is death. Douglas out of season, empty cafés, and bars, walks along the seafront in the rain. A frozen black Irish Sea, bubbling black Irish coffee drowned in canned whipped cream. There's not even the aforementioned escape. My eyes filled with grit and salt grains whipped in from the sea. I reach for a handkerchief in the side pocket of my suit sports jacket, though I never carried a handkerchief. Instead I find a letter from Ingrid. It reads: "The future lay amongst the stars. When I look out there, I always feel there was someone watching me. And yet, when I looked to Earth, it called to her like a child calling to its mother."

"Don't you remember?" she wrote, "When you were eight and you lived by the park and you stayed out late one night in September? It got dark and your friends went home but you stayed a little longer, waved them off goodbye, went and sat on a park bench, watched the sun go down. Do you remember you heard something behind you, something rustling in the deep undergrowth where the blackberries grew? You turned your head and saw a glimpse of just an eye and black hair around an ear."

I had told her of the stone a long time ago, but had never told her of the girl with the dark hair, so how could she know? I did not remember it fully myself, I kept that memory at bay, hidden like a prized fighter in the shadows of a ring, but now the remembrance came back, slowly flooding my imagination, adding to it, pulsing through me.

"And you went in there, didn't you? You got up and walked in to the darkness and there she was, stained deep red around the lips from eating blackberries. She was a girl your age. And you stood before her not knowing what to say. Her knees were scuffed with dirt. She put an arm around you, kissed you. The stone passed so quickly between your lips you never noticed.

She ran away crying. You went home, and in the night had hiccups."

"I remember," I say out loud, and stand up in the Italian sunken garden on the seafront in Douglas. Sodium light glared down now, it was dusk, seagulls swirled around in search of unlikely chips fallen from invisible wrappers. I look around. There was no one. A dot of two people possibly struggling with a wayward inside-out umbrella far down the concrete promenade. A window being firmly closed after being torturously cleaned on the outside by a landlady at a pub behind. A man in a cap and a boy on a bike, barely able to stand in the frame bought too big to let him grow into.

I go back to the letter. She wrote, "That stone slithered down inside you, fell into your stomach and grew, covering with moss and slime. The next morning there was a stain of black on your lips and your head was dull with clanging broadswords clashed on armoured helmet.

You thumbed a lift and sat in the back of a car, the girl with the black hair sat next to you. Fringe cut short, the rest falling down either side of her ears. Jeans, jumper, trainers. Jeans that flared out a bit with a woven yellow flower patch on her right thigh. Her heavy eyes were fixed on the trees and countryside outside. Then the girl rested her head on your lap, shut her eyes, folded her hands under her head. You carried the girl's sleeping body down the narrow track over blistering gravel into the lodge. In the morning you caught the ferry to Raasay. The sound was thick and purple. An otter climbed onto the ferry and licked its belly fur. The stone moved and you gripped the blue boat rail. The pain was intolerable. The captain steered the boat towards the shore, black extinct volcanos, Cuillin Hills, behind, expectant for carrion. The girl peed with her dress held up in a cold pool on a hill in Raasay. A track led down the hill, the girl kept pace with you. Brambles, ferns, the rush of a waterfall unseen. The path led through a copse and on the other side were the foundations of stone cottages, clearance relics. The girl pointed onwards, below you Loch na Mna, a blue oval, silent.

'Now we wait,' the girl said, and you sat behind a small wall of stones. She went off, scurrying across the steep hills. Returned with wood to build a fire.

'Who are you?' you asked.

'I am here to help you,' the girl replied, 'the stone you carry is a lodestone, formed by the striking of rock by lightning. It was not meant for you.'

'What is in the water?'

The girl thought for a moment and then replied, 'An each-uisge, a water-horse. It means to cut you open and take the stone.'

'Why did you bring me here?'

But there was no answer.

Night came, sparks trailed up to the stars from the fire. Then there was a slow deep guttural moan from the loch. The girl said, 'I am the blade,' and pushed you on your back. You could not move. The stone anchored you to the ground. Then a shrieking came from the loch. The water bubbled. A fold of wave rushed to the shore. In the faint glow of firelight the creature surfaced; a mangled head of snout and mane, twenty-foot-long neck of throttled sinew, steam bursting out through wide nostrils, slithered towards you. You backed away, arms and legs working to escape, but the girl grabbed you by the jacket, held you fast, yanked up your shirt, exposed your belly, the stone inside pulling at your skin to be set free. The girl held her hand up high and then suddenly plunged it into your belly like a blade. The creature, as rapid as a lizard, broke the bank and was upon you, thick claws pinning your legs. The girl pulled at the lodestone, freed it, brought it out covered in starshine, sticky in thick moonlight. She held it up to the creature. Massive jaws came down, the girl stepped aside quickly and the creature bit the earth. The girl took out a short sword from beneath her clothing, stepped back, raised the blade, and chopped down cutting the head of the monster off. The creature's body writhed and twitched, spasmed and crawled, headless, towards you, blood oozing from its neck covering you, and then collapsed across your body, shuddered one last time and lay still, sliding back slowly into the water from where it came. The head, its huge jaws agape, sat on the bank of the loch. The girl, covered in blood and bile, her face and mouth sticky with red, turned and walked away, black hair bent looking for the track away."

We landed with no way to return. This was a new land, an island on a new world. What was behind us was the past. We were a small group, enough to forge a community, to prosper, but our means were limited. The fuel that had brought us this far was all spent. The landing craft were just hunks of metal, soon to rust and bury themselves in the soft sand, a little salvage here and there, but if there was to be any sort of progress made we would need a form of energy, something to power home-made vehicles, to transverse this new world, to explore and settle in this new home.

We built houses in the sand for now, just a few needed to house us, eight in all, built a crude telescope to look back to where we came from, fashioned a means to record our knowledge so the advancements we knew would not be lost. We inscribed stones, used crystals and quartz, but it was slow growing. Imagine trying to do anything without a constant power supply? We had no microscopes, no means to test anything, to study. Everything was trial and error.

Even the simplest things, a plate to eat from, a cup to drink from, a pot to cook in, things we take for granted, had to be reconstructed from the beginning, ones we had brought with us fell into disrepair. Find the clay, make the pot, maybe inscribe a pattern in it, build a forge, feed the fire with driftwood and seaweed (there were no trees), reach the right temperature by constructing and using bellows, then fire the pot so you can cook food to eat.

Sometimes we got so bored we would experiment, throwing different wild herbs in the pot. We discovered one that gave us hallucinations; we climbed the mountains and sat up there hallucinating, watching the lights in the sky, the shifting magnetic disturbances much like our own back home.

We were thrown back to a time when our own civilisation foraged for food. We planted crops and hunted with the few weapons we had, but the crops failed. Ice had swept down from the north and we had to move on. We knew there was a mainland, we had seen it coming in when we landed, we headed south. Others went east, where they began work on new buildings. Our community was growing, babies were born, children grew. All aspects of the society that we had lost from home resurrected themselves, including some that turned out to be divisive.

There was a flourishing of superstition, in a world dependent on the weather, the cold, the storms, some started to believe in omens and prophesy, not something unknown in our own time. Temples were built, there was ancestor worship. A man or woman would die and their house would be turned into a shrine by their children. Ritualization occurred, a series of steps and acts needed to be played out and then the storm would abate or good weather would come. And of course, if it worked, it became a system by which to live.

But we still hadn't discovered a way to get past this Stone Age life. Sure, we managed to make metal at some stage, we had religion, ceremony, with the Gods we worshipped, changing over time. We had clothing from the skins of animals and then weaving. We had tools made from antlers, axes, swords, bows. But no real power. It was that we sought. A source of energy that had eluded us.

Before we left for the mainland we held a tribal council, looking for ways to increase our potential as a people. We knew there were indigenous people on the mainland, much the same as us, humanoid, hunter-gatherers. If we were to pass through their lands, or even settle there, we needed some way of showing our supremacy, so we would not be killed outright, or stabbed in the back at a future date.

We felt we had a destiny, that we should develop, improve, leave something behind. And we were desperate to find out what had happened to our home planet. Had everyone perished or could we reach out, communicate with those we had left behind. The only natural form of energy was the sun, the waves, and lightning. We chose lightning. We set up metal lightning rods. Tried to capture the power of the lightning strikes. It took many years of experimentation. We could catch a strike, but turning it into useable energy was difficult. Then we discovered certain types of rock could hold a charge, we could use them as rudimentary batteries.

By incorporating a bipolar transistor, a relay of lightning rod to another rod, and employing orthostates, large megaliths, polished on one side, we could arrange them around the rods and capture energy; the rocks would heat up and create piezoelectricity from the stress and heat.

When that power was unleashed and focused we saw the beginnings of a new cult arise. A priesthood and their apprentices, who would walk into the lightning, test their courage; those that survived felt that they had transcended this world, escaped to another. They said that in their brains, the pineal gland, excited by the lightning surge, opened wide the last chakra, that of the fontanelle, and the apprentices became what they should have never ceased to, Guardians of the Light.

We saw all this and became afraid of the power hierarchy. We left, taking our newfound devices with us. We heard stories of the collapse of our first community, the loss of power turned kings into paupers. Stripped their authority. But we pushed on and travelled through the mainland, crossed seas, set up new power stations in new lands.

The emotional trauma that we held as a people stripped from our homeland stayed with us. We tried to diffuse these feelings, threw ourselves into our work. But some of us succumbed. There was talk of sacrifices that groups were practising in secret. We kept pushing south, the ice floes behind us, looking for a new place to make home, a new land that could provide us with a place to continue our work and find solace in our shared sense of destiny.

And we found it. A broad plain, high ground, with lightning strikes happening at regular intervals. A river nearby to bring in materials, huge stone slabs that had been left behind from the glacial retreat of a previous ice age. But we needed the correct quartz-filled stones to make our design perfect. We brought them over land and by river. We set the stones in a circle and eventually, over hundreds of years, built lintels, arranged them in a way to provide the best possible use of them, to hold the power, set a current going that travelled around the top of the circle. We, ourselves, were surprised by the results.

On our home world there had been experiments with super conductors and creating a continuous band of current that would last for eternity. There were experiments that showed a change in gravity in the centre of the circle. Some postulated that this circle of energy stretched up in a cone, theoretically went right out into space. That somehow, a vortex could be created, that we might even be able to use it to travel home, or at least use it as a radio telescope to send messages back to where we had come from.

But then the indigenous people who had been shocked and baffled by what they understood as our magic, treated us as deities. We became their new Gods, and the temptation to live out that life became too much for some. We gave into corruption, to ego; the irony being, we had created a means of power to cure ourselves of nostalgia but had succumbed to the power of holding that knowledge. Huge festivals were arranged; we had employed the local population to help move the stones, now they used the machine we had built as a place of pilgrimage and sacrifice.

Young boys and girls were brought forth, taken on ceremonial routes, tied to our lightning posts and suffered the deaths of heroes. We built roofs over our machines, tried to hide them away, but it only made it worse. Initiation ceremonies were organized, with parents gladly giving up their offspring in an attempt to appease the Gods.

Some of us left, headed south. They built pyramids as another form of energy device, using water and passageways, directing signals to the stars. Most of us stayed. We lived lives of Gods, and a priesthood was formed. By keeping the knowledge secret, people created higher archives of understanding, created a class system. And finally, the original ancestors of the members of that first crew that fell to Earth slowly died with their knowledge and their hope, and our destiny was lost in time.

But their transmitters lived on. Their attempts to harness lightning, to find a way home, to reach out and call their planet had a long-lasting side effect. For the beacons they devised were locked onto by a people trying to escape their own, different planet, and they used these ancient megaliths and pyramids to transport themselves across the galaxy, to find a new home on Earth. They became known as the Greens, though their name was the Prinshj People, and it was through their secret order that the earth might be saved from destruction.

So, you should view this fleeting world as a star at dawn, a bubble in a stream, a flash of lightning in a summer cloud, a flickering lamp, a phantom, and a dream.
— Diamond Sutra

I walk on another part of the island, in the north, on the point of Ayre, around another lighthouse, striped red and white, along the sand dunes in the National Wildlife Reserve, watch the diving gannets plunge into the sea like kamikaze pilots, watch them tuck their white flowing scarves in, head into the wash of oil and metal ship decks as wave crests. I walk between the sand dunes and pop my head up to see the heart of the sea pumping out in the gold blue. The diamond cutters shaping the day. Down in the sand I burrow to find a locket like the one I found at the bottom of the river when I was a boy and inside is a diamond, I realize at that moment, in the wind of the morning and the shattering of the fridges that fall from the sky, I am dead, and there is a life beyond, and that when I die I shall see everyone again, that my wish will be granted, and the diamond mind of all of us can save us. And I know now that a diamond will save us, and I wake clutching a tiny diamond as though I had brought it with me and I had been saved by something that pulled me back. And that I can never be pulled back again.

I awoke from my death dream in a small caravan with curtains at the windows covered in green and pink flowers. I had no idea how I got there, but I knew now why. The door to the caravan opened and a figure stepped in, dressed in dungarees, hair tied up, her eyes shone, Alice.

We built a platform in the methane lake in the Humber River as it pooled before colliding with the North Sea. Out on Spurn Point a lighthouse flashed its beam at intervals. The spit of land to our left curved out to meet the sea. We bought lumber and metal from Hull, strapped it down to the back of a pickup truck we'd bought. Hull had emptied out or hunkered down. News had spread fast, they knew there was something coming.

I sunk a series of poles in the lake bed, fixed cross-beams, fusing them together with fire from my hands. Alice watched from the shore as bubbles and smoke rose and broke the surface.

She helped by pushing out planks of wood strapped together with thick rope. I tied them to the metal struts. A pontoon was made just above water level. I swam down and forced more metal poles into the lake bed. Alice handed me poles from the shore. I built a structure below. I worked diligently, though I didn't reveal to Alice what all of it meant. She asked but I was hesitant to explain the whole scenario. My mystery annoyed her but she went along with the project, delighting in doing something that had a purpose. She also didn't trust my recovery. She thought I hid pain from her.

I told Alice about diamonds, showed her one in the palm of my hand, tiny and resting in the crevice of my heart line. I said they concentrate my power, that I can use them to make bolts of plasma.

Alice asked, "Where does the power come from, are you a superhero?"

I laughed, stripped to the waist, scuba goggles around my neck, the shape of the bullet hole like a red pulsar in the eye of my Koi carp tattoo, "No. Not an alien. It was when they took me. I was given over for experiments, for a price, for a punishment."

"I don't like to think of it. What kind of people experiment on people?"

"The bad kind. The bad kind who think they are doing good."

"I don't understand. There's a lot of things I don't understand," she said, handing me another metal pole.

"What do you want to know?"

"You have all the answers?"

"Some."

"I want the big answer to the big question."

"You want the big answer?" I asked.

"Sure, you're the big man."

"I don't have it." I raised my hands in a shrug.

"And what about this, what meaning does this have, what's going to happen?"

"I don't know yet, I don't know everything, I know the boy must come."

"When?"

"Very soon. We must prepare."

"I guess I'm on boiling the kettle and fixing lunch duties as I don't have hands like flamethrowers, then?"

"Ah, well, no. I mean, I can do that."

"Seems like there's not a lot of room for a woman in this scenario?"

"Can you test the platform?" I pointed to it sitting on the water fifty yards out.

"Test it for what?"

"It needs to hold, go jump on it or something."

"Well, better than domestics. Anyway, how do I get out there?"

"I bought a blow-up dingy, it's in the truck. You didn't see me loading that thing in?"

"Does it have a paddle?" Alice asked, ignoring his question.

"It will have a paddle."

"I'm glad," said Alice in low voice, and then she looked at me, in a way I understood.

10

Irma

We met at a hotel on the edge of Hull, and sat around a large table in the restaurant. Alice had the chilli, Gerad, a grilled cheese sandwich, me, the pan-fried chicken, Sami, the trout, Mike, nachos, and Alice, the jumbo burger and strawberry shortcake.

Max didn't eat, didn't need to of course, but he needed to recharge, which he did later that night in his room, staring at an intricate pattern in the wallpaper.

Alice gazed at Sami, across the table, the brother she never knew. Their eyes met once but Sami didn't want to prolong the connection, there was something that he knew which required him to act towards his sister in a way not connected to feelings, nothing emotional, that's what Alice surmised. She tried to talk to him, but he gave a scant account of the last few days, and before that it was a mystery, apart from a time spent in Lisbon, Portugal. They all met as strange friends, an estranged family, nobody very hungry or wanting to talk. Mike downed beers quickly. Alice and myself were situated at either end of the table, we ate silently. Alice looked up once and I caught her eye.

When the food was finished Alice plucked up the courage to ask Sami what it was that he kept secret. There was a hushed silence around the table.

Sami said, "It is something I was asked to carry, it has been hard, it hurts, but I will be free from it soon."

Gerad put his arm around Sami's shoulder. Sami thought of Taza. Taza in hospital, surviving the gunshot and recovering from his wound.

Our trip to the hotel had been one of few words, my taciturn manner didn't help. What was she doing here anyway, that's what Alice was asking herself. It was great to see Dad, but, what now? On a wild goose chase, following a man across the country, just because her eyes lit up? Alice sighed. What help could she be anyway? She noticed a look between Gerad and me, but didn't understand its significance. There was an understanding, but a sadness also.

On the way Mike had driven through Salisbury and called at the house where he had dropped Isaba off. The man in the suit trousers answered the door.

"Remember me?" asked Mike.

"No," answered the man.

"You will when I'm gone."

The man was closing the door on Mike's face when Mike put his right boot in the door jam. The man looked horrified, then angry. He turned his head back into the house, "Isaba, call the police right now!"

There was no response from back in there. Mike heaved the door open. The man made to hit Mike, but it was a feeble attempt and Mike just put up the palm of a hand, covered the man's face with it and pushed him back into his soft carpeted floor. Isaba appeared and as she walked out she gave the man a good hard kick in the shins. Mike led the way to the truck and they drove with Isaba back to Mike's place where he told Isaba to make herself comfortable and he'd be back in a day or two. He'd find a way for her to live without slavery, whatever it took.

He had taken Rufus straight from the compound to hospital, but on the way, Rufus had asked to be taken home. His injuries were slight and he was feeling he would be better surrounded by what he knew. He added, "The apples won't pick themselves." And Mike nodded and understood that his father would recover just fine.

We all slept the night in the hotel, the foyer had a pool and fountain with sculpted whale tails poking out of the water. The night was humid and none of us slept well. I wanted to travel back to the caravan at Spurn Point that night, but Alice said she'd rather spend the night in a proper bed, so I set off without her. She thought it awkward I had hired a tiny caravan, one with only a double bed. In the end I had slept on the foam mattress bench seat whilst she had the bed. But then, in the middle of the night, she woke suddenly gripped by a fear and hired a taxi and went out to me in my caravan. She knocked on the door and I let her in. The night was close. I was withdrawn, Alice trying to break through my resistance. What did she really mean to me? I poured us both a drink of whiskey that we drank from plastic cups. We sat side by side on the thin cushion. A wind gathered up and rocked the caravan, the windows shook in their mountings. Alice wasn't expecting anything, she was cool. I reached into my pocket and pulled out her skull and crossbones earring.

"Yours?" I asked.

"Don't know, maybe." Alice reached for her ear, it was missing.

"I found it."

"Aha." Alice took it from my hand.

"You should go back."

"Back where?" asked Alice.

"To the hotel. Or home."

"After all this? Why did you bring me along anyway? What use am I?"

"You're the only person who believed me. Believed in me."

"I haven't got a lot of belief in anything," she kind of blurted it out, "anyway, what do you care. You want to send me away. You want me with you. You don't know what you want. I thought I was happy but you made me sad."

"I'm sorry, it wasn't my intention."

"Oh, fuck it." Alice stood up. I caught her hand.

"What now?" asked Alice.

She was standing there, standing, and not leaving, and I touched her and she had not burst into flames, which was a start. She didn't pull away. In fact, despite herself, she looked at me and couldn't hide herself.

"Stay," I said.

"And what then?" asked Alice.

I dropped hold of her hand, got to my feet, kissed her and the night was long.

The air is thick with a heavy, impending storm. Gerad is crouched over Sami on the long grass at the edge of the water.

Gerad readies himself and puts his hands together. Sami lays out on the grass, his shirt pulled up. Gerad pushes his fingertips into Sami's belly, deep inside, catching something and pulling at it, extracting the 'star' — a diamond the size of a football from Sami's stomach.

Sami is in great pain, but relived to finally give up the precious cargo he has travelled so far with. The diamond came with them, from their own planet, many years ago, and has been handed down through the priesthood.

Gerad gently hands the diamond over to me. I wait in attendance. Alice places her hands on Sami's stomach, healing the wound. The real power she had hidden. For, her eyes open a lens on the interior, her hands heal the exterior. How she healed me. Now I realize. Why my death dream was mixed with her past, her future, the future of us all.

Alice watches as I take the diamond, wash it in icy water. I know now why I was made this way, who the experimenters were, the aliens, preparing me for this, what my life has been bent towards. There is no better feeling, to understand my place in the jigsaw. The preparations they made to protect this Earth, their new home, so sacred in their rituals.

I squeeze the diamond between my hands, stare down into it. There is a deep, bright spark of light inside. My hands press on the uncut edges. The diamond moulds to my hands, becomes part of me, neither a diamond nor hands, but the same, and I know they are the same. I squeeze until the power comes. I lift my hands up. A stream of fiery plasma shoots from the palm of my hands, flashes across the surface of the lake, igniting the rich methane that seeps from it, and hits Max, who is stood on the platform in the middle of the water. It hits him in the chest. His arms bend back.

Max feels the onslaught. The plasma beam jolts his whole being. He is made from pieces, but he stands as a saviour. There is nothing that separates him from humans except death, and here he was looking death in the face, here he was needed to direct the force of the beam.

Alice watches as Max takes the force of the blow. Sami sits up, watching the spectacle. Gerad is nearby, he is nervous, he studies me and then Max. There is something wrong, the beam has not enough force, not enough for their purpose.

Gerad looks up towards the sand dunes. Alice sees something. Across the lake. Top of the dunes. A figure with flame red hair. And she knows who it is. Alice runs, through the long grasses, through bracken and ferns, around the edge of the water up the dune hills. Not again, it cannot happen again.

Gerad looks at me, I turn and stare at him, my hands burning hot, holding the beam directed towards Max. And then I nod, knowing there is no other choice. Gerad takes a silk handkerchief from his pocket and raises it in the air waving.

Francesca on top of the dunes sees the signal. She fixes a silver-tipped arrow in her bow string.

Alice hurtles across up the dunes, she fights to pump her legs to drive her harder. She knows.

Francesca aims the arrow across the lake at my heart, a range of a hundred yards, but she can make it. My arms are held out in front, but she has the angle to bypass them and hit my heart full. Out of the corner of her eyes she sees something, Alice, running towards her. She keeps her aim steady.

Alice sees Francesca, her sister, sees her aim — John, the man she has fallen for. Her mother's thoughts are in her head, telling her to stop. She knows she is watching from the lighthouse. But she cannot stop, never could. Not now. She runs at Francesca. Runs at her because she has the power that can stop the madness, stop someone hurting me ever again. And in that moment, she knows, there is nothing without pain, and nothing without love and the two twine together like a twisted rope. She is without fear, without all that has held her back. Her X-ray eyes help her see what is deep within. Pure love. She will die today. She flings herself at her sister, throws all of her being into that jump. And fails.

Francesca releases the arrow. It flies across the lake and hits my heart and in an instant my heart explodes and my whole body becomes alight, burning bright, and the plasma beam enriches, expands. I become a chalice that directs the flame across the lake, ignites the methane, creates a diamond-methane nuclear fusion beam, that hits Max who spreads his arms. The plasma beam exits through his hands, upwards in a channel, spreading out across the surface of the planet, creating a halo of energy that forms an anti-gravitational field.

Uley watched from the lighthouse, as, from the sky, suddenly, the meteorite hurtled to the ground and then, just as the rock is about to hit, a beam of light covered the surface of the earth. Uley, her eyes shut, channelled her force towards the asteroid.

And the asteroid stopped, one inch from the ground, held in stasis over the thick mud flats of the Humber Estuary.

Earth fell silent.

Hopi mythology says: "In the final days we will look up in our heavens and we will witness the return of the two brothers who helped create this world in the birthing time. Poganghoya is the guardian of our North Pole and his brother Palongawhoya is the guardian of the South Pole."

"In the final days the Blue Star Kachina will come to be with his nephews and they will return the earth to its natural rotation which is counterclockwise. Not far behind the twins will come the Purifier — the Red Kachina, who will bring the Day of Purification. On this day the earth, her creatures and all life as we know it will change forever."

The meteorite cracked, a jagged crack that spread from its tip, dividing in two. Slowly, the two pieces fell apart and were attracted to opposite geographical poles, drifting across the land, to rest, held above the Arctic and Antarctic.

Uley's eyes opened and in them the image of the meteorite grew smaller.

Irma married and had children. She tried desperately not to think of Max and Tom. She wanted to leave the past behind, where it belonged, in a small box she kept under lock and key in the pit of her stomach.

Then one day she saw an article in a magazine. She must have picked it up by accident at the supermarket checkout; she wouldn't have bought such a thing, maybe it had slipped inside another magazine. Maybe her son, Max, had pulled it out and it had tumbled into her shopping.

The exploitive splash of an article concerned a beast seen roaming in the forest on Dartmoor, a man unlike others, a Big Foot, a Sasquatch. There were lurid reports of the beast attacking animals and people, of picnics being disturbed by a looming giant, of blood-curdling screams heard in the night by local farmers. Wild ponies were said to shy aware from one part of the forest. And she knew. The stimulus for her action came with synchronicity. Teresa, her daughter, was playing with an old box of toys brought down from the attic, and there in her hands was the walkie-talkie that she had spoken to Max with many years ago.

She drove the next day and stayed at a pretty B&B on the edge of the forest. At dusk she set out on foot, found a remote spot, and switched on the walkie-talkie. She spoke softly asking if he was there. She knew there was a chance the receiver was still embedded in Max, but she didn't know for sure, and as each night ended without success she sank a little closer towards that terrible small box, chanced to open it a few times and feel the wave of guilt and remorse flood over her. In bed, with the contents of the box laid out in front of her, she cried silent tears until there were no more tears and her heart shut down and she was overcome by sleep.

On the fourth day, after she had phoned her mum to check on the children, Irma stepped out into the quickening darkness and took up her position on a small hill overlooking a shallow valley. She could hear a stream tinkle below her, the wind had died down, and the air was crystal and sharp. She turned on the walkie-talkie and said,

"Max? Can you hear me? Max?"

There was the static answer she had heard on all the other previous nights and then, just as she had resigned herself to the fate of never knowing, a faint voice crackled through, "Bright, bright."

Irma stayed very still, a cold ripple spread down her spine and ignited the small box in her stomach.

"Max?"

"I'm here." The voice was stronger, it was him. "I want you to know I am so sorry for my actions," he said. "I am not a man, I am nothing."

"Please," she replied, "please listen to me, it was my fault, my life, my choices, I am sorry. And I'm scared for you."

"Don't be. There is nothing for me now, except to know if you are happy. Are you happy?"

"I can't answer that. I don't want to."

And he was gone, voice lost in the crackle. And never spoke again though she visited again, and eventually moved to Dartmoor, bringing her family with her.

Irma was two hundred and eighty now. She couldn't quite believe her age. She was still active and would walk down to the shops in the valley. Occasionally she would wander out to the forest, but she never took the walkie-talkie with her. Her husband was dead and her children grown up with children of their own. She lived alone and was happy in her way.

One day, one day after Max had saved Ruth from death he went with her to the forest in Dartmoor. He saw Irma walking slowly along a path, and so as not to astonish her, sat on the stump of a tree and waited, asking Ruth to wait for him. Ruth asked why he hadn't gone before, but all Max would say is that she had her life to lead and he had his. He had saved the world but not himself, and so he'd left everyone in peace. And even though the world had endured, everything returned to the same, all in their right place and no lasting change for peace everlasting. And then he saw Ruth and Lilly and it reminded him of the love he once had.

Irma knew who he was as soon as she saw Max from a distance, and for a moment she hesitated as to whether to go and meet him. He was still the same and she was old. Max stood and walked to her. He smiled, "There was never a fourth wish, but if there was let it be mine. I wanted to see you again. And thank you."

"Thank me?" asked Irma.

"Please do me this one favour, this one last favour and go forward with a happy heart, a knowing kind heart, and know I am learning that this resemblance of a life has only one meaning, change."

Max turned to walk away.

"Max?"

"Yes?"

"I loved you."

"I love you still and always will."

Irma walked home. She switched on the radio. A song from the past they both knew was playing, their favourite, Elvis Presley, "Love Me (Treat me like a fool)", came on. She thought she could hold on, gripped the sideboard, but there in her kitchen she cried, knowing she would never see him again, and let the music take the pain away.

After Houdini's death, his wife, Bess, held a yearly séance, waiting for a prearranged code from her dead husband to tell her there was life after death. She went every year but heard nothing. She gave up in 1936 saying, "Ten years is long enough to wait for any man."

In Eastern Arnhem Land the Marrakulu Clan act out the parts of their Yellow Ochre Ancestors when someone dies. They drag digging sticks behind them and hold sacred woven-string dilly bags, gripped in their teeth. They dig for ochre, testing it under their arms and across their chests. The bags collect the ochre and contain the anger of the bereaved.

She wrote, "There are patterns to our love, like a fern curls up inside itself, or an ice crystal forming, cracking under the weight of expectation. There is a window in my cell. It looks back to Earth, I am swamped with a great longing for firm earth, for my feet to hold fast, for non-regulated air in my lungs, for the catastrophe of life, with all its faults, to burn down all the libraries of the world, with all the commentaries, with all the thoughts, to have only one thought, or no thought.... I am homesick, nostalgic. I don't even know if you are receiving these messages... There has always been a question that we've never answered up here. With all the developments, all the progress, all the aspirations: what are we here for? I don't mean in the philosophical way, I mean, here, in space. What is the purpose of all of it, what have we learned? ... We haven't been enlightened by looking outwards, by exploring space, mining asteroids. Where did the mission go wrong, in the largest sense? Right now, decisions are being made without me, we are making for a new home. Can we call somewhere home without roots, without the smell and tastes of home? Time will tell."

After twenty-three years, that seemed like just one sleep, Ingrid and Tom, a guy who worked maintenance on the ship, and the cat called Fluffball awoke from stasis, the only survivors onboard the ship that now orbited their new home, a new planet. All were dead but them, they were alive and the others had perished. Tom and Ingrid laid wreaths on each capsule before it was shot out into space. There were no words said. Just a process.

It might seem churlish to bring judgement to their coldness to the others who had died; there was nothing they could do but surge forwards. This was frightening to them both. And so, they made plans to activate the shuttle that would send them down to a planet they neither knew could sustain life.

She wrote, "This is my last message before we set off for our new home. I cannot stop thinking of that story I read in that book called *Zen Inklings*, about the butcher in Japan who all his life, cut up meat. He had started as a boy, scrubbing the chopping board, then moved onto cutting out the entrails, then to killing itself, cutting the throats of pigs. One day, a day like any other, he was slitting the throat of an animal, pulling out the stomach, his hands deep in the blood. Outside, it was a bright autumn day and he could see, through a window, flowering grasses in a meadow. He looked at his hands in the blood and the guts and a feeling came over him. He was at one with the meat. I know, it sounds so odd. He stood that way until nightfall, hands in the meat, eyes on the grass, and at dawn he left, never to return, he never killed an animal again. He walked up into the mountains and there he stayed. He wrote a poem which became famous:

'Just yesterday, the soul of a demon,
This morning, the face of a bodhisattva.
A demon, a bodhisattva...
There is no difference.'"

On the new planet Fluffball pounced and in that jump was the stretched-out paws of an eternal time lock, signifying the end of past, the beginning of now. She had caught a bird, played with it for a while, patted it between paws, and so the cycle of need and learning began to quicken the heart once more.

**ROUNDFIRE
BOOKS**

FICTION

Put simply, we publish great stories. Whether it's literary or
popular, a gentle tale or a pulsating thriller, the connecting theme
in all Roundfire fiction titles is that once you pick them up you
won't want to put them down.
If you have enjoyed this book, why not tell other readers by
posting a review on your preferred book site.

The Cause
Roderick Vincent
The second American Revolution will be a
fire lit from an internal spark.
Paperback: 978-1-78279-763-0 ebook: 978-1-78279-762-3

Don't Drink and Fly
The Story of Bernice O'Hanlon: Part One
Cathie Devitt
Bernice is a witch living in Glasgow. She loses her way
in her life and wanders off the beaten track looking for the
garden of enlightenment.
Paperback: 978-1-78279-016-7 ebook: 978-1-78279-015-0

Gag
Melissa Unger
One rainy afternoon in a Brooklyn diner, Peter Howland
punctures an egg with his fork. Repulsed, Peter pushes
the plate away and never eats again.
Paperback: 978-1-78279-564-3 ebook: 978-1-78279-563-6

The Master Yeshua
The Undiscovered Gospel of Joseph
Joyce Luck
Jesus is not who you think he is. The year is 75 CE. Joseph
ben Jude is frail and ailing, but he has a prophecy to fulfil ...
Paperback: 978-1-78279-974-0 ebook: 978-1-78279-975-7

On the Far Side, There's a Boy
Paula Coston
Martine Haslett, a thirty-something 1980s woman, plays hard
on the fringes of the London drag club scene until one night
which prompts her to sign up to a charity. She writes to a
young Sri Lankan boy, with consequences far and long.
Paperback: 978-1-78279-574-2 ebook: 978-1-78279-573-5

Tuareg
Alberto Vazquez-Figueroa
With over 5 million copies sold worldwide, *Tuareg* is a classic
adventure story from best-selling author Alberto Vazquez-
Figueroa, about honour, revenge and a clash of cultures.
Paperback: 978-1-84694-192-4

Readers of ebooks can buy or view any of these bestsellers by
clicking on the live link in the title. Most titles are published
in paperback and as an ebook. Paperbacks are available in
traditional bookshops. Both print and ebook formats are
available online.

Find more titles and sign up to our readers' newsletter at
www.collectiveinkbooks.com/fiction